BLOOD SPOTS

BLOOD SPOTS

BLOOD SPOTS

LIN LE VERSHA

This edition produced in Great Britain in 2025

by Hobeck Books Limited, 24 Brookside Business Park, Stone, Staffordshire ST15 0RZ

www.hobeck.net

A CIP catalogue for this book is available from the British Library.

ISBN 978-1-915-817-69-3 (ebook)

ISBN 978-1-915-817-770-9 (pbk)

Cover design by Jayne Mapp Design

https://jaynemapp.wixsite.com

For Julie

ARE YOU A THRILLER SEEKER?

Hobeck Books is an independent publisher of crime, mystery, thriller and suspense and we have one aim – to bring you the books you want to read.

For more details about our books, our authors and our plans, the chance to enter competitions, plus to download *Crime Bites*, a free compilation of novellas and short stories by our authors sign up for our newsletter at **www.hobeck.net**.

You can also find us on Twitter **@hobeckbooks** or on Facebook **www.facebook.com/hobeckbooks10**.

PROLOGUE 1989
MONDAY 28TH AUGUST 11.30PM

The body, still warm, lay in a heap, hidden by a tarpaulin, waiting for its final resting place...

The moon disappeared behind a cloud, leaving Naz blind, scrambling down the cliff, falling down the last few feet of the treacherous pathway and landing on his knees. Luckily, it was sand.

Why had he returned to the party anyway? The reeling figures on the beach were well beyond drunk – wrecked or paralytic would come closer to describing their raucous laughter. Screams from the skinny-dippers and triumphant cheers for the shadow staggering across the sand with another armful of booze, depressed him further.

All the adults involved in the final performance of *A Midsummer Night's Dream*, had seen sense and after a polite glass or two, had disappeared – all except Beverly, their Director, who must have felt responsible for them. She sat on a large tree trunk beside a male shape that Naz couldn't identify. They were knocking it back too.

Why ever had he got himself involved in this clusterfuck of

a play? He rolled the newly acquired word around his mouth, saving it for the more extreme moments in his life, such as now.

He knew the answer – Lucy. His Lucy – or she was – until Beverly imported the sexy French Hugo to play Puck. All the girls had thrown themselves at this sex bomb with his Gauloises deep voice, but his Lucy had laughed, called them sluts and said she was happy with him – until she wasn't. Now she'd left everything to go with Hugo to Paris – just like that. He'd seen the taxi, and that was that. It was over.

Now all their plans were smashed. It would have been perfect – Lucy in drama school in London and him up the road in Oxford. He sighed, kicked a stone into the waves and vowed he'd have nothing to do with the thesps ever again.

Two skinny-dippers, desperate to find their clothes, bashed him out of the way and he almost fell onto the bodies tangled around the fire, their faces glowing in the flames.

"Oy! Piss off! That was my hand!'

Now with a soggy back to add to his misery, he shivered as he stumbled towards the cliff path, about to go home and be miserable, when he felt an arm snake round his shoulders.

'No, you don't mate.'

Naz jumped. 'Marcus! What the fuck!' Skidding on the loose pebbles, he fell back into his best friend's arms.

'Don't even think about it. You're staying, mate.'

'I've had enough – I only—'

'We're all sick of hearing you only did this because of Lucy. But look, mate, she's gone. Jess and me could see it coming and you deserve better than that little tart.' Marcus shoved a bottle of beer in his hand. 'Now let's have some fun.'

'I don't—'

'For fuck's sake – sit down with me and enjoy yourself for once. We're going to conjure up some spirits. Anyway, what would you do if you went home?'

Marcus was right. What would he do? He slumped down on the sand beside Marcus and stared around the swaying circle, their faces washed pale in the moonlight. He attempted to concentrate on the Ouija board set out by Kate, who'd played Titania – the first of Hugo's conquests.

A fierce look from Kate made him add his finger to the pile of the others on top of the glass. It wobbled a bit and moved towards the circle of the alphabet before settling between "Yes" and "No".

'Whoever is pushing that, stop now!' Kate threw a poison glare at Marcus.

'Not me!' He lifted his finger away from the pile and the wobble continued.

'See?'

'Let's try again.' Kate moved the glass back on top of the gruesome skull at the centre of the circular board, which appeared to wink in the flickering firelight.

Naz squeezed his eyes to re-focus – how could an empty eye socket wink? He must have had more than he thought. In the sudden silence as they all concentrated on the board, he became aware of the crashing waves as the tide was moving up the beach and the eerie hoot of an owl from above on the cliff made him jump.

'I'm scared! I don't want to do this.' Paula, who had played one of the fairies and had always fancied Marcus, whined and grabbed his arm.

'Don't be so wet. Have another drink.' Marcus pushed a bottle towards Paula, who took a gulp, still grasping his arm.

The six of them, fingers outstretched on the glass, waited for Kate to start. She milked the moment, closed her eyes, raised her left hand to touch her temple in concentration and bowed her head.

'Got a headache?' Marcus draped his arm around Paula,

who giggled at his wit and snuggled even closer to him. A good job Jess wasn't around.

'Shhh!' Came from all sides, while Kate ignored him. She raised her head, looking up towards the graveyard high up on the cliff above them, her face a ghostly mask in the moonlight. 'Is there anybody there?'

They sat in silence, waiting.

'Yes, it's me.' came a voice from above.

Paula screamed, thrusting herself against Marcus.

'It's me. Can't you see me?' Jess climbed down from the cliff path, jumping the last part and dislodging a few stones which rolled towards the board. 'What on earth are you lot doing?'

Kate, who was a little scared of the brilliant Jess, stammered. 'We ... we're communing with the spirits.'

'Communing? What rubbish! I thought we were having a party.' Jess stood on the edge of the circle. Several fingers were lifted off the glass.

Kate, annoyed at having lost her position as the centre of attention, shouted back at Jess. 'You're only criticising 'cos it wasn't your idea!'

Jess dithered on the outside of the circle, apparently unsure of what to do. She was saved by the ever-loyal Marcus. 'It'll be a laugh, Jess.' He slid his arm from around Paula and beckoned to Jess. 'Come on – join us.'

Jess, hand on hip, stared hard at Paula, who got the message and shifted on her bottom along the sand towards Naz, leaving room for Jess to take her place, which she did with a theatrical flounce. Marcus put his arm around her shoulders, and Jess nestled into him. Seeing them made Naz even more pissed off. His arm should have been around Lucy, now instead she was – he wasn't sure where exactly – but she wasn't here with him, was she?

He tuned into Kate's voice. 'Right, put your fingers on the glass again.' They all obeyed her, even Jess. 'That's right. Now, where were we?' She took a deep breath, closed her eyes and in her most dramatic voice demanded, 'Is there anyone there?'

A long pause. The silence was broken by a gasp from someone as the glass moved towards the word 'YES'.

'What's your name?' Kate asked.

After a pause, the glass slid towards the letters at the edge of the board, shifting between M, L, K and J. Surely someone was moving it? Naz couldn't see who. He knew it wasn't him. Marcus was the obvious one, but his finger was on top, and he could feel Marcus was relaxed.

A ripple of fear spread through the silent group as the glass appeared to move of its own accord and the joking and grinning stopped. They were all serious now, with a few looking a little scared. The glass returned to the centre to settle on the skull for a few moments, before moving to Y, then U.

'Told you it was rubbish. We should ignore it.' Jess's voice rang across the circle.

Kate smiled, pleased that Jess was getting involved at last. 'Could it be, "why you" to someone called M, L, K or J?'

'Quite a lot of choice there!' Marcus voiced what Naz had been thinking.

'Could it be Kate? How spoooooooky is that?' The dramatic whisper from Jess made Paula giggle.

'Shh. It's moving again.' Kate waved her free hand at the interruption, and the glass continued travelling around the board.

K – N – O

It stopped.

'Keep your fingers on it.' ordered Kate.

It swept across the board to the letters W – H – U

'Does it mean who? Know who?' Kate asked, in control

again. No one replied as they were distracted by Paula squealing and burying herself this time into Naz, who nudged her away a little.

'Not great at spelling, is it?' Marcus took a swig from the bottle Jess had found.

'Where are you?' Kate demanded.

'U – P.'

'At least it's in heaven. We don't want one from hell – they're no end of trouble.' Several of them nodded at the wise words of Kate, now their spirit expert. 'Have you got a message for us?'

The glass shimmied around the board before coming to a stop. All of them froze, not daring to move, peering at the circle of fingers attached to the glass. Slowly, it slid towards the letters. No jokes now, but intense concentration.

F – N – D

'FND? What does that mean?' asked Naz.

'Foundation? Fund? Fucking Nothing Doing? You choose.' Marcus, about to lift his finger off the glass, received another hard stare from Kate.

'Maybe it means FIND. But where?' Kate's voice had become a whisper, as if the spirit was standing behind her shoulder, listening.

The glass appeared to hover above the surface of the board and again stopped.

They froze, waiting.

The waves pounding the beach were getting closer, the fire dying down to embers pushed the darkness over them flattening them into black silhouettes.

'Is that it?' Jess grabbed the bottle from Marcus and took a gulp. 'Anyone else want a drink?'

'Put your finger back, it's not finished!' At Kate's urgent cry, Jess replaced her finger and at once the glass moved.

D – E – D

'Who?' Kate's asked, looking up at the sky. At once, everyone was shocked into an uneasy silence.

The glass skidded crazily across the board, pulling their fingers with it before flying up into the air and onto the sand.

'Who did—'

A piercing scream drowned out her voice.

2019

CHAPTER ONE

FRIDAY 19TH JULY: 6.30AM

'Come, Benson!'

Annoyed that he'd run off again, Sue stopped walking and turned in a complete circle, scanning the field and hedgerow. Her wellington boot sank deep in the mud and made a satisfying squelch as she tugged it out of the gluey muck. Her yellow Labrador was always running off – he didn't behave like this in training sessions, did he?

She slid down the steep path to the broad, which appeared to be getting larger each time she walked past it and there, doggy-paddling across it, was a very happy Benson. He scrambled out and shook himself, showering her with a perfect arc of droplets.

Despite the soaking, she smiled at his obvious delight. 'Come on, let's go to the beach.' Her jeans would soon dry, and it was a joy to be out so early with the entire beach to herself. Benson thought so too! He ploughed through the sand, chasing the ball towards the tiny waves, folding over with a whisper. How different to last night.

The wind had smashed into her cottage for hours and she'd

hardly slept. The rain was so powerful it had forced its way through the gaps in the old sash windows, which she'd soaked up with tea towels along the sills. To have such a wild storm in July was rare – but it wasn't that rare now, was it?

Recently, the weather patterns had been totally disrupted, and the winter storms happened at any time of the year. On her way down to the beach, she'd climbed over an uprooted oak tree lying across the footpath, its enormous root ball reaching up into the air – it must have been several hundred years old. While ahead, the beach was littered with small pieces of drift-wood, plastic bottles and old cans trapped in a wide swathe of seaweed. Why couldn't the ferries realise that the rubbish they dumped overboard didn't simply dissolve?

The crisp sky was cloudless, a perfect blue, which gave the brown Suffolk sea hints of the Med. She picked her way through the stinking mess of seaweed and walked along the edge of the waves towards Covehithe, relishing the sunshine.

Turning back to look up at the cliffs, she was horrified to see how much of it had come down in the storm, now piled in enormous heaps of rocks on the beach. The usual egg timer trickles of sand appeared to have bred overnight and created an orange mist in the breeze.

Two trees, now teetering over the cliff, roots hanging in the air, appeared ready to topple down at any moment. A jagged gash penetrated deep into the cliff wall, invading the field and revealing more condemned vegetation. At least there weren't any houses falling over the edge, unlike so many further up the coast in Norfolk.

Benson was having a wonderful time fetching the ball, making perfect Vs swimming in the placid sea. Sue wished she'd had the nerve to come down in the middle of the storm to see for herself the dramatic waves that had pounded the cliffs. But she could well have been blown away like the bright yellow "Cliffs Are Dangerous" notice, now facing the sky halfway down the beach.

Sue must have been below Covehithe church when she tripped over an enormous flat stone and smashed down, face flat on the sand. The grit in her mouth got stuck between her teeth and she tried to spit it out. If only she had a bottle of water.

Benson, desperate to help, jumped on her back 'Ouch! That hurt!'

She shoved him off by turning over, hauled herself up – not an easy job in the shifting sand – and, shielding her eyes, focused on the top of the cliff. She couldn't believe what she thought she was seeing.

It looked like two off-white arm bones stuck out from soil at the top of the cliff, and further along a skull, stared out to sea through empty eyes. The sun, higher than when she'd set out, spotlighted the bones sharply against the terracotta cliff.

She rubbed her eyes in case she had imagined it. But no, the bones were still there when she opened them. Could it be a prank? Kids wanting to scare people like her? Even if it was, she ought to tell someone to remove them.

Pulling her phone out of her pocket, her hands shaking, it took two attempts to push the right numbers. When she got through, her high shaky voice surprised her.

'Police, please.'

CHAPTER TWO

FRIDAY 19TH JULY: 8.30AM

'SORRY LOVE, THEY'VE FOUND A BODY.' Chief Inspector Hale switched off his phone and, standing up, speared the last piece of bacon off his plate.

'Where?' Steph Grant struggled to force down a sigh. That was their trip to Latitude gone then.

'Covehithe. The storm last night washed away part of the cliff – a dog walker spotted it. I'll need to go. Sorry.'

Trying hard to keep her face in neutral, Steph picked up the empty plates, throwing a piece of bacon rind to her dog, Derek, who snapped it in mid-air and gulped it.

'Maybe we could go later?'

'Maybe – but you know how these things are. Perhaps you could ask Caroline, so we don't waste the tickets.'

'No. Spending two nights glamping with Caroline isn't quite the same, and it was your birthday present.'

As soon as the line-up had been announced in January, she had booked a luxury yurt at the Latitude Festival, on the outskirts of Southwold. Derek was to stay with the dog lady while they spent the weekend wandering around the maze of stages.

Using the online Clashfinder, they had revelled in working out a schedule which included George Ezra, Stereophonics, comedians Mark Watson and Frank Skinner, with a spattering of jazz and one or two plays that looked promising. It had been exciting planning the weekend together and, as the last few weeks had been relatively quiet, she dared to think it might actually happen.

Damn that storm. Apparently, they'd had a month's rainfall in the last two days and many local roads had been closed because of flash flooding. But why couldn't the cliff have waited until Monday to topple down?

Hale took the plates from her, placed them back on the table, pulled her towards him and hugged her, resting his chin on top of her head. 'I know how disappointing this is – for me, too. But you know what it's like. I'll see what's happening and I'll phone you.'

Leaning back, she swallowed the sharp disappointment and smiled up at him. 'Well, there'll be another year.'

She watched him as he pulled on his jacket, grabbed his phone, then froze. Frowning, he flicked back his dark brown hair, now with grey bits, which constantly flopped across his forehead while he looked around, then patted his pockets.

'They're in the bowl by the door.'

He grinned, spotted them, and rolled his eyes. 'Oh, that's where they are! Speak later.'

Watching him drive off, she couldn't help smiling that this capable police officer never knew where he'd dumped his keys. Still, if that was his major flaw, she was doing all right.

Stacking the dishwasher, she kept herself busy to stop moping about what might have been. Desperately disappointed but realistic; after all, she had lived that life herself for thirty years in the Met and Suffolk police.

Her boss for twelve years, they got together when Philip Hale, known to everyone as Hale, had investigated a murder at Oakwood Sixth Form College, where she was receptionist and PA to the principal. She'd always got on well with him and she and her late husband, Mike, had regular Friday night curries with Hale and his wife Sheila. When they met again, Hale had recently divorced, and she was feeling stronger after her husband's death a couple of years earlier. After going on several dinner dates, she realised she was having an unexpected love affair.

In his late fifties, a few years older than her, Hale was fit, in all senses of the word, with the most beautiful go-to-bed eyes and crooked smile. She had convinced herself she would continue her life alone, sharing her days with Derek – her rescued black and white collie cross, but now she was thrilled that Hale was there too.

The phone interrupted her thoughts. 'Hello ... No, he's been called in for an emergency, so I'm here ... That sounds mysterious ... Right, I'll be over in about twenty minutes.'

Caroline, the Head of Art at the college and her best friend, must be a witch to phone on cue like that. She lived on the other side of Oakwood with her partner Margaret and their white fluffy dog Marlene, who got on well with Derek. She postponed cancelling the dog lady until later, not wanting to face up to her disappointment quite yet.

Walking into the bedroom, confronted by their overnight bags, packed and ready to go, her mood was crushed once again. Caroline was fun, but no compensation for the delicious weekend she and Hale had planned. She reprimanded herself – at least she was going out and, after all, he was only doing his job.

After her shower, she deliberately pulled out a pale blue blouse and beige linen trousers from her wardrobe, which were certainly not Latitude garb. Anyway, after that thunderstorm the site would probably be a mud bath, so perhaps it was a good thing they weren't going.

She blow-dried her short blond curls, which, after her recent visit to the hairdresser, framed her face, and then did her make-up. The moody blue eyeshadow she'd bought especially for the weekend complemented her eyes, and the blouse helped, too. Not bad! Standing sideways towards the mirror, she breathed in and stood taller. Perhaps she should return to that aerobics class? Maybe – after the summer.

With Derek in the back, she drove across a sunny Oakwood onto the common, trying not to mourn the missed Festival. Gazing at the cloudless blue sky sweeping away into the distance, she found it hard to believe last night's ferocious storm had happened, until she had to stop twice to wait her turn to edge past three enormous tree branches that blocked the road.

Some of those branches, which must be quite heavy with summer leaves, had remained fixed to the tree for well over a century. Now the frequency of storms with sixty and seventy miles per hour winds was increasing, presumably because of global warming. How depressing. She sighed, then deliberately smiled, to give herself an injection of serotonin to lift her mood and by the time she drew up outside Caroline's, she was positively sparky.

As she was getting Derek out of the back, the front door flew open, and Caroline dashed down the path to hug her.

'Darling, I'm so sorry your weekend has been ruined. I know he can't help it, but that man of yours works so incredibly hard. You'd think they'd give him one weekend off!'

'Derek, get down!' Steph pushed him away from Caroline's

swishy red dress, where he'd joined in the hug. 'It's the job and there was an emergency. He had to go in.'

'Well, it means that I can have you all to myself this morning. Coffee's ready and Margaret has baked the most scrummy chocolate and ginger cake and – wait for it – I have the most spectacular news!'

CHAPTER THREE

FRIDAY 19TH JULY: 10.15AM

SETTLED in the conservatory opposite Caroline with a mug of nutty coffee and a gigantic slice of Margaret's scrumptious cake, they watched Derek chasing Marlene around the flower bed of bright pink hydrangeas and white roses, until she let him catch her and lay on her back, waving her legs in the air.

'What a tart that dog is! Now, darling, I have the most amazing plans for us.'

'Really?'

'Don't sound so suspicious. It'll be so jolly!'

Margaret came in and sat beside Caroline, making the wicker sofa crackle. 'She's right. It'll be just the thing to give the summer some – some structure. And this time I'm involved too, so I'll keep you both out of trouble.'

Margaret had been Caroline's partner for over twenty years, which Steph found amazing, as they were polar opposites. Caroline, her long curly grey hair always escaping from some arty slide, wore floaty dresses topped with dramatic scarves and never looked as if she was the other half of Margaret with her twin sets, sensible shoes and short grey hair.

'I'm the music director, you know. A great honour. Terrific score – original by Duke Special – composed for the 2009 National Theatre production.' Margaret shifted to let Marlene jump upon her lap to escape Derek's over enthusiastic attention. 'Not my usual thing, but I'm having a rather a good time arranging it for our college orchestra. I'm sure you'll appreciate it, Steph. You are so musical.'

Steph smiled at this enthusiastic Margaret. Whatever it was she was talking about had obviously energised her and she looked much better than when Steph had last seen her at the end of term. Margaret, a talented pianist and music teacher, had to halt her popular recitals when her Parkinson's shakes made her hands unreliable.

'It's great to see you two so excited, but please, will you tell me what you're going on about?'

Caroline winked at Margaret. 'We are *all* going to be in a production of *Mother Courage*.'

'All?'

'We'd hardly miss you out, would we, darling? I'm designing the set and costumes, and Margaret is the musical director and you—'

'Me?'

'And you will be our stage manager.'

Had she heard what she thought she'd heard?

'Sorry? Me? But I know nothing about stage management.'

Caroline waved her hand dismissively. 'Oh, come now, darling. You know how to manage people – you're the best I know – and you're so organised. That's all you need to do a brilliant job.'

'Come on, Caroline. You can't be serious.'

Margaret leaned forward and patted Steph on the knee. 'Now, don't be modest, my dear. You'll do an excellent job. We both thought of you immediately. Rehearsals start on Monday

with curtain up at the end of August. We'll do three performances over the bank holiday weekend and, most exciting of
all, a TV company is coming to film it as – guess what? Jessica
Marlowe will play Mother Courage!'

'Jessica Marlowe, the film star?'

'Film star, stage star, advertising star – you must have seen
that shampoo advert? That's her! She's returning to Oakwood,
where it all started. She was in *A Midsummer Night's Dream*
the summer before she left college for drama school and is
returning to do this production in aid of the local hospice. We
both taught her, you know.' Margaret was full of it. 'She wants
to give something back to the next generation of actors and
musicians and, of course, be filmed doing it.'

Steph felt flattered for a few moments that they thought
she could be part of their latest project. She had no idea what
Mother Courage was, but if they were involved, she was sure it
would be good, and even she had heard of Jessica Marlowe but
... and it was a big but ... why should she put herself in a position where she could fail?

Since she'd left the police force under a cloud and
collapsed for a year, she'd worked hard at building herself up
again. Did she really want to risk putting herself in a role she
knew nothing about?

'I'm really flattered you've asked me and said such nice
things, but I'm not sure I'm the right person.'

Caroline re-filled Steph's coffee mug and offered another
fix of chocolate cake, which she declined. 'We'll have a hoot,
darling – it'll be delicious fun. Beverly Elkin is the director,
and she certainly knows what she's doing—'

'Not that vicar at St Mary's that everyone's always
complaining about?' Steph couldn't believe it. Hadn't Caroline
moaned to her about the over-the-top, showy end of term
service at the college, where Beverly Elkin was also chaplain?

Margaret frowned. 'Gossips always criticise tall poppies. She's immensely talented and experienced—'

'Beverly was the county drama advisor in her earlier life and did some wonderful productions with our gifted drama students.' Caroline took Steph's empty mug. 'You'll love working with her—'

'She launched Jessica's career, you know. That's why she's come back to work with Beverly thirty years on.' Margaret's enthusiasm had transformed her – she'd even spoken over Caroline!

Caroline placed her hand over Steph's. 'Do say you'll do it, darling.'

As Steph opened her mouth to reply, her phone rang – saved by the bell. It was Hale.

'Excuse me.'

Both women nodded as Steph stepped onto the billiard green lawn to take the call.

'Yes ... I'm at Caroline's ... Really? That's great! I'll drop Derek off on the way home and see you there.'

All at once, the sun shone brighter, and the birds sounded chirpier. 'Derek, come!'

She walked back into the conservatory to be met with Margaret and Caroline's questioning expressions. 'Sorry – have to go. It looks like we'll be going to Latitude after all. Sorry to dash.'

They both followed Steph out to her car. After loading Derek in the back, she stepped back and bumped into Caroline, who threw her arms around her. 'Lovely to see you, darling, and really pleased you're going to Latitude. See you on Monday at the first rehearsal. I'll phone when you get back to give you all the info.'

'No promises, OK?'

'Have a good weekend. I'll phone on Sunday night.'

CHAPTER FOUR

AFTER THE NEWS THAT MORNING, Steph found it hard to believe they were on their way to Latitude. She squeezed Hale's thigh and grinned across at him.

'Oy! Careful, you don't want us to crash!'

Steph removed her hand. 'Just wanted to make sure I'm not dreaming.'

'Is that why you pinched so hard?'

The afternoon sun flickered through the trees as they made excellent progress towards Henham Park and their glam yurt – until they hit the queue inching into the site. Steph checked the site map. 'It says here to go to Red Gate 2 – must be for posh people only.'

'Rather a lot of posh people then.' He leaned his head out of the window to see how far the queue stretched, filling the car with dust and petrol fumes, so shut it again. 'Let's be grateful. I'll stop moaning. After that call, I didn't think we'd get here at all.' He patted her knee.

'You're not the only one. Remind me once again of the arrangements you've made with the team.'

Should she tell him she hadn't listened to a word he said when he'd come back to the flat? She'd been too busy making sure they'd got everything, that it would all fit in his car, and if they dashed away as quickly as possible, it would magically stop further phone calls to pull him back on duty.

'As I told you ... and I know you weren't listening to me—'

'That's not true—'

'The parts of the skeleton we have are ancient – not ancient–ancient but pretty old. At least thirty to fifty years, at a guess. Not much left to help us identify it. They think it's a female from the few scraps of nylon lace left, which look like they're from pants and a bra – we also have two of those metal hoop things.'

Steph grinned. 'Do you mean from an under-wired bra?'

'Probably. Oh, and we also have a bracelet – silver but badly tarnished– a chain with a heart.' As they weren't moving, Hale switched off the engine.

'Anyway, the bones appear to have been scattered by rabbits and earth movement and are being carefully searched for and removed by the forensic scientist and her team. We'll have to wait until at least the start of next week for her initial thoughts and probably a lot longer for them to find the rest. It may be some time before we know when it was buried, how old it is and receive confirmation it's a female.'

The queue hadn't budged for about ten minutes. This time, Steph put her head out of her window to see if she could spot the reason for the hold-up on her side. The sun blazed in through the windscreen and they were getting hot, despite the blast from the air con. What an amazing change in the weather. Torrential rain one day, then searing hot sun the next. It felt like they were in the tropics. 'Can't see anything. What is it they say on the traffic news – "sheer weight of traffic."'

'Nothing we can do about it.'

The boom of the bass guitar and the drums from the main stage drifted in through the open window and gave her a ripple of excitement as she felt the rhythm vibrate through her body. It was going to be a fabulous weekend.

Shutting the window to give the air con a chance, she turned to him. 'Surely if it was buried in the cliff and revealed by erosion it would be much older than forty years? Hundreds perhaps?'

'No, I don't think so. You see, great chunks of that cliff have fallen into the sea each winter and now, with the powerful storms we've had over the last few years, the erosion is speeding up.'

Hale moved forward a few car lengths before grinding to a stop again. 'At least we're moving. Johnson, who's lived here all his life, reckons as a kid they'd walk across two fields from Covehithe church to get to the edge of the cliff. Now it's a few metres. It could have been buried way back in the field and the cliff edge has just reached it.'

She screamed in surprise as a man in a yellow jacket knocked on their window.

'Ticket, please.'

Steph handed the printout to him, which he scanned and returned.

'You vant de-yurts?' His Eastern European accent made it difficult to take in what he said at first. She must have looked puzzled, so he continued. 'Glamps, yes?'

Steph smiled. 'That's right.'

'We stop traffic – come out – along there – first left.' He flapped his hand, beckoned them out of the queue and pointed further down the hedge. 'Twats in wrong place.' He waved at the cars in front of and behind them.

'Thanks.'

Hale checked there was no oncoming traffic, swerved the

car out of the queue and drove alongside some grumpy looking drivers stuck in the heat. One red faced, sweaty man made a V sign and shouted something Steph was pleased she couldn't make out.

She felt Hale tense and held her breath, desperate that he shouldn't get out to take issue with the aggressive man. He was off duty, after all. He didn't. As promised, a second yellow-jacketed man waved them into the entrance and checked their print-out again before they joined another long queue. At least they were inside the park.

'You couldn't do anything?'

'Not until the remains are removed and examined. There was no other evidence underneath or around the bones and we can't start looking at mispers until we have a rough idea of the approximate years we're dealing with. The team has the weekend off, apart from those on the rota for this place, which, now I come to think of it, is most of them.'

'Best behaviour then.'

The car crawled forward, past a field of fluorescent pink sheep dyed especially for the festival, ignoring the chaos and concentrating on nibbling grass. They parked the car, went through security, and with their wristbands fixed, headed for their yurt.

Inside the canvas tent, the sifted light felt cool but every-where was dominated by the powerful odour of soggy hay, giving Steph a sneezing fit. The yurt must have been put up after the storm, with the tarpaulin trapping the damp. Rolling it back they exposed the grass, hoping that it would dry out and stop the dank rotting smell impregnating their clothes.

Exhausted, and finding it hard to believe they had made it, they collapsed onto the double bed – a mattress with a pillow and duvet on the ground. Lying on their backs, eyes shut, they soaked in the jumble of sounds – music and laughter and hubbub.

'Perhaps we should stay here for a while and ...' Hale embraced her, gave her a long, passionate kiss while gently feeling through her blouse for her breast.

As she emerged breathless, she pushed him away a little. 'I can't believe we're actually here. Let's explore first. We do have the whole weekend.'

'Oh.'

'Let's get our stuff put away in that chest.' She pointed to a dark wooden chest that looked as if it had come off a pirate ship, its black metal hoops reaching over the lid to a hasp on the front with a reassuringly modern padlock.

Hale sighed, rolled onto the floor, and picked up his bag, which he stuffed into the chest. 'In the rush, you never told me what Caroline wanted.'

'Apparently, she and Margaret are involved in a production of some play – *Mother Courage*, I think it's called? They want me to be the stage manager.'

'But that's great! You'll do a great job.'

'No, I don't think so.'

'Rubbish! You must do it.'

She wriggled his bag around, squeezing hers on top, shut the lid, locked it, held out the key to him, then thought better of it and fixed it to her jeans belt.

'Just what you need, another one of Caroline's projects! It'll keep you out of trouble until the term starts again!'

'You may think I get long holidays, but I'm actually working in college for much of it.'

'But rehearsals will be in the early evenings and weekends, surely?'

'How do you know that?' Suspicious, Steph moved in, held his shoulders and eyeballed him. 'She's got to you, hasn't she?'

How dare they talk about her!

He raised his hands in defence. 'Only to get me to persuade you – honest.'

About to attack him, she froze when the phone in his pocket rang. Their eyes met and both sighed – he frowned. 'I'd better.'

Listening intently, he stepped outside, turning up wind from the music and putting his hand to his non-phone ear to block out the wall of sound. He took small steps in a circle until he'd found the best reception, then faced outwards, towards the mass of brightly coloured tents filling the next field. Surely it couldn't be yet another emergency that demanded his attention?

Apart from the occasional 'Umm' and 'I see', Hale added little to the conversation. Finishing the call, she heard him say, 'Right. Until then.'

Thrilled he'd escaped a call out, she hugged him from behind. 'You're not needed then?'

He turned to face her and kissed the tip of her nose. 'No, it'll wait.'

'What was it?'

'A fuss about nothing. Come on – let's get going. Don't want to miss Marcus Brigstocke.' He picked up their knapsack, scanned the inside of the yurt and closed the flap. 'Well, what are you waiting for?'

'Nothing. Let's go.'

His arm draped around her shoulders, they set off towards the pulsating wall of sound and the heaving mass of thousands of revellers.

He grinned at her and squeezed her shoulder. 'Great to be here. And for the whole weekend.'

She smiled back, but something had changed.

CHAPTER FIVE

SATURDAY 20TH JULY: 7.30PM

A HUSH FELL over the diners as Jessica wove her way through the tables, apparently unaware of the stir she was causing. But Naz noticed she took a longer route to their seats than the one indicated by the maître d'.

Although she ignored the nudges and eye movements the diners made towards her, Naz was relieved when they slipped into their seats at a secluded table inside the bay window and opened the enormous menus handed to them by the obsequious waiter.

Naz had chosen The Ugly Duck, a Michelin two-star restaurant on the Norwich side of Oakwood, hoping no one would recognise them – but how wrong was that! As a well-known solicitor in Oakwood, he was used to receiving waves and nods when he went out to local restaurants and pubs, but this was way off his patch. He had obviously underestimated Jessica Marlowe's fame and chided himself for his stupidity. Of course, he should have known that a West End actress and star of several Hollywood films would be recognised, but then he didn't go to the cinema much, did he?

'What are you going to have?' Jessica lowered her menu and smiled across at him. 'What a relief to see a bog-standard English menu again.'

'The lobster's good here and I thought I'd start with their carpaccio of beef – but maybe you'd prefer the tasting menu?' Naz hurriedly checked the notes at the bottom of the menu. Should he have booked the tasting menu before they arrived?

He was relieved when she replied, 'Beef followed by lobster sounds perfect. And I'll have real chips with it. I can always starve myself at the end of August.'

'I thought you LA stars only ate omelettes made with egg whites and then left most of that!'

'Well, I'm not in LA now and I'm starving.'

The impeccably dressed waiter in full evening suit, magically appeared at their table to take their order. He congratulated Naz on his choice of the 2016 Chateau Latour, which cost a second mortgage, but hey – he didn't often have a date with a celeb. 'Oh, and two glasses of this, please.' He pointed to an expensive champagne on the wine menu before handing it back to the waiter, who bowed even lower.

'Do you come here often?' Jessica handed her menu back to the waiter, who melted away. She laughed and pulled a face. 'I can't believe I've just said that!'

'I bring clients here occasionally. It's good to be out of Oakwood and I thought you might like to see how Suffolk cuisine has improved since you left.'

'I have been back a few times since 1989, you know, but just quick visits to see family between shoots or rehearsals. Enough about me. Now tell me about your life since that dreadful play. You never got married?'

Naz felt surprised when Jessica phoned out of the blue and suggested they meet for a catch-up dinner. He had suggested The Ugly Duck and their taxis drew up at the same time. After thirty years, he was amazed to see how young she looked, but didn't all the stars "have work done"?

Her long black hair was caught up in a complicated arrangement held together by a diamond slide, which glinted in the last rays of the sun, now dipping behind the trees. A few strands had come adrift to frame her face, which didn't have a single line, even around her eyes.

Her intense blue eyes, an unusual shade of turquoise, sparkled across at him and she had that mysterious, come to bed smile on her lips he'd seen in her adverts. Now admiring her designer midnight blue silk dress, with a crescent moon diamond brooch on her left shoulder, he felt flattered to be seen with her.

'No, never found the right woman. Got engaged at Oxford but we drifted apart ... you know.' He frowned – why had he felt the need to mention Oxford? 'And since then, I've been busy building up the practice.'

'So, I hear.'

'Really? What have you heard?'

The waiter returned with their glasses of champagne. Jessica lifted hers towards him. 'Cheers. Here's to rekindling old friendships.'

He clinked his glass against hers and sipped the champagne, appreciating the honey-nutty taste of the vintage he'd chosen.

'Umm! That's good.' She placed her glass on the table, running her fingers up its stem, and looked deep into his eyes. 'Now, what have I heard? That if anyone wants anything legal in East Anglia, you're the best person to see.'

'I don't believe that for a minute! And is that why you've contacted me after all this time? For legal advice?'

For a moment, a slight blush touched her cheeks, and she lowered her eyes. When she raised them, she gazed into his once again and reached across the table to touch his hand. 'No, not legal advice and let's be honest, Naz, what you're really asking is why have I contacted you after all this time?'

Now it was his turn to blush. 'Well, it did cross my mind.'

'As I said, I plan to stay here for at least six weeks and I need some stimulating company from a good-looking man while I'm in the back of beyond, doing my duty.'

'I see. And what duty's that?'

'You remember that dreadful play we did the last summer after our A Levels?' He nodded but waited for her to continue. 'Well, Beverly wants to do a reprise.'

'She's doing *A Midsummer Night's Dream* again?'

'No, it's *Mother Courage* this time with me in the title role, but at Covehithe again, and I shall be here until the end of August. I had a gap in my diary so said I would.'

'Right.' He took another sip of the champagne, pleased that he'd chosen it.

'Beverly's doing it to raise money for her pet charity, and you know how persuasive she can be. She pushed the guilt button about how my career was launched here, and wouldn't it be great PR to return to raise loads of money for the children's hospice?'

Their first course arrived and, after admiring the delicate arrangement on their plates, they gave it their full attention. Naz felt surprised but had to admit he felt flattered by Jessica's bold approach to him. He hadn't seen her for ... what? Thirty years? And now she appeared to be suggesting they get together for a few weeks – no strings. Well, he wasn't going to object to spending time with this beautiful woman and he'd be happy to go along for the ride.

He topped up her wineglass. 'It's good of you to come back for what is essentially Am-dram. Way out of your league, I'd have thought. You know, Beverly continued to do a play each year until she stopped being the Suffolk drama advisor and became a vicar.'

Jessica laughed loudly, attracting attention from the table to their left, where a couple appeared to be leaning in trying to overhear their conversation, so she lowered her voice. 'When I heard she'd become a vicar, I was amazed at first, then I thought, of course, she would. Typical. Suits her perfectly – the robes, the theatrical setting, the drama, the adoring audience.'

'Yes, the Reverend Beverly Elkin has an idiosyncratic style which is not to everyone's taste, but the drama continues. People go to watch her perform each Sunday and she does a lot for that hospice.'

They concentrated on savouring their beef carpaccio, which was excellent. She waited until he had finished and smiled up at him. 'That was good. Tell me, Naz, have you continued to act?' She gave him *that* look again, which made him feel ... well, deep down, rather good.

'Good heavens, no. I only did *The Dream* as I wanted to spend time with Lucy. Didn't have ambitions in the theatre like you thesps.'

The waiter removed their plates with an extravagant twirl to be replaced immediately by two others who served their main course. Once again, the plates resembled edible paintings, and Naz was pleased he'd chosen this place as Jessica appeared impressed by the service and the food.

They ate in silence as they cracked the shells and pronged the flesh out of their lobsters. Seeing Jessica had appeared to finish hers, leaving half the lobster and most of the chips, Naz gave up teasing the final shreds of flesh from the claws. 'Did you get that grant thing in the end?'

Jessica sighed. 'Yes, I won it. I can hardly believe the power Beverly had over us. We needed her reference and the Suffolk

Award to pay for drama school then. Now they do degrees and get grants like all universities and people like her don't decide who gets the money to study drama. How we all danced to her tune!'

Naz picked up the bitterness in her voice. 'It certainly made things rather nasty between you all, didn't it?'

'Looking back, it's surprising that we didn't all gang up on Beverly but instead turned on each other.'

'How do you mean?'

'Well, I was the last one standing then, and now I'm the only one left to tell Beverly her fortune!'

CHAPTER SIX

MONDAY 22ND JULY: 5.00PM

STEPH EMPTIED the final load of washing from the machine after their weekend at Latitude. It had been terrific fun, but she felt a little deflated – or was it disappointed – as Hale hadn't appeared to be there much of the time. Several times she'd had to repeat herself as his mind appeared to be elsewhere and he sank into patches of silence as if she wasn't there. All the time she'd known him, he'd never been moody and always shared his thoughts.

But then, he often detached himself in this way when he was in the middle of a complex or frustrating case, trying to work out his next steps. However, the body on the cliff had yet to be identified and he couldn't do much to move it on until the forensic report came through, so it wasn't that.

Then there was that weird phone call, which had lowered his mood dramatically. He kept saying he was fine, but she knew he wasn't. He was stressed about something and not ready to share it, and her imagination was working overtime. Maybe it was a health problem. How many months was it since he'd had his last medical? She jumped as the doorbell rang, interrupting her calculations.

As soon as the door opened, Caroline thrust a Union Jack cake tin into Steph's hands. 'Love from Margaret – another of her creations she said you must try.'

Steph followed her into the sitting room. 'This wouldn't be a bribe, by any chance?'

'A bribe? Whatever gave you that idea, darling? Anyway, you know you want to do it!'

Steph prised the lid open to reveal a magnificent coffee and walnut cake – her favourite. 'Thank you. We should declare this open – cup of tea?' Steph flicked the switch on the kettle and spooned tea into the pot.

'Please, darling. You know you'd make an excellent stage manager, and Beverly was thrilled when I told her you're on the case.' As Caroline grinned and plonked herself in an armchair, the flat door opened, and Hale appeared. What was he doing home early? He stopped and frowned, apparently puzzled to see Steph standing with her mouth open, holding a cake tin.

'What's in that tin?' Hale bounced across the room and peered into the tin. 'Coffee and walnut cake? Fantastic! I'm ravenous.' No kiss then.

He moved beside Caroline, grinned down at her and kissed her cheek. 'You've persuaded her?'

'No need. She was desperate to do it.' Caroline winked up at him.

'Stop ganging up on me, you two.' Steph poured the hot water into the pot.

'Anyway, really pleased to see you, Caroline. I was going to phone you.'

'Haven't been speeding again, honest.'

Steph handed Hale two plates loaded with generous slices

of cake – one for Caroline, the other for him. He returned to carry Steph's plate to the coffee table, then sat in the other armchair.

Caroline finished a mouthful of cake and delicately wiped her lips. 'Now Hale, how can I help you?'

'It's to do with the body – or should I say skeleton – we found on Friday on the cliff by Covehithe Church.'

'The one that was in Saturday's *Chronicle*? I brought it over in case you haven't seen it.'

'What? They're quick off the mark!' Hale sighed; his earlier smile replaced by a frown etched deep into his face. He had missed it while they were at Latitude, but she was surprised one of his team hadn't shown him. 'I wonder if we have a leak?'

'More like their new reporter with "o'er weening ambition". Always sniffing around after a story. Has his eye on Fleet Street or Wapping or wherever it is they produce the nationals nowadays.' Caroline pushed the paper towards him on the coffee table.

Hale took a photo out of his jacket pocket. 'Anyway, forensics suggests it's a female about seventeen to twenty and she's been buried in the earth, or rather the sand, about twenty-five to thirty years.'

Steph brought over a tray with the mugs of tea and placed it on the newspaper.

'Mind out!' He grabbed the paper from under the tray, placing it on the floor beside him.

'Golly – that was quick. It usually takes weeks to get that far.' Ignoring Hale's outburst and Caroline's puzzled expression, Steph passed round the mugs of tea.

'It would if we had to run a radiocarbon test, but we may not need to. Jenny put it through the hospital scanner and from the bone density has calculated her age. But the real find is

29

this.' Hale handed Caroline a photograph which Steph, leaning over, could see was of a fine, black chain, probably tarnished silver, about bracelet size with a delicate heart hanging from it.

Another shot revealed the back of the heart, where some faint engraved marks had been cleaned up, making them difficult to read until the final one, the letter C. Below it were some figures, again hard to make out – possibly a faint 9.88.

'We think, given the bone density, this could be an eighteenth birthday present to the girl from her parents or perhaps a boyfriend.'

'Wow! What luck! You could have been months trying to trace her without this.' Steph's voice conveyed the wonder of the find and hoped her enthusiasm would include her in the conversation.

'The problem is that we have gone through all the mispers – sorry, Caroline, missing persons – from September 1988 to 2000, the latest we think the body could have been buried and can't find anyone with the surname beginning with C or with a birth date around 1970. Nothing on file locally or the national missing persons' database. Surely someone would have missed her? Parents? Boyfriend?'

'You'd have thought so.' Caroline handed the photo over to Steph.

'Any chance of cleaning up the other initials or the full date?' Steph squinted at the picture of the back of the heart, turning it to the light, before handing it back to Hale, who appeared not to have heard her.

'I wondered if any of your students disappeared around that time. You and Margaret were working at the college then? If any girls had disappeared around 1988, you'd have noticed, wouldn't you?'

Caroline frowned. 'The answer is yes, and probably. But I

can't recall anyone disappearing – although in a college of sixteen hundred, I may not have been involved if she wasn't in my tutor group or didn't take art or music. Sometimes students disappear because their parents re-locate, or they drop out.'

'I presume if she was in education locally, she would have been at the college? There aren't any school sixth forms around here, are there?'

'Maintained schools locally don't have sixth forms – they all come to the college at sixteen, but independent schools do in Norwich, Ipswich and – oh yes – and Southwold. She could have been in one of them.'

'I can check the college records if that would help.' Steph offered, bringing over the teapot for top-ups.

'Thanks. I can send Johnson round to the independents.'

'Even though it's the summer holidays, there should be someone in the office.' Steph contributed. Hale folded the photo and replaced it in his pocket.

Caroline smiled at her. 'You'd know all about that! And don't forget, a large proportion of the sixteen to eighteen-year-olds weren't in education then. She could have been working.' Caroline finished her cake.

Steph returned to the kitchen area to make another pot of tea.

Hale sighed. 'You're right – I hope our luck holds and we find a local eighteen-year-old who disappeared, but why did no one report her missing?'

CHAPTER SEVEN

MONDAY 22ND JULY: 6.00PM

The Oakwood Chronicle – Saturday 20th July 2019

Storm Lena Unearths Body – Joe Denny

Storm Lena, the most powerful storm to hit East Anglia for over ten years, caused chaos on Thursday across Suffolk and Norfolk, even unearthing a body on the Suffolk coast.

A serious incident was declared across Suffolk when Storm Lena flooded the A12 at Yoxford and Woodbridge and at several points along the A14, creating a two-metre-deep ford in the Woolpit stretch.

Both major roads remain closed, along with the Orwell Bridge, causing gridlock around Ipswich. Countless B roads were also impassable and red flood warnings remain in place all along the coast.

Abandoned cars on the flooded roads made it difficult for emer-

gency vehicles to rescue families from their homes, many from their upstairs windows or their roofs.

Shop keepers in Lowestoft town centre attempted to keep the waters at bay with sandbags, but the water rose too high and too quickly for many of them to save their stock. The flood reached the height of the platforms at the railway station, and there will be no trains to Norwich and Ipswich for several days.

Students and teachers were stranded at Sir Thomas Mills School in Framingham, and they only escaped late last night when local farmers brought in their tractors and trailers to rescue them.

Southwold Lifeboat Station recorded winds of 67mph at 6.00pm as the River Blyth broke its banks and flooded 18 houses in Walberswick.

"This is the first time it's been this bad here since the great storm of November 2007." Chris Woods (47), the landlord of The Bell, wearing fishing waders, struggled to save his stock. "There was no warning from the weather forecasters neither. We won't be open again for months, not until this foul-smelling mud is gone."

Further along the coast in Hemsby, Norfolk, the authorities evacuated five houses when the coast road disappeared as another three metres of cliff were eroded in the storm. It is expected that Great Yarmouth Council will serve demolition notices on the houses which will make a record number of twelve demolished this year.

"I was told my house would go over the cliff eventually, but not

until at least 2050, which would've been long enough to see me out. Now I'm homeless." A shocked David Simpson (71) of the road known as The Marrams, Hemsby, stood staring at his house, teetering on the edge of the cliff. "Anyone who says this global warming isn't happening is cracked!"

On Friday morning, while walking her dog on Covehithe beach, Sue Hewitt (53) of Church Farm, Covehithe came across a shocking sight – parts of a skeleton hanging over the top of the cliff. The high winds, driving rain and the unusually high tide had undermined the sandstone cliffs and caused a large section to collapse onto the beach, exposing the remains, which must have been buried in the field at the top of the cliff.

"I looked up and couldn't believe it. A skull and arm bones were hanging over the top of the cliff. It looked more like a horror film than a peaceful walk. It must have come from the graveyard." Mrs Hewitt contacted the local police, who sealed off the area while a forensic team was recovering the body for examination. She commented, "I told the police they'll need to dig up all those bodies in that graveyard or we'll be hit by falling skeletons every time there's a storm."

A source close to the local police force believes that someone buried the body in the field approximately 40 years ago, and the erosion of the coastline has now exposed it. Asked if it could have come from the graveyard beside Covehithe Church, the police source believed it hadn't and the find could lead to an investigation of a suspicious death.

The Chronicle's meteorologist says he's surprised by the ferocity of the storm and the damage it caused, but warned us with

*climate change and global warming, storms like Lena will be
more frequent and not limited to the winter months.*

*If you were stranded by the storm in your workplace or school,
experienced damage to your property or have any information
about the remains at Covehithe, send your comments and photos
to J.Denny@OakwoodChronincle.co.uk*

———

A FURIOUS HALE threw the newspaper on the table where it
skidded onto the floor. Derek dashed across to snatch it, but
Steph got there before him and started to read it. Before she'd
got very far, Hale grabbed it out of her hand and pointed to the
photograph beneath the fold with the caption *Remains found
at Covehithe.*

'How did they get that photo? That's what I want to know,
and how did he get his information?'

'He must have been contacted by this Hewitt woman at
the same time as she rang the police.' Steph took the paper
back and looked at the photo, which showed a skull and the
arm bones hanging over the edge of the cliff. 'Gruesome! And
you're right, it must have been before your team arrived as
there's no sign of anyone else up there.' Steph continued to
read the article. 'Have you seen this last line?'

'Make my day. What does it say?' Hale threw himself in
his usual armchair.

'He's asking for information from anyone who knows about
the remains.' She ran her finger along the line of print and held
it out to him. 'See? There.'

'He's what! Who does he think he is – Poirot? That's the
trouble with so many TV detectives, everyone thinks they can
join in.' Hale sighed and rubbed his temple as if trying to ease a

headache. Derek rested his head on Hale's thigh, waiting for attention, but was promptly shoved out of the way. 'That's all we need. Loads of amateur detectives tramping all over the scene to solve something we have yet to determine was unexplained.'

'I'm sure—'

'What a total prat! Caroline's right. He's a young, ambitious journalist desperate for a sensational story. And if I find out who his "police source" is, I'll flay him or her alive.'

Steph handed the exploding Hale an open bottle of lager and sat opposite him. He gulped a few mouthfuls and sighed again. 'Now I'll have to spend time finding out how he got this photo and the information and shut him down before he does any more damage.'

Steph waited until he'd finished the bottle, then fetched him another one. It was unusual to see him in this state, whatever the provocation. All the time she'd worked and lived with Hale he'd been well known for his calm, controlled approach, however difficult the situation. He'd always said that losing it didn't help anyone and anyway, was this newspaper report really that bad?

Surely, he'd had to handle worse leaks to the press, and it wasn't a wise move to upset journalists. In the past, he'd made sure he'd worked alongside them, keeping them informed – giving them enough for their story but ensuring they didn't interfere with his investigations. The diplomatic balance he'd managed to achieve was admirable. Now it sounded as if he was going to blow it.

'Maybe sleep on it, eh?'

'You think I can sleep after this – this interference? No, I'll be off to see him first thing tomorrow and have a few words with his editor.'

'Who has changed, by the way. It could be this new

woman – Hilary something, I think – has been putting pressure on him. Local papers are having such a struggle to sell copies with all the news online – she's probably trying to keep the paper from a slow death.'

'They'll wish for a speedier death when I get hold of the two of them.'

It was best to move off this subject as soon as possible and try to restore the calm. 'Now, what about supper? I've got some fresh salmon from the fish hut in the harbour – salmon with salad?'

Hale frowned. She waited. Did it really need that much thought? He hauled himself up and out of the armchair. 'No, you're all right. I seem to have lost my appetite. I think I'll have an early night.' He walked towards the bedroom, turning as he reached the door. 'Keep the TV down low, please.'

No chance of her following him then. 'Don't worry, I was going to continue reading my book club book – we have a meeting next week.'

Hale made a 'Humph' sound, walked into the bedroom, shutting the door with a loud click. She sat in the sudden silence, her stomach churning.

CHAPTER EIGHT

FRIDAY 26TH JULY: 5.00PM

MOTHER COURAGE WOULD BE STAGED inside the ruins of Covehithe church, but the first few weeks of rehearsals would be held in Oakwood Church Hall. This was the first time Steph had been inside the Victorian hall which resembled so many others built in the same period.

A well-worn grey wooden floor, it may once have been oak, led up to a stage mottled with a mass of chips showing through layers of brown, black and beige paint from previous attempts to smarten it up and one dusty curtain, originally dark red now a grimy pink, dangled from a broken cord. The windows didn't need curtains as the grime smeared over them created an eerie light when the sun tried to shine through them. All surfaces felt dusty and a damp, rotting wood smell wafted through the air each time someone opened the door. Steph had the urge to wash her hands and to avoid touching anything.

Steph gazed at the crowd milling around the hall, greeting each other, chatting or laughing. Having read the play, she knew it had an unusually large cast of thirty-eight and calculated that at least ten of the people there were backstage staff.

She recognised many of the group, who ranged in age from sixth formers to a huddle of friends aged about sixty-five. It was certainly going to be a real community production.

Beverly, wearing her dog collar, stood on the floor in front of the stage, her voice floating effortlessly over the huddles of chatting actors and backstage staff. 'Welcome everyone! Now, please bring a chair from the stacks at the back and come and sit up here in a circle.' Steph obeyed and grabbed a chair, at least they looked clean.

At last, after much dragging of chairs and re-arranging them from a three-sided rectangle into a circle, everyone was sitting, waiting for a smiling Beverly to begin. 'Welcome everyone to—'

The door slammed at the back of the hall, and all heads turned to see who was late. Jessica Marlowe posed, as if waiting for applause, then sashayed confidently across the silent rehearsal hall to greet Beverly with an extravagant cry of joy. 'Darling! Mwa! Mwa!'

Overawed, the cast appeared shocked by the arrival of this Hollywood film star. They knew she was coming to join them, but the reality of seeing her in the flesh was overwhelming and they couldn't take their eyes off her – several sat open mouthed, gawping at her.

The double air kiss created sufficient time for everyone to appreciate Jessica's elegant figure and to show off her perfectly groomed curtain of black hair, which moved just as it did in the shampoo advert. Even dressed casually, in jeans and a large fluffy ivory pullover – cashmere probably – she looked amazing. Steph estimated Jessica's rehearsal clothes cost more than her entire wardrobe.

Jessica's extravagant turn allowed her to scan the group of actors and techies and give them a chance to admire her. The awed silence of the star-struck cast hadn't inhibited her in the least but pushed her performance up a notch. Everything Jessica did appeared to be designed to keep her at the centre of attention and she moved in a series of snapshot poses, just in case someone was grabbing a photo with their phone. She threw up her arms when she recognised Caroline, sitting beside Steph.

'Caroline! Darling! How wonderful! You haven't changed at all.'

She thrust herself at Caroline, enveloping her in an enormous hug, topped with the ritual air kisses. The boy sitting next to Caroline blushed as he was bestowed with a perfectly bleached white smile, got the message and went to the back of the hall to collect another chair so Jessica could sit beside Caroline.

'Darling, we must catch up after this rehearsal. I want to hear all your news. You look sensational – you must have a picture in your loft. I mean—'

The entire room focused on this exchange as they soaked in the lyrical voice of Jessica Marlowe in their hall, in their lives, in this play. Even Steph, sitting close to her, was overwhelmed by a compulsion to fix her eyes on this great Oakwood legend.

Beverly cleared her throat and smiled across at Jessica, who smiled back at her, bowed her head in apology and flicked her hand towards her as if granting Beverly permission to speak. 'Sorry, darling. Do carry on.'

Steph smothered a smile as she observed the power play between the two women. Until that moment, Beverly had been the queen bee, now she had a rival.

'As I was saying, everyone ...' Beverly paused until she made sure that all heads had turned in her direction and away from the star. 'Welcome to this first rehearsal of *Mother Courage and her Children* written by Bertolt Brecht in 1939. It is set in the thirty years' war in the early seventeenth century, which left Europe devastated.'

Beverly paused to send a beaming smile across to Jessica. 'We are privileged and thrilled that Jessica Marlowe, one of my most successful drama students, now a West End star and the toast of Hollywood, has returned to her roots to play the lead role in my play.'

Beverly made an extravagant sweeping movement with her hand and arm, welcoming Jessica to the group, who stood up and bowed her head, acknowledging the thunderous applause and whoops of delight. Lowering her head further, Jessica brought her hands together in the namaste gesture then placed her right hand on her heart as she humbly appreciated their adulation.

At last, holding up her hand, Beverly indicated the star worship was over, and they should listen to her again. Jessica resumed her seat with the grace of a dancer. 'Mother Courage, although a peasant, is an intelligent, wily, successful business-woman who survives through trading goods from her cart.'

Beverly scanned her audience, evidently ensuring she had their full attention. 'We see her rise to affluence and her decline to poverty as her three children, one by one, are taken by the war. Yet she battles on as the eternal pragmatist or black marketeer, depending on your point of view.'

'You will see as we rehearse that I intend to create the horror, the brutality of war, and its terrible impact on all those who are forced to live through it. The short scenes will be punctuated by the evocative music of Duke Special, under the direction of our own Margaret Durrant.'

Steph felt a dig in her ribs as Caroline grinned at the deafening applause and catcalls that met this mention of her partner. Margaret sat in a corner, surrounded by her small band of musicians, apparently trying to ignore the applause, but as it went on, she smiled and raised her hand in acknowledgement.

Jessica had remained silent throughout Beverly's impressive speech, which left her audience enthralled. It felt good to be part of something so exciting, as Beverly stressed how each one of them was vital, however large or small their role, and how the next few weeks would be hard work but worth it.

'Right, enough waffle. Let's get to work. Actors, stay where you are for our first read through. Technical team, you will work under Steph Grant, our stage manager. Please stand and give everyone a wave, Steph. She will now take you to the back of the hall and organise your work schedule.'

Steph was horrified. Work schedule? What on earth was that?

CHAPTER NINE

FRIDAY 26TH JULY: 5.20PM

Caroline grabbed Steph's arm, hissing in her ear as she propelled her to the wall which had received Beverly's imperious hand gesture. 'All you have to do is to get everyone to introduce themselves and to explain what they'll be doing. I'll draw a plan of the arena while you're doing the intros, which you can show them, then tell them to give you a description of how they will organise their area by the next rehearsal.'

'Why ever did I agree to this?'

'Oh, come on, you'll be fine. I'll help.'

Caroline's script worked and Steph appeared to get away with it. No one walked out or rolled their eyes, and the members of her newly acquired team left the hall with their jobs well-defined. Not that difficult, after all.

Steph was relieved. 'Thank you so much for your help, Caroline. I couldn't have done it without you.'

'Of course you could, darling. How's Hale, by the way? He seemed rather grumpy last time I saw him – so not Hale.'

'Interesting you should notice it too. He was upset by the article you mentioned – you know, about finding the body on the cliff. He appears to have declared war on the young reporter and his editor. Came home in a dreadful mood saying if they interfered with his investigation again, he'd charge them with perverting the course of justice.'

'That doesn't sound like him – mid-life crisis?'

'I don't know I—' Raised voices from the actors' circle made them turn to see the cause of the row between Jessica and Beverly that was getting louder with each exchange.

'Yes, I know only too well, you're a professional—'

'And directed by Peter Hall, Trevor Nunn and Scorsese – to mention but a few. I think I know a little of what I'm talking about!' Jessica emphasised the names, pausing after each one and rising to a dramatic crescendo on the third.

'But this is an amateur cast, and they find it helpful.'

'With respect, Beverly, we didn't even do your exercises in drama school – they're massively out of date, darling.' Jessica's breathy voice emphasised each word, lingering over the vowel sounds.

Steph noticed most members of the cast nodding their approval of Jessica's challenge. Beverly was losing the battle, and it appeared from her expression she knew it.

Pulling herself up to her full height and using her most authoritative tone, Beverly attempted to re-claim her position. 'If you feel that strongly, Jessica, then I suggest you miss the improvisation sessions and arrive in time for the breathing, voice and warm-up exercises. I assume even you professionals lower yourselves to our level and do those before a performance?'

Before Jessica could bite back, Caroline stepped forward. 'Will the techies be able to come to the warmup, please? It does bind us together as one team.'

'Of course.' Beverly beamed at Caroline, turned her back on the scowling Jessica who was frantically searching in her bag for something, and addressed the group. 'An excellent read through of the first scenes, thank you, all of you. Please put these rehearsal times in your diaries.' She bent down to pick up a blue plastic folder and handed the printed schedules to the actor either side of her to be passed around the group. 'Scene Five here tomorrow, starting at five – five thirty for those who would prefer to skip the exercises.'

Jessica, head held high, slung her bag over her shoulder, threw her photo smile to everyone in the room and glided out of the hall to an awed silence. As soon as the door clicked shut, an excited chattering filled the hall as the actors grabbed their bags and walked towards the door, only to have Beverly shout over the babble. 'Sorry – please, will you stack your chairs against the back wall?'

The actors obediently turned around to collect and carry their chairs as instructed, punctuating it with 'Thanks Beverly'. When the dust they had churned up had settled, the hall was clear – apart from a single chair.

Beverly frowned. 'I suppose she's used to everyone running around after her. Well, if she thinks I'm going to, she's got another think coming!'

Caroline picked up the chair. 'I'm sure she'll be fine. We had a lovely group of backstage staff, didn't we, Steph?' Caroline nudged Steph with her eyes.

'Yes, everyone knows what they're doing, and I'll send you a list of props that you might have or ask the cast to bring in.' Steph hoped she sounded in charge.

'And I've found someone to make Mother Courage's cart, and I'll paint it. I think it will be brilliant.' Caroline added.

'Thank you, darling.' Beverly pushed her script and notebook into her large leather satchel and walked towards the door. Steph grinned at Caroline, who had definitely been out darlinged in this company!

Beverly held the door open and took out a large iron key. 'And great news! Rahman Solicitors will sponsor us for all the production costs, which means one hundred percent of the ticket sales will go to the children's hospice.'

'I've worked with Naz Rahman.' Steph spoke to Caroline, but Beverly frowned at her. 'Have you? When?'

'When I was a police officer, he was often the duty solicitor. And very impressive too.'

'You must remember him, Caroline, in the same year as Jessica?' Beverly locked the door.

Caroline nodded. 'He was a lovely boy. I'd forgotten he was in *The Dream*.'

Beverly dropped the antique key in her bag. 'Yes, he was rather forgettable.'

Caroline rolled her eyes at Steph, who bit her lip to stop giggling.

Beverly leaned towards Caroline, and making sure no one else was around, whispered. 'Oh darling, I hope I haven't made the most enormous mistake of inviting Jessica Marlowe to work with us again. She is so opinionated.'

'Well—'

'If she shows me up again in front of everyone, I shall do something I'll be sorry for!'

CHAPTER TEN

FRIDAY 26TH JULY: 7.30PM

'You've got a visitor, Naz. Shall I show her in?'

'Please, Hazel. Good heavens! Look at the time, you must get off home.'

Naz closed the file he had been reading, added it to the pile in his in-tray and stood, ready to greet Jessica. The three evenings he'd spent with her over the last week had made him the happiest he'd felt for ages, and last night, she didn't go back to her hotel.

Jessica flew across the room, threw her arms around his neck, and gave him a lingering kiss. Over her shoulder, he spotted Hazel's amazed expression and knew it would be around the office first thing on Monday – if not before.

'Let's get out of here. I thought we'd go to The Rialto, that new place off the High Street. We can walk from here.' Naz leaned over his antique mahogany desk to pull his jacket off the back of his chair.

'Sounds good to me.' Jessica reached out her hand to him.

They walked hand-in hand past a gawping Hazel, out onto the High Street, quieter now the shops had shut, towards the new restaurant in Church Street. Naz admired the handsome couple reflected at him in the supermarket window, out for a Friday evening.

In his business suit with uniform white shirt and college tie, he made a good match for Jessica, in her stylish ivory pullover and tight jeans – her clothes always understated and in excellent taste. Flattered to be with seen with her, he noticed several people recognising her signature shiny black hair swinging below her shoulders as the breeze caught it. He hadn't felt so content and alive in a relationship for years.

As soon as the thought entered his head, he banished it. She had made it clear he was the man she had chosen for a few weeks' fun before returning to her life in London or LA. No, he must be realistic and stop the romantic fantasising.

'Rather classy for Oakwood, isn't it?' Jessica was right. The pale grey and white striped blind, which shaded the outside tables surrounded by pots of bay trees sculpted into tiny pyramids, could have been lifted from a smart London street. Oakwood was certainly improving!

Inside, the upmarket elegance of The Rialto continued. The gleaming pale wood floor, the ivory tablecloths and the light brown cane chairs created an authentic reminder of his last visit to Venice.

As Naz smiled at her across the table, ignoring the now familiar nudges of other diners and sipping Aperol spritzers, a holiday mood enveloped him, but he noticed Jessica was irritated. 'Anything wrong?'

'No, sorry ...' She finished her drink, plonking the glass on the table. 'It's that woman. Already she's driving me mad.'

'But it was only the first rehearsal today?'

Jessica thrust out her empty glass to a passing waiter. 'Another for you?'

Naz nodded, and the waiter collected his glass too. 'What happened?'

'You'd think after all I've achieved; she'd have the grace to listen to me. She expects me to do those silly exercises she forced us to do when we are at college – you must remember them?'

'How could I forget the night we spent in Henham Wood? We all got soaked to the skin in the torrential rain pretending we were in Greece.' Naz closed his eyes and pictured the group of miserable young actors huddled around a pathetic campfire.

'She wouldn't even let us have tents. "You need to experience a night in the woods as the young lovers did to develop your emotional memory – to make your performance authentic. In *A Midsummer Night's Dream* they slept on the forest floor, the tree branches were their tent." – I can hear her now.'

Naz laughed at her perfect imitation of Beverly.

'All we had were sleeping bags and after an hour they were soaked.' Naz shuddered at the memory. 'But the amazing thing was, we did what she told us – didn't even question it.'

'I bet kids now wouldn't put up with her whims.' Jessica threw an imperious look at the waiter, who was chatting to a pretty waitress instead of picking up the tray with their drinks. He caught her glare, lowered his head and moved towards her at speed.

Naz enjoyed watching this performance he'd never dare create. 'But you lot would've done anything to get that award – and she knew it.'

The waiter placed their drinks before them on the table and they gave their order for the risottos for which the restaurant was famed, even after three weeks.

'Cheers!' Naz held up his glass, and she chinked hers to it.

'If it hadn't been for that bottle of brandy, we'd have died from exposure.'

'That sexy French guy brought it – you remember – he played Puck. What was his name?'

'Hugo.' Naz frowned as he recalled the searing hate he'd felt for him at the time.

'He worked his way through all the girls, didn't he? He was so rude and left the last night party early – missed that scary seance run by – now what was her name?'

'The girl who played Titania – can't remember her name.' Naz recalled the acute misery he'd felt at the so-called celebration.

'Kate, that was it. Bossy Kate. That's right, Hugo left early to whisk Lucy off to France—' She gasped. 'Oh sorry, Naz.'

Naz took a large gulp of his drink. 'Don't worry. Got over it years ago. Hugo really turned on the French charm for her, didn't he?'

Jessica smiled. 'Who could resist that deep, deep gallic voice?' Her sexy French accent penetrated the sudden silence in the room, causing the diners at the two nearest tables to stare at her once more. Jessica smiled in apology. 'But I was surprised that Lucy fell for it. I thought she was mad leaving you for him. He was so ... so obvious. Although if she'd stayed, I'm sure she would have got the award and what would have happened to me then?' She touched his hand, her head on one side, her voice sympathetic. 'You must have been really upset when she walked out like that. You were incredibly close.'

'At the time I was devastated – first love and all that – but water under the bridge. I hope she's a happy Madame living with her French clown.'

Jessica laughed 'Of course, he went to the famous French clown drama school, didn't he? We were all in awe of him – he was so cool and sophisticated with his Gauloises and brandy.'

'And Beverly couldn't get enough of him, could she?' Naz was relieved the serious note had dissolved.

Jessica sat up straight and assumed her Beverly voice. 'I can hear her now – "The most exquisite Puck I've ever had!"' The couple on the table beside them swung around at her powerful stage voice.

'She didn't! She must have been twice his age!'

Jessica leaned forward, aware that others might be listening. 'My dear, the way she fawned over him was enough to make us change our minds about the direction she faced.'

'Sorry?'

'Come on! Surely, you've heard the rumours?'

Naz frowned. 'Rubbish. She almost got married a few years ago to another man of the cloth.'

'Makes my point – *almost*.'

The waiter returned with a bottle of Barolo, which he poured for them, and their risottos. After savouring the first mouthful, Naz was convinced the restaurant deserved its excellent reputation. Even Jessica tucked in.

Their conversation had transported Naz to those last few months before he'd left for university and a period in his life he'd forgotten about, or perhaps repressed. His deep mourning of Lucy's betrayal had pushed him into a painful depression, which had lifted eventually when replaced by the distraction of moving to Oxford and the novelty of student life.

He glanced at Jessica, enthusiastically eating a few forkfuls, before delicately lifting her napkin to blot her lips. Was she performing for him or the other tables? He rather liked the stir she caused and the reflection on him as her chosen escort, but would he tire of her perfect performance?

She hadn't always been so perfect, had she? She hadn't mentioned that she'd quit early on that appalling night in the woods after dramatically storming off, wanting the "authentic experience" to be alone in the dark wood. They'd let her go, but when she hadn't come back, they'd searched for her for at least an hour in the pouring rain before giving up and collapsing in a drunken heap.

Only in the morning, when a furious Beverly came to collect them, did they realise Jessica had run away and spent the night in the dry at Beverly's house, claiming they'd bullied her. He recalled how he had loathed her for her deceitful behaviour and her determination to come out on top, whatever the cost.

Marcus, the talented lighting technician also a contender for the Suffolk Drama Award, was convinced she'd done it to suck up to Beverly and to increase her chances of winning. No one spoke to her much after that, and even the sexy Hugo ignored her.

The eighteen-year-old Naz was well below her league, but now here he was. Was he star struck, flattered, or had she really changed? He glanced at her plate, her meal almost half eaten this time.

She met his eyes. 'You're miles away, Naz. Everything all right?'

'Yes, fine. This place is good, isn't it?'

Jessica reached across the table and placed her hand on his. 'Yes, but it's the company that makes it special for me. Thank you for saving me.'

'Saving you from what?'

'The most miserable few weeks of my professional life.'

'Sorry?'

'Making it possible to survive working with that witch in this dump – not this restaurant – but Oakwood. Do you know, I'm sure some of the people here are wearing the same clothes they were when I left!'

Naz frowned at her change of mood. 'But I thought you said it would be good PR.'

'Oh, it will certainly be that. It's just I don't know how I'll get through the next few weeks without killing her.'

'That sounds a little dramatic.'

'Ignore me, Naz. But if she continues to treat me as she did all those years ago, she's going to be in for a shock. I know her little secret. I know where the bodies are buried, and she'd better watch her step!'

CHAPTER ELEVEN

MONDAY 29TH JULY: 7.00PM

STEPH HAD FINISHED REHEARSAL EARLY, leaving Beverly to work on some new movement ideas with the soldiers. Caroline thought it was safe for them to go as Jessica had already left, so there was no danger of a row turning nasty. She'd dashed off, collected Derek and was planning to go for a walk on Southwold beach when her phone rang. It was Hale.

'No, finished early and collected Derek. Why? ... That would be great. Shall I pick you up on the way? Ten minutes and I'll be there.'

It was a beautiful, sunny evening, and a walk was just what she needed to clear her head and now she had the bonus of Hale. Perhaps a walk would do them both good. The dark smudges under his eyes and his perpetual frown had been worrying her, and he still hadn't told her what was wrong. Whenever she got close to asking, he changed the subject, buried his head in work or went to the loo. Perhaps this walk would give her the opportunity to find out what was bothering him.

When she arrived, Hale was standing outside the police

station, glaring at someone walking away up the High Street. He smiled when he saw her, climbed into the car, leaned over and kissed her. 'Thanks. Great timing. I need a walk after today, I can tell you.'

She drove off towards Southwold, aware that he was scrolling through his phone. 'Really? Not a good one?'

'The worst. No, that's not true, just frustrating. You know, one of those days where however hard you work, you seem to go backwards.'

'I know that feeling, all right. But for once, peace broke out at the rehearsal. Beverly and Jessica seem to have called a truce, and we got through the scene early.'

Steph decided not to push any further while they were driving but to wait until they were walking and anyway, he was concentrating on messaging someone on What's App, and they drove the rest of the way in silence.

As usual, they parked in the harbour car park and as soon as they opened the hatchback, Derek dashed off through the dunes. Steph handed Hale the ball thrower and a tennis ball, which he catapulted toward the sea, much to Derek's delight. The beach was deserted, and the tide was going out, giving them some firm sand to walk on. For once, Hale grinned as he repeatedly chucked the ball into the sea for Derek to retrieve.

They stood on the edge of the foam, laughing as he crashed through the waves after the ball and swam back, his tail heli-coptering with joy. At last, Derek picked up the ball and ran off with it rather than dropping it at Hale's feet – a sure sign he was getting tired.

Amazed at this miracle, they walked behind him towards the town huddled around the famous lighthouse, which bizarrely was on land and worked all day. Now, against the darkening sky, the flashing light was bright and cut through the clouds. The moment had come.

'Is everything all right?' Steph bent down to pick up a hag stone – a pure white stone with a hole in the middle to add to her collection hung on a string outside their back door.

'Fine. Well, apart from making zero progress identifying this body from the cliff.'

'Really?'

'We know it's female, late teens or early twenties, and has been there since the late nineteen eighties. If we believe the date on the charm – and we are assuming it was for her eighteenth birthday – could well have been her twenty-first – she would have been born in 1970 or 1967.'

'Right.' Steph sneaked a sideways glance at him. He was stressed – his jaw fixed and the little vein in his temple stood out. 'Well, that narrows it down.'

'You'd think so, wouldn't you? No female in that age range reported as missing around that time. And I've had the DNA tests back today – no luck, I'm afraid – no match anywhere.'

'Could she be foreign? Trafficked?'

'Unlikely from the DNA. She had excellent teeth with no dental work, which gives us another dead end. But what they have found is a fracture on the back of her skull. She was murdered, which has upped the game, and now I have the boss on my back demanding results.'

They reached the row of beach huts where Derek had to be put on his lead. 'Shall we go on, or turn back? We could always go to The Harbour for a beer.'

Hale sighed. 'Sorry, Not tonight. I want to go home, have a few glasses of wine, then an early night.'

'Come, Derek!' As Steph called out, Derek stopped digging a hole to bury the ball and his head jerked up, his ears alert. As they turned back towards the harbour, he dug out the ball and raced after them, claiming his usual position as leader.

Steph slipped her arm through Hale's, and they pushed

into the wind, squinting against the flying sand. The grey clouds had merged into a dark lead mass, and it felt as if it was about to rain again. 'Did Caroline get back to you about dropouts from the college?'

'Yes, she did, but nothing there.' Hale sighed and frowned. 'And Johnson spent ages trawling through all the local independent schools' data from thirty years ago. They also reported no missing girls.'

Steph picked up the ball Derek had dropped and put him on his lead, giving him a chance to dry out before jumping into the car. 'How frustrating!'

'You can say that again! Apart from that silver heart, we have sweet F.A. to go on and the pressure to get results has not been helped by that cocky little journalist.'

'Oh?'

'He's been sniffing around again. He disappeared when he saw me come out to meet you this evening. I haven't found out who he was waiting for, but when I do, they'll be skinned alive.'

CHAPTER TWELVE

As SOON AS she opened the door into the gloom of the church hall, Steph knew she'd walked into yet another row. The last few weeks had become more and more charged with the increasing tension between Beverly and Jessica.

She moved towards Caroline, who was painting strips of wood destined to become Mother Courage's cart, and whispered, 'What's going on?'

'The usual. Today it's about Brecht's intention in the final scenes. Getting way above me, darling. I'm only a simple painter, after all.'

Steph moved closer to the stage, where a small group of actors stood patiently observing the exchange between the two women. The tension felt like a solid wall.

Jessica, beautifully dressed in jeans and a grey linen shirt, swooshed her hair and posed with her hands on her hips, smirking at Beverly. 'And do tell me, Beverly, how exactly have you discovered Brecht's intention? Has he taken you out for a drink recently?'

Several of the actors, now an entranced audience, struggled

to stifle their sniggers at the battle, which was now a familiar part of each rehearsal, with many of them appearing to have sworn allegiance to Jessica.

'Don't be ridiculous, Jessica.'

'Well, stop talking about his intention then. He's dead. It's up to us to interpret what he's written. Anyway, even if he was alive and we could ask him, he probably wouldn't know what he meant when he wrote it. Believe me, I've worked with enough writers and should know!'

James, one of the soldiers stepped forward. 'Look, can you two have this fascinating discussion after rehearsal? We want to get on with the final scenes. Some of us have homes to go to.'

'Hear! Hear!' the Peasant's Wife shouted.

Irritated, Beverly turned away from Jessica, frowned and opened her script. 'Right, let's go from the start of Section 11, page 84, where you soldiers approach the cottage. Now, this time look more threatening and aggressive – you plan to kill them, not drop in for afternoon tea!'

Jessica, realising she wouldn't be on stage until Section 12, picked up her script from the floor and slumped noisily in the chair beside Steph.

'You see, she's done that deliberately! She said we'd do the scene between me and Peasant's Wife first, and I could go early. Now she's doing the longer one that leads up to it. Typical!'

Steph took out her notebook and script, ready to take down the props needed for the scene. 'Sorry, I must listen to this.' She opened her annotated copy of the script and tried to concentrate, nodding at Jessica's constant mumbling beside her.

'That woman always has to have the final say. A power trip. That's all this is. This scene will go on for about an hour and that's if she doesn't make a fuss. And then what? I only have a page of dialogue after that and anyway, Margaret isn't here for me to go through the song, is she?'

Caroline leaned over. 'Margaret said you're going to go through all the music on Saturday, after you've blocked all your moves.'

Jessica sighed. 'Sorry, Caroline, I'm not having a dig at Margaret, just frustrated at that woman. She keeps me hanging around needlessly. Anyone would think I was a student again, not a grownup.'

'Shame she doesn't behave like one, then!' Caroline whispered in Steph's ear.

Jessica put her head in her script and muttered to herself, apparently learning her lines. Steph swallowed her giggles hoping Jessica hadn't heard, while Caroline returned to her painting.

'Stop! Stop everyone!' Beverly pranced into the action and the First Soldier stepped back from attempting to kill the Peasant's Son. 'Steph, have you noted we need a spear and a knife here?'

'Yes, the spear's in the script. It's on the list, but not the knife.'

'Sorry, I've added the knife. I think the threat to the boy needs to be more intimate – you know, a throat sliced through rather than a distant stabbing.'

Beverly narrowed her eyes and stood back from the actors grouped around the kneeling boy awaiting death, his parents being held back by the Lieutenant. 'That stage picture isn't quite right. James, stand behind the boy not with your spear but with your knife about to slit his throat – yes, that's better – and parents grip on to each other terrified and further upstage—'

'Have you thought of moving them all downstage centre? Let me show you.' Jessica zoomed into the group of actors and, grasping their shoulders, manoeuvred them into a tighter shape closer to the front of the stage. Jessica's arrangement was so much more effective, highlighting the potential tragedy of the kneeling boy.

'What do you think?' Jessica turned to a red-faced Beverly, who said nothing.

Jessica directed her questioning gaze to Caroline, who took a deep breath. 'I think both positions have merit but, speaking as an artist, I see what you mean. Our attention, along with everyone on stage, is focussed only on the boy and really emphasises his danger.'

Was Beverly about to explode at Caroline? From the expressions on the soldiers' faces, they certainly thought so. A mumble from one of them broke the silence 'She's right, isn't she? She knows what she's doing – she's worked with De Niro.' Several murmurs suggested his fellows agreed with him.

Taking them all by surprise, Beverly smiled beatifically at Jessica and spoke calmly. 'You're right. That works so much better. Thank you, Jessica.'

She nodded, still smiling at Jessica, and turned to the actors. 'Soldiers, please go back to when you enter in front of the thatched cottage and go as far as this, then I can see how you get into your new positions.'

Jessica returned to her seat, evidently pleased that Beverly had accepted her suggestion. Caroline rolled her eyes, said nothing, and got on with her painting. The rehearsal continued with several false starts as Beverly worked on the actors' body language and voices to increase the threatening behaviour of the soldiers towards the peasant family.

Looking at the clock, Beverly held up her hand. 'OK everyone, time we finished. Thank you all of you, a good rehearsal. See you tomorrow, five-thirty sharp to finish Sections 11 and 12.'

The soldiers and peasant family gathered their bags and walked towards the door, laughing and arranging to go on to the pub for a drink. Beverly shoved her script in her bag and came over to Jessica.

'Jessica, that was so helpful. Thank you so much for your advice and I'm so sorry we didn't get as far as scene 12. We shall tomorrow. Good night both.' She waved at Caroline and Steph. 'Don't be here too long, will you? Just pull the door to when you leave. I'll pop by and lock it later.' With that, Beverly swung her bag over her shoulder and swept out of the hall. The door slammed behind her.

Jessica glared after her. 'See what I mean? She did that deliberately! By slowing down that scene, she made sure we'd never get to mine and wasted my whole evening.'

Caroline stood up from her painting and cleaned her hands on an old tea towel. 'Surely not, Jessica. She accepted your suggestion, and it took them some time to get it right.'

'But then she punished me by making me sit here all this time. I've had enough! If she continues to carry on like some – some power-crazed old woman, I'll walk out! I've got other offers, you know. If I thought she'd put me through this, I'd never have come to work with this – this amateur.'

She picked up her bag and appeared to be leaving but, after taking a step, swivelled round. 'What did she say? "That works better." Damn right it does! I know what I'm doing after all these years. When will she accept that I'm no longer eighteen?' She closed her eyes, taking several deep breaths, and appeared to be trying to lower her blood pressure. 'Sorry. I shouldn't go on, but she is *so* difficult. Have a good evening, Caroline, Steph. See you tomorrow.'

Jessica made one of her balletic turns and gracefully left the hall, ensuring that the door closed quietly behind her.

Caroline let out a deep sigh. 'Oh! What a drama!'

'Do they have to be at daggers drawn constantly? Why can't they simply get on with it?' Steph shoved her notebook and script in her bag.

'Darling, they are true thespians and are fighting for their creative space.'

'I'd say it was simpler than that. It's two women bitch fighting. We're lucky they haven't scratched each other's eyes out yet. But give them time. I have the most awful feeling this will not end well.'

CHAPTER THIRTEEN

WEDNESDAY 14TH AUGUST: MIDNIGHT

Naz found it difficult to concentrate after eleven o'clock, even with fizzy water rather than his usual whisky, but he had to finish working on his brief before he collapsed in front of some rubbish on the box to help him calm down before bed.

The court case the next day would be tricky, and he had to be on top of the mass of evidence to ensure the jury grasped his argument, which was pretty complex in this fraud case. Somehow, his client had acquired nine bank accounts. Naz found it a challenge managing his two and a tiny part of him admired his client for his financial juggling skills. The doorbell made him jump. What? Whoever was it at this time?

He opened the door to find Jessica leaning against the porch wall, grinning. Without a word, she fell into his arms, looking up at him, a pleading expression on her face.

'Naz, darling, save me from myself, I beg you.'

The amount of alcohol he breathed in overwhelmed him, and he stepped back a little.

'Oh, don't reject me, Naz!'

Holding her up, he guided her to the sofa in front of the hearth and helped her to stumble to it.

'May I get you anything, Jessica? Coffee? Water?'

Frowning in deep concentration, Jessica spent a long time apparently considering his offer before reaching out and grasping his hand. 'Coffee, darling. Suspect I need it – too many teensy little G&Ts.' She held up her finger and thumb showing a tiny space and attempted to peer at him through it. Groaning, she slumped back, closed her eyes, but opened them immediately, grabbing the sofa arm. 'Oops! Dizzy!'

Naz went out to the kitchen to make the coffees. Since Jessica had been back, she had become a regular visitor, latching on to him – was latching the right word? Over the last few weeks, she had spent most of her time at his cottage when not rehearsing. Despite being officially booked into The Crown, she said she preferred being with him and he had not objected.

He had to admit he found it flattering to walk into a restaurant or pub and have people recognise the film star and assume he must be someone special too. They had become close, but he wasn't kidding himself. At the end of August, she'd return to her life in Hollywood or London – he was a convenient distraction, a holiday romance.

Did he feel used? He asked himself that a lot, but decided he liked being with her. She made him laugh and was great fun to spend time with so he would enjoy the ride as long as it lasted. But he wasn't expecting her tonight and there was that unfinished brief waiting on the desk.

Jessica appeared to be asleep when he carried the tray back into the sitting room. Should he wake her? He left her coffee on the lamp table beside her, carried his cup over to the desk and got sucked back into the complicated mire of fraud.

A few minutes later, a murmur made him glance over to

the sofa and see Jessica was sipping her coffee. 'Thank you. Lovely coffee. Talk to me.'

Naz brought his cup over to the armchair to the right of the sofa and smiled at her. 'What would you like to talk about?'

'Don't know. The past?'

'What about it?'

A dribble of coffee worked its way down her chin, falling onto her ivory polo neck. Naz stood.

'Don't leave me, Naz.'

'I'll just get a cloth. You'll stain your pullover.'

'Don't bother. It's old.'

It looked new, cashmere probably, but he obeyed her and sat back down.

'I saw Jason tonight.'

'Jason?'

Jessica dumped the cup on its saucer but missed and it tipped over at an angle, dripping coffee onto his red Persian rug. Oh well, it was dark, and it wouldn't show. Frowning, she concentrated on fitting the cup back on the saucer. 'There!' Looking up, she examined him intensely. 'Jason, you know ... Jason!'

'Sorry—'

Jessica was becoming impatient. 'For fuck's sake, Naz. What's wrong with you? Jason Strong, Marcus Strong's nephew. You know, Marcus?'

'The Marcus who did the lighting in *The Dream* and crashed his bike?'

Jessica hiccupped. Naz hoped she wouldn't throw up. 'Yes, that Marcus.'

Marcus had been one of his best mates. He was a brilliant lighting technician, and it was thought he was the favourite for Beverly's drama award. Naz had helped him to hang the lights for the play and had been impressed by his vision and calm expertise.

His death on his motorbike had hit them all. At their age, they were still immortal and only old people died. They all crammed into St Mary's church for his funeral and several of his friends had given up their bikes and scooters after that.

Jessica held her breath, appearing to have defeated her hiccups. 'Jason's the mirror image of Marcus, isn't he? Just as he was ... was then.' She took a gulp of coffee, and another dribble joined the growing stain on her polo neck.

'Is he?'

'Thought I was talking to Marcus most of the evening – same voice, same smile ...'

'Oh? I've never met Jason.' Naz glanced at his watch, making sure Jessica couldn't see. That brief needed a lot of attention, and it was getting on.

'So tragic! Marcus died like James Dean ... So young ... So beautiful.' She drank some more coffee. 'And he kept wanting to talk about the crash ... asked if I knew anything.'

'And did you?'

Jessica shook her head. 'He's convinced it wasn't an accident ... thinks someone killed Marcus ... my beautiful Marcus.'

'But it was an accident, wasn't it?'

CHAPTER FOURTEEN

THURSDAY 15TH AUGUST: 12.30AM

'IT WAS AN ACCIDENT, WASN'T IT?' Naz repeated as he fielded the cup just in time as it toppled off its saucer. He should have given her a mug.

'But I haven't finished!'

'I'll get you a top-up, shall I?'

'Please, darling.'

When he returned with a replacement mug and more coffee, Jessica's eyes were full, and she was dabbing at her eyes with the sleeve of her pullover.

'Why so sad?' Naz handed her a tissue, and she blew her nose, dropping the tissue on the floor. He stopped himself from picking it up.

Jessica drank more coffee and narrowed her eyes as she examined him. 'This evening, I was back in that summer. We were all so happy then, weren't we?'

'Were we?'

'Life was ... yes, less complicated, and it was great doing *The Dream*. The perfectest time of life, wasn't it? Wish I could go back there now. Don't you?'

All Naz could recall was the constant stress of exams and how he questioned everything about himself. His face, his body, his brain – nothing seemed to be quite right, and all the others were so confident and so sure of themselves. And then there was Lucy ... he'd never got over Lucy.

'I loved Marcus ... I did ... I could love Jason in the same way.'

'But he's at least half your age!'

'So sad, the way Marcus went and died and left me. At least now, there is Jason.' Another large swallow of coffee and she'd finished it. Once again, Naz rescued the mug from being dropped on the floor.

He knew he had no right to be jealous or even to pry, but could it have been Jason she'd been seeing on those evenings where she'd been evasive about what she'd been doing? She must have seen him at least two or maybe three times recently.

She threw her arms out in a super dramatic gesture and yawned loudly. 'Need sleep now.'

'Good idea and I need to finish this brief.'

After several futile attempts trying to haul herself off the sofa, Naz stepped in, grasped her hands and pulled Jessica up to her feet, where she wobbled while she got her balance.

'And there was that Puck man – the sexy Frenchman – such a seductive voice.'

Naz guided her towards the bedroom.

'He was gorgeous and so ... so experienced.' She giggled and stroked his bottom. 'But he took Lucy to France, not me.' A sudden stop – she turned and grabbed his shoulders. 'Oh, Naz, I'm so sorry. You and she ... you must have been so upset.'

Naz tried to be gentle as he nudged her into the bedroom. He could do without all this digging up the past.

'But you are happy now, aren't you? You're happy with me, aren't you?'

'Of course, I am.'

She pulled him down beside her on the bed and leaned her head on his shoulder.

'Perhaps I should give up all the travelling ... going and coming ... and coming and going over the pond.' She waved her hands back and forth across them both, making him sway along with her. Please don't let her throw up here. Not in his bedroom.

Seizing his chin, she forced his face down towards hers and stared into his eyes. 'Perhaps I should stay here with you in this dinky little cottage and cook supper for you when you come home from work.'

Naz smiled down at her. 'You know that would drive you barking mad. Your life is on the stage or in front of a camera. Now let's get you ready for bed.'

'Ooh, that sounds fun, Nazzy darling!' The kiss she gave him was well off target and, as she slurped across his face, once again he turned away to breathe fresh air.

'But I could be happy living here with you and go to London on that little Noddy train. I could still act. Couldn't I?'

Naz wasn't sure. Was it the gin talking?

'We could have babies – we would make lovely babies together, Nazzy. Not too late.'

Once again, she grabbed his chin and tried to focus on his eyes. 'You do love me as much as Lucy, don't you?'

Not waiting for a reply, she slobbered over his cheek. 'Jason is so sweet, so sexy. Almost as good as Marcus. Marcus was good at ... you know! But you – you do love me, don't you, Naz? Lucy was a silly little tart – didn't deserve you – but I do, don't I?'

She kissed him again and stroked his thigh, moving her hand up his leg. He held her hand still and patted it.

'Lucy wasn't a good girl you know – I told you then someone was threatening me – you remember?'

'Yes, I do—'

'I know it was Lucy – she threatened me – hurt me. Pushed me off the stage in the dress rehearsal to stop me performing, but I did it anyway.'

'Come on – you can't know that.'

'I know it was her. Lucy wanted that award so bad she sent – what are they called? – poison pen letters, that's it – told lies about me to Beverly – told Marcus I slept with Hugo.'

'That was years ago. Time to move on and time you went to sleep.'

'No, you must listen. Lucy went to Paris with Hugo.'

'Yes, I know.' Why couldn't she stop rubbing it in? Naz tried to undo her arms which encircled him.

'It was my fault she went. Lucy hurt me so much. That's why I told her you were two-timing her and sleeping with Titania for months and months.'

'What?!'

Jessica started hiccupping again. 'Sorry. I didn't mean to hurt you, just her. That's why she went off with Hugo. I'm so sorry Nazzy. You do forgive me, darling ... don't you?'

Why had she thrust him back to that awful time? Was Jessica really to blame for the months of misery he'd endured after Lucy fled with Hugo? He'd never felt the same about anyone since.

Pushing her away, he tried to stand, but Jessica clung to him. 'Lucy was bad – she wanted that prize – knew I was the best – I deserved it, not her. I was the best, wasn't I?'

Naz glanced at his watch – he'd had enough of this. It would take at least another hour to finish the brief, and he was finding her rambling upsetting. Jessica grabbed his hand, squinting at his watch. 'What's time? Numbers moving.'

'Close to one o'clock and you should be asleep.'

She hung her arm around his shoulders and pulled him towards her. 'Soon be morning and another fucking awful day with that fucking stupid cow.'

Pulling his head round once again, Jessica stroked his face. 'Shh!' She placed her finger on his lips and glanced around the room to make sure no one was listening. 'A secret – I will tell you a secret.'

'What?'

'No, not yet. Not time yet. But it is a big secret, a very, very big secret.'

At last, Naz managed to undo her hands and helped her to lie back on the bed, but she sat up again, grasping his shoulders.

'Beverly's wicked ... so bad. I give her publicity for her crappy play. She's a basilisk – gives looks could kill. She wants me out of the way, I know she does. But you'll look after me. You'll stop her killing me, won't you, Naz?'

'She won't kill you. Now time for bed.' Naz helped her to lie on the bed, where she stayed this time.

'No, she can't kill me, can she, if I tell everyone her secret first!'

'What secret?'

No reply. She was out of it.

He pulled off Jessica's shoes, struggled to peel off her trousers and polo neck, then covered her with the duvet. Naz sighed, turned the light off and returned to his desk.

He stared at the page but couldn't concentrate. Pictures of Lucy pushed themselves into his head and the pain he had squashed deep down for decades had been dug up by Jessica's drunken ramblings. How did he feel about her? Confused was the answer. One moment Jessica was trying to re-live her past by seeing Jason, pretending he was Marcus, the next proposing a life with him. He must be realistic – he was just a way of filling in the time while she was here.

And what had she said about Lucy? If it was true, it was Jessica's fault he'd suffered. He hadn't been aware how raw Lucy's betrayal still made him feel, and it had all been Jessica's fault.

Underneath all that rambling, he was convinced she knew more than she was saying. Jessica knew some secret from the past and it appeared she'd come back to do something about it.

CHAPTER FIFTEEN

FRIDAY 16TH AUGUST: 6.00PM

STEPH WAS RELIEVED that at last, a week before the performances, the rehearsals moved from the hall to Covehithe; originally a large medieval church that was now a ruin.

Apparently, when the local population declined, the enormous building had been allowed to crumble after being replaced by a smaller thatched church built against the far west wall. The ruins had no roof but still retained the large perimeter of the walls, most of which supported empty window spaces. The largest and most dramatic wall was at the east end, facing the sea where the altar would have been.

Raked seating had been installed on three sides of the space for about two hundred people, and they were to perform *Mother Courage* on the flat grassy area in front of the east window. The weeds and brambles had already been scythed, and the rabbit holes in the acting area filled in.

Two scaffold towers carrying clusters of Fresnel lights had been erected on each side of the performance area, with a lighting bar stretched between them holding spotlights. Max, the lighting technician, had worked with Beverly from her days as drama advisor and, although he now needed Jason, a younger apprentice to help him climb up the ladders, his lighting designs were apparently legendary.

Max and Jason had been in the day before to construct the towers and the bar, hang the lights and to make sure the path from the car park in the farmyard opposite was well lit. All they had left to do during this rehearsal was to angle the lamps on the action from the two towers.

Beverly had decided that in line with Brecht's philosophy, the audience should see that the performers were actors, playing roles so they would be on stage all the time. She had arranged for straw bales to be brought in for them to sit on at the back of the action for the performances, but until then they would use blue plastic chairs, which looked bizarre against the natural flint walls.

Steph hoped moving out of the hall might dilute the animosity between Beverly and Jessica, which had become embarrassing as each woman pushed for control at every rehearsal. Beverly would organise some complex movement for a crowd scene, only to have Jessica make an alternative suggestion, moving the actors around as she explained her ideas, leaving the cast confused with no idea where they should go.

The arguments were even worse when it came to Jessica's performance. Beverly wanted a low key, flat delivery, while Jessica went all out for the drama queen version. The cast was now used to ignoring the pauses in rehearsal while the two of them bickered, leaving Steph or Caroline to mediate. Beverly arrived at each rehearsal taut, ready to lose her temper at the slightest mistake on stage, but until now she'd kept well away from the backstage crew.

Caroline had been right, Steph found it easy to function as stage manager, transferring her skills from managing police officers to the volunteers helping with make-up, creating costumes and props, or painting the set. They responded well to her leadership and had met all the deadlines she had set.

Steph parked her car as close to the entrance gate as possible to help Caroline unload pieces of Mother Courage's cart from her boot and assemble it for the rehearsal. Beverly came into view in deep conversation with the chap who played the chief soldier, and her forthright directions penetrated the closed windows.

'No, you listen. You are an officer, a lieutenant and responsible for them the whole time and you must keep them in line. You understand?'

The poor man stood before her; his head bowed.

'You understand?' She repeated, this time even louder and waited until he looked up at her and nodded. 'Yesterday, a couple of them were sniggering all the way through the third scene and not concentrating on the action.'

The soldier sneaked a look around, presumably to see who might be listening.

'Are you listening to me?' Beverly's screech alerted everyone within the walls of the ruin to witness the dressing down. 'Well, are you?'

The soldier blushed and mumbled. 'Yes, Beverly.'

Beverly's voice continued at the same decibel level, much to the fascination of the entire cast and crew. 'You must be more assertive. I want you to drill them as if you're their sergeant major and keep going on at them until they obey your slightest frown. They are a lazy lot and need pulling into line. Understand?' She paused.

The soldier stood sullen and silent while a rebellious muttering of discontent rose from his cohort of soldiers a few yards away.

'Well, do you?'

'Yes.' He nodded his head and, walking towards his men, spat on the ground.

'Getting into his role then!' Caroline laughed.

Steph shook her head in wonder. 'Do you know before doing this stage manager job, I would never have believed that adults would put up with the stuff she shouts at them?'

Caroline laughed. 'Oh, this is mild compared to what she got away with when she was drama advisor – but that was in the twentieth century – wouldn't be allowed now.'

'Why did they put up with it?' Steph watched Beverly check her notebook and head for the next unfortunate victim who needed her coaching.

'Because she built on their talent and she had an amazing reputation in the theatre world for developing some big stars – well, like Jessica – and she wasn't the only one. Beverly had a wide network of contacts in the professional theatre and helped her students even after they left drama school. They put up with it because in the end the plays she produced were outstanding – always won local and even national drama competitions.'

'That's as maybe, but let her come near me and put on her parts and—'

'She'd never interfere with you. You're doing an excellent job, and she knows it and anyway she daren't question your authority. Haven't you noticed she steers clear of your crew?'

'Well, now that you mention it—'

'Come on, we'd better get this cart assembled or we'll be next on her list.'

As they moved towards the pile of wood, a howl of rage fixed them to the spot, along with everyone else in earshot. 'Jason, just who do you think you are? How dare you come so late to rehearsal!'

Beverly bore down on Jason, who had tried to creep behind

the church without Beverly seeing him. What a mistake! It was one thing to be late, quite another to try to avoid offering the humblest apology and seek Beverly's forgiveness. Head hung down and red-faced, Jason absorbed her anger. 'So, you think your time is more precious than anyone else's, do you?'

Jason raised his head a little. Surely, he wouldn't try to answer her question? That would be tragic. Thank goodness he remained dumb. 'Max needs you, NOW!' She bellowed, then in the quietest voice imaginable, 'And don't you ever come late to my rehearsal again.'

Released at last, Jason scurried over to Max, who patted him on the back with a sympathetic expression on his face. Everyone else got on with what they'd been doing before Beverly's eruption, but there remained a strange tension in the air, as if something was about to happen.

CHAPTER SIXTEEN

FRIDAY 16TH AUGUST: 6.30PM

CAROLINE AND STEPH made quick work of building Mother Courage's cart from the flat-pack version Caroline had painted and set it in the centre of the acting area on a white dot made by spray paint used by builders to mark out underground pipes. Jessica, as Mother Courage the profiteer, would spend much of the play on or around her cart selling black market provisions to the soldiers in the war.

Steph looked up at the lighting bar above the cart, which had been hung with a row of lights the day before. Jason was halfway up the left tower adjusting the lamps, estimating where their light would fall, while Max sat at the lighting board. He spotted her moving the cart precisely over the white spot. 'Steph, could you sit on that truck please, then I can see if the angles work?'

'Sure.' Steph moved towards the cart and was about to sit on it when a shadow zoomed past her.

Jessica swooped in. 'No, do let me try it. You don't mind, do you, darling? It will help me get into my part.' She clambered onto the cart and sat in the middle of it, looked around the acting area and the cart in relation to the audience. 'No, no, no! Definitely not! This is in the wrong position! It should be further upstage to keep the eyes of the audience on Mother Courage all the time.'

Jessica clambered off the cart and pushed it a little to the right and further back. Taking a few steps away, she narrowed her eyes to check how far it was from the centre of the acting area. She frowned, then made a quick dart towards the cart, gave it another little shove and stepped back once more to check she would be in the eyes of the audience constantly. Happy, she climbed back on the cart, stretched her arms out wide and threw a self-satisfied grin towards Beverly, who was watching this performance, her face like thunder. 'There, darling. See? Perfect.'

Beverly strode over and stood beside Max, now on the ground beside the left tower. 'I disagree. That white spot there —' She strode over to stamp on the white spot on the grass and dragged the cart with Jessica on board back to its original position. 'There. That spot indicates exactly where I've decided it should be. Just below the lighting bar.'

'But I shall be in shadow in that position. You must know, darling, actors should never perform directly below the Fresnels.'

'But—'

'Darling, please! The audience wants to see my whole face. I do know what I'm talking about, you know.' All conversation was halted, and all eyes focussed on the Hollywood star and her challenge to Beverly.

'Yes, but now it's in the way of—'

'In the way of nothing, darling. I ask you, how am I expected to act when the lights are directly above my head? I need to be further behind the bar and a little more to stage right.'

Jessica, taking Beverly by surprise, jumped down, seized the side of the cart and pulled it back to where she wanted it, forcing Beverly to let go, before climbing back with a broad smile of victory. A whoop of support came from the direction of a group of soldiers, but further audience participation was quelled by a piercing stare from Beverly.

'Max, darling, please shift the angle of that lamp on the tower, stage left, it needs to light up my face. As it is now, it will miss me entirely.' Jessica waved her hand at the offending light.

Beverly stepped towards the cart and, with a great effort, nudged it back towards the white spot. 'No, Jessica. Max and I discussed this. The cart must be dead centre under the bar.'

Jessica, apparently annoyed at being moved, climbed off the cart, pushed it back where it she wanted it and climbed aboard, folding her arms. 'Max, darling, let's just try it and I'll show you what I mean. I think you'll find I'm right, darling. After all, we don't want this to be a deal breaker, do we, sweetie?' She leaned over the side of the cart and stroked Beverly's arm as if she were a small animal. 'If you're right, we'll move it, darling. Promise.'

She blew an air kiss towards Beverly, who looked ready to explode. Was she going to hit Jessica? Steph tensed, ready to pull them apart as the animosity between them was almost visible. Beverly, red faced and biting her lip, sighed, turned and nodded to Max who, raising his eyebrow, gave the signal to Jason to adjust the light Jessica had indicated.

'Here?' Jason re-adjusted the lamp that had come on as if by magic and Jessica, now in its full beam, bestowed an enormous smile on Max and raised her thumb.

'Super, darling. Don't you agree, Beverly darling?' Beverly shrugged her shoulders and walked away while Max turned off the lamp so Jason could tighten the screw on it.

'Right Beverly, we're switching them all on now! You can get down now, Jason.'

Jason clambered down the tower, jumping the last few feet to the ground, steadying himself by holding onto the scaffolding, which juddered. As Max moved the sliders on the control board, bright light flooded the acting area. A loud crash and a piercing scream made everyone freeze. Jessica lay in a heap on the cart. A lamp had fallen off the bar and hit her.

CHAPTER SEVENTEEN

FRIDAY 16TH AUGUST: 6.45PM

FOR A MOMENT, everyone froze, staring at the cart in an eerie silence, broken only by the distant crashing of the waves on the shore. Jessica hadn't moved. Was she dead?

Steph got to her first, followed by Beverly. Leaning into the cart, Steph felt for Jessica's pulse and saw that she was breathing, shallow breaths, but at least she was alive. 'Call for an ambulance!' Steph yelled at Beverly. 'Quick. Tell them she's breathing but unconscious.'

For once, Beverly did what someone else told her and she stepped away while making the call, not taking her eyes off Jessica.

All the actors crowded around, staring at Jessica's limp body, horrified at what had happened. After the stunned silence, their whispering became louder as they all had theories on how the lamp had fallen.

'Someone had it in for her.'

'Well, we know who that is don't—'

'Come on, you can't think—'

The lieutenant at the end of Beverly's sharp tongue,

appeared to have successfully acquired the skill of crowd control and ordered them to stand back. 'Let her have some air. Let's all go into the chapel for a drink while they sort it. You too, son.' He put his arm around Jason's shoulders, who was trembling and looked as if he was about to faint, and herded most of the cast away towards the church.

The silence stretched as Steph and Max stood over Jessica's unconscious body, willing her to open her eyes.

Max leaned in and extracted the lamp from the damaged cart, being careful not to touch Jessica. It hadn't quite gone all the way through the wooden slats on the cart floor but had splintered several of them and hung by its bracket from one of the smashed pieces of wood.

'Look Steph,' he held it out to her. 'No safety chain. I put them all on yesterday and on the ones I put up today. I always put chains on them. I wouldn't leave it up there without a chain, not even for a minute.'

'I know, Max, and if you look there—'

Max, now holding the lamp, twisted it towards Steph, who pointed at the bracket. 'See there – no, don't touch anywhere else – see the screw has been undone, so it wasn't fixed to the bar, just dangling there. It could have fallen at any time.'

'And that lamp was right over the white dot where her cart would be parked. If Jessica hadn't moved it, that lamp would have crushed her skull.'

Still no movement from Jessica. There was no blood as far as Steph could see, which was a relief. But Jessica remained unconscious in a crumpled heap, taking shallow breaths.

Beverly joined them. 'They're on their way. Should we move her? She looks so uncomfortable.'

Steph stepped in front of her, raising her hand to stop her from touching Jessica. 'No, leave her Beverly. Luckily, she's fallen into the recovery position, and we have no idea what damage that lamp did or if she's impaled on one of the wooden slats. I can't see any blood, but we don't want to make it worse. How long did they say they'd be?'

'They're sending a first responder.' As she said it, the scream of a motor bike rebounded off the walls. A tall man pulled off his helmet, took a large bag out of his pannier, and ran towards her.

'What's her name?'

'Jessica.' Steph recognised him and knew he was good. 'A stage lamp fell on her and knocked her unconscious.'

He gently examined her, then turned away and made a phone call. Steph took Beverly aside. 'Max is convinced that someone took off the safety chain and unscrewed the bracket overnight.'

'Whoever would do that?'

'Whoever it was, intended to hurt her.'

'No, surely it was an accident?'

'Having seen Max's safety precautions, I don't think it was. It was only Jessica moving the cart that saved her from immediate death. This could be attempted murder. I'm going to call the police.'

Beverly opened her mouth but before she could say anything, Steph continued, 'I suggest you take the rest of the cast and sit in the church.' Steph pointed to the gaggle of peasants watching the drama from the raked seating who had resisted the lieutenant's orders. 'Make them a drink while they wait for the police. No one is to leave until the police have spoken to them.'

'Attempted murder? Rubbish. It was an accident!'

In her "don't mess with me voice," Steph pulled herself up to her full height. 'Beverly, I said, from what Max has told me, this wasn't an accident, but it could be attempted murder. I was in the police force for thirty years, so I know what I'm talking about.' Speaking quietly but slowly, underlining every word, she took a step towards Beverly. 'Now please take the cast into the church and keep them calm.'

For once, Beverly was speechless and took a few steps towards the church, then hesitated and looked back at Steph, who spoke quickly. 'I'll stay here with Max and wait for the ambulance, so Jessica won't be left alone. You are the only person who can manage the cast now. Many of the younger ones will be scared stiff and need you to re-assure them.'

Beverly sighed, and without another word, rounded up the horrified peasants from the edge of the raked seating and herded them into the church. Max stared at Jessica, hugging the light close to his body. Steph moved to stand beside him. 'Without touching the lamp anywhere else, do you think you can put it on the ground just here?'

Max, now a grey colour, lowered the lamp as if it might explode and placed it on the spot Steph indicated. 'It wasn't us, Steph, honest. I know Jason and me put the chains on them all when it was hung, and we'd never have left the bracket undone like that.'

'With any luck there'll be fingerprints on the lamp or even on the bar and we'll find out who did it.'

Max didn't look comforted by her words and slumped down on the ground beside the cart.

'Come on, Max, you go and sit over there on one of the cast chairs. I'll join you in a moment.' Steph helped Max up and stayed beside him as he shuffled to the nearest chair where he sat, head in his hands, looking totally miserable and suddenly very old.

A blue light bounced off the flint walls of the church as an ambulance pulled up as close to the cart as possible. A bedroom window opened in the pink cottage opposite, and a head appeared, presumably to find out what all the fuss was about.

With the help of the first responder, the two paramedics fixed a neck brace on Jessica and edged her onto a stretcher. Steph glanced at the bottom of the cart. Thank goodness – no blood. The shattered wooden slats didn't appear to have pierced Jessica's body, but despite being moved, she hadn't stirred.

'Are you going with her, love?' The first responder put his arm on Steph's shoulder. She knew she and Max would be the best people to speak to the police and Beverly would be the obvious person to go – but she should stay with the cast. She'd also be a key witness.

Caroline, carrying a tray with mugs of something hot, emerged from the church porch. Of course – Caroline. She'd be the best person as she'd taught Jessica and when she woke – Steph clung to "when" and not "if" – she'd be with someone she knew well.

Steph dashed down the path and, to Caroline's surprise, grabbed the tray and put it on an ancient coffin-shaped grave-stone. 'Please, will you go in the ambulance with Jessica? I need to be here, and so should Beverly. I'll sort out your car if you give me your keys and I'll get Margaret home if you get stuck in A&E.'

'Right. Tell them to wait while I get my bag, and I'll go with her.'

Steph dashed over to the ambulance, where Jessica was being connected to some tubes and an oxygen mask. 'Caroline Jones will go with her. She's just fetching her bag – Ah! Here she is.'

Caroline climbed up the steps. 'I'll give you a ring. Have you phoned Hale?'

'Just about to.'

CHAPTER EIGHTEEN

FRIDAY 16TH AUGUST: 7.15PM

JUST AS HALE's car drew up, accompanied by a police car, Steph's phone rang.

'Hi Caroline, everything all right? ... That's great news! ... Sorry, what was that? ... Yes, I'll tell Hale, he's just arrived. Let me know how she gets on.'

Hale strode across the grass to join Steph.

'Attempted murder? You're sure?'

'Look for yourself. Here's the lamp that fell on Jessica—'

Hale leaned over the lamp 'Wow! That's quite a weight.'

Steph pointed up to the bar and the space where it had been. 'You can see that the safety chain has been taken off and if you look at that clamp—' she pointed at the long screw. 'That should have been done up tightly around the bar, but it's been undone. Look at all the others with chains and their clamps firmly closed.'

Hale scanned the lamps, checking them. 'It could still have been an accident.'

Steph shook her head. 'I've worked with these guys, and they are so safety conscious you wouldn't believe it. And this light fell directly onto the cart where Mother Courage spends most of her time during the play. This was no accident – it was carefully planned.'

Hale looked up at the bar. 'Phew! That would have come down with an amazing force—'

'And if Jessica hadn't shifted the cart, it would have been much worse.'

'What?'

'See that white mark on the grass?' Steph pointed to the white smear.

'Yes.'

'That's where Beverly said the cart should have been, but Jessica moved it. That meant the lamp fell to the side of her, not on top of her head.'

'You're right. Does sound like it could be a murder gone wrong – thank goodness.'

'And Caroline has just told me Jessica has come round in the ambulance and keeps saying, "Not again, this is happening all over again. I shouldn't have come back." I wonder what she means?'

'Perhaps Caroline will find out more?'

'I'll text her.'

Max, his face even greyer, came up close to join them. 'We put the lamps up yesterday afternoon, but we made sure each had a safety chain, and they were all firmly fixed. You must believe me.'

Desperate to convince them, Max swivelled from Steph to Hale. 'Nothing like this has ever happened before, and I've been doing it all my life and Jason does what I've taught him.' Steph put her hand on his shoulder. 'We always double check everything. Someone has undone it.'

'We'll need a statement and to take your fingerprints and Jason's for elimination. We'll get someone up there...' Hale pointed to the bar '...and see if there are other fingerprints beside yours. Anyone else go up there?'

'No. Only me and Jason.' Max turned to find Jason had come out of the church and beckoned him over. 'Over here, Jason.'

Hale glanced behind Max and nodded at Jason. 'And you both built the scaffold towers?'

'Yes. Me and Jason. There may be others like the delivery people who touched them, but they usually wear gloves.' The panic in Max's voice made him sound desperate.

'You go over there with Sergeant Johnson who will take all the details.' Hale pointed to the front row of the audience seating then turned towards Steph, who smiled at Johnson as he ushered Max with Jason in tow to the seats.

Hale turned to Steph. 'Where's everyone else?'

'I told Beverly to take them into the church and keep them calm.'

'Well done. We'll both go into the church and have a chat with her while the other two talk to the cast and find out if they saw anything. It sounds as if it was an overnight visitor, doesn't it?'

'The people in the pink cottage might have seen something. John and Oonagh Wells – they own the farm and have been great – they've given us their yard as a car park.'

As they entered the church, everyone stopped chatting and stared expectantly at Hale and the two uniformed police officers behind him. Steph decided it would be less dramatic if she spoke, so stepped forward. 'This is Chief Inspector Hale of the Suffolk police, and he will investigate what happened. The good news is that Jessica has regained consciousness. These officers will need your contact details, and please tell them if you saw anything – anything at all that might explain how this happened.'

Leaving Hale by the door, Steph moved towards Beverly and beckoned her to come with them. They returned to the acting area where Steph arranged three of the cast chairs upstage behind the cart, and they sat down.

'Nothing like this has ever happened before. I'm shocked – horrified. I don't know what to say. I'm convinced it was an accident – who would want to harm Jessica?' Beverly appeared to have lost her confident command and was now subdued and very pale.

Steph frowned. 'Apparently, Jessica is claiming that something like this did happen before, and she shouldn't have come back. Do you have any idea what she means?'

Beverly sighed, lowered her head, paused, then looked straight at Steph. 'I can only think she is referring to the last play we did here in August 1989 when she played Helena in *A Midsummer Night's Dream*. There was some – er – awkwardness between her and some other members of the cast.'

'1989? That's thirty years ago. How old was she then?'

'She'd just taken her A Levels, and it was our summer production before she went to drama school. It was a brilliant production, with amazing reviews. She was part of a very talented cast – but as I say, she experienced some difficulties.'

Hale took out his notebook. The movement distracted Beverly and she looked at Hale, but Steph made eye contact with her again. 'Well, Jessica appears to think this has something to do with what happened before. What were these difficulties, as you call them.'

'Jessica mentioned something to me at the time about some nasty letters and – yes, of course, she fell off the stage – she said she was pushed. I sent her to A&E but when she came back, she said she was fine to carry on and I thought that was the end of it.'

'Apart from that play, could she be referring to anything

else? Of course we'll speak to her, but if you can think of anything now, it would be helpful.'

'No, nothing that I know of.'

'And are there any overlaps with that play thirty years ago?'

Beverly looked around the acting area. 'Well, we did it here. Different staging. We built a raised stage, and the audience was in a central block but faced the same way—'

'No, I meant were any of the actors or technicians in both plays?'

Beverly frowned. 'Me, of course, Caroline did the set and Margaret the music. And the actors playing Bottom and Starveling are in this cast, but I think that's all. Just Jessica and the two of them.'

'Could you give me a programme or cast list from that play and any contact numbers you have for those involved?'

'Yes. I'll let you have them as soon as I get home.'

'Thanks.'

Hale put his notebook back into his pocket. 'When the contact information from your cast has been given to us, you may all leave. We'll need to examine the lighting rig, so I'm afraid you can't use the acting area. And we'll also need an official health and safety inspection before you can return.' Hale stood. 'Can you come to the station for an interview tomorrow, first thing.'

'Why?'

'From what I understand, it was only Jessica moving the cart from the white mark that saved her life.'

'What?' Beverly looked puzzled, then the blood drained from her face as she stammered. 'You mean ... You can't think I've had anything to do with this?'

'We don't think anything at the moment, Beverly. We'll talk tomorrow. Meanwhile, Steph and I will go to the hospital to see Jessica.'

'Please send her my love and tell her I'll come in later, if she can receive visitors.' Beverly stood and started to walk towards the church but appeared to change her mind and returned to them, looking rather wobbly. 'You don't really think this is ... you know ... attempted murder?'

'I'm afraid I do.'

CHAPTER NINETEEN

FRIDAY 16TH AUGUST: 8.45PM

'Sorry, they've sedated Jessica, and you won't be able to talk to her until tomorrow at the earliest.' Caroline shook her head apologetically as Steph and Hale arrived outside the ward to give her a lift home.

'How is she?' Steph asked as they walked down the empty corridor towards the car park.

'Aware that it was a miracle she wasn't killed. She's in shock. It grazed her shoulder and arm on the way down and hit the side of her head. They want to keep her in overnight, as she was concussed and needs to rest, but she appears to have escaped with only minor injuries.'

'That's great news. Let's get you home.' Steph looped her arm through Caroline's.

'Is Margaret all right?'

'Fine. We took her home on the way here.'

As they got outside in the car park, Hale walked beside them. 'You said earlier that when she came round, she claimed it had happened before?'

'She was pretty incoherent, but she kept saying it was the

94

same place, and she'd almost lost her life then and now they'd come back to finish it.'

'Did she say who had come back?'

'No. But I did ask her why she didn't go to the police, and she said whoever it was threatened to kill her younger sister if she did.'

'Man or woman?'

'She didn't say.'

'We'll have to come back tomorrow when she's awake.' Hale unlocked the car, and they climbed aboard.

For some time, they travelled in silence, watching the last rays of the sun flashing behind the trees. As they were turning off the A12, Caroline on the back seat leaned in between them. 'Oh, I forgot. She said she wished Beverly hadn't asked her to come back and re-live the dream or nightmare.'

Steph half turned to her. 'Yes, Beverly said something similar to us before we left. She thought it might be linked to *A Midsummer Night's Dream* in 1989. She said you were involved.'

'Yes, I designed the set. Very different staging to this one, of course, but it was a great success.'

Now it was Hale's turn to turn his head towards the centre, but, keeping his eyes on the road, raised his voice so Caroline could hear him. 'I gather she's done lots of these shows. Does she always use Covehithe?' Hale turned right on the Oakwood road.

'No, This is only the second time. After *The Dream*, she used the college theatre for her summer shows when she was Drama Advisor until she took early retirement in 2004.'

'Was that when she trained to be a vicar?' Steph handed Caroline a packet of Polo mints over her shoulder.

'Thanks. Yes. This is the first play she's put on since then.' Caroline passed the mints back to Steph. 'Although some of her parishioners say she puts on a weekly show – twice each Sunday.'

'Really?' Steph took the Polo mints and stowed them in the glove compartment.

'How sad all this is!' Caroline sighed. 'You know Jessica was Beverly's greatest star and I think she wanted the play to be a celebration of thirty years since she launched her career.'

'It would give Jessica some good publicity too, wouldn't it?' Hale drew up outside Caroline's house.

'Fancy a coffee?'

Hale got out and opened Caroline's door. 'That's very kind, but we ought to get back. Early start tomorrow.'

As Caroline put her key in the lock, she turned back. 'I think I've got a programme or a review somewhere from 1989 – I'll scan them and send them over to you.'

'Thanks, Caroline. That would be really helpful.' Hale got back in the car, waved, and they set off for home.

Steph observed him for a few moments. Apparently feeling her gaze, he turned to face her.

Steph smiled. 'Are you OK? You seem a little distracted?'

'No, I'm fine.' Hale sounded irritated that she'd asked.

Steph opened the glove compartment and replaced the Polo mints. 'Did you get that thing sorted?'

'What thing?'

'You know, the thing that came up when we were at Latitude.'

'Not sure I know what you're talking about.'

'That phone call.'

'I can't remember any phone call.'

Steph frowned. 'The one you took just after we arrived. Outside the yurt. It seemed important.'

'So important, I can't actually remember it.'

They drove in silence the rest of the way. She felt something was going on and it was weird that he didn't want to share it with her. And now, whenever they were together, he was detached – as if he was somewhere else all the time.

A sick feeling crept up from her knotted stomach and she breathed in deeply to hold back the panic. Her phone beeped. She looked down to see an email from Caroline thanking them for the lift and with two attachments.

'What's that?' Hale pulled up outside her flat. It was all right for him to ask, wasn't it?

'Caroline's sent us the attachments. Must be the stuff from the other play.'

As soon as they'd calmed a starving Derek by providing him with a late supper, Steph opened her laptop and downloaded the attachments. She'd been right. It was the review. As she opened it, Hale sat beside her so they could read it together.

The Oakwood Chronicle – 27th August 1989

Another outstanding production by Suffolk Drama Advisor

Arts Editor – Bill McDonald

Last night inside the atmospheric ruins of Covehithe church, we were transported into a magical fairyland by the creative direction of Suffolk Drama Advisor, Beverly Elkin (39), in her annual production with the cream of her Suffolk drama students. Transported to Athens, where the human and supernatural worlds collide on midsummer eve, we were treated to an outstanding production of "A Midsummer Night's Dream".

As the gentle evening light gave way to darkness, the stage, built in front of the huge gap where the enormous east window would have been, featured Caroline Jones' imaginative set which made the most of the darkening clouds to create an evocative backdrop to the drama in the wood and the Duke's court.

Right from the start, Lucy Craddock's sensitive performance as Hermia captured our hearts as she faced being forced into an arranged marriage to Demetrius (Duncan Patterson) by her brutal father. In an act of rebellion, she and her lover Lysander (Nazim Rahman) elope to the forest followed by the rejected Demetrius and the lovelorn Helena (Jessica Connell) where they become the playthings of the mischievous Puck (Hugo Dubois), on loan from the prestigious clown school in Paris.

Hugo's gymnastic performance was perfectly suited to the part as he darted between the four lovers and Oberon and Titania (the king and queen of the fairies) and the mechanicals, rehearsing a play for the Duke's wedding, spreading his malevolent mischief and creating magical chaos. His undisputed talent will guarantee his future in the French or English theatre.

James Wyatt's hilarious Bottom had the audience in stitches as he persuaded the queen of the fairies to fall in love with his ugly half donkey-half-human monster, tempting her to scratch parts of his anatomy I am too embarrassed to mention here!

The tension and interplay between the four lovers created the outstanding element of the drama. Helena's spaniel-like submission to Demetrius was taken to the extreme as she crawled on all fours carrying Demetrius' lost shoe in her teeth. Both she and the bewitching Hermia were the standout performances from the Suffolk contingent and we look forward to seeing their names in lights in the West End.

———

Steph got up to let Derek out into the garden. 'Sounds like a great success.'

'It's a shame he doesn't mention all the cast.'

'They'll be on the programme. I'll open it.'

The scanned programme wouldn't download and on Hale's third attempt, a pop-up box informed him of a corrupted file.

A look of annoyance flashed across Hales' face. 'Typical!'

'I'm sure Caroline didn't intend to corrupt it.'

'I didn't say she did.'

'I'll get Caroline to re-send it tomorrow. It's too late to phone her now.'

Hale grunted and checked his watch. 'Really?'

'Or if it won't work, I'll go round and get the original programme.'

Steph sighed and went to the kitchen to find a quick salad supper from the fridge.

Hale joined her and reached over her shoulder for a bottle of lager. 'And when we've got that cast list, we need to ask them all what happened in 1989 that appears to have led to attempted murder thirty years later.'

CHAPTER TWENTY

SATURDAY 17TH AUGUST: 9.30AM

STEPH KICKED herself that she hadn't phoned to check they could visit before setting off on the forty-five-minute drive to the hospital. Throughout the journey, Hale remained quiet, and Steph hoped he wouldn't blame her if they were turned away.

As they approached the ward, she tensed, preparing herself for any moans, but why should she take the blame? He could have phoned first, couldn't he? They tuned in to the conversation between a tall man and a fierce-looking ward sister, who blocked the door to Jessica's room and appeared to be telling him off. Steph peeped through the porthole in the door and saw a deathly pale, unconscious Jessica looped up to a mass of tubes and beeping machines.

'Well, when do you think I can visit?' His patient tone of voice belied his irritated expression at the monologue he had endured.

'Difficult to say. At the moment, she remains in a medically induced coma and can't receive visitors. And who did you say you were?' The ward sister frowned, looking even more antagonistic as she scrutinised the man.

'I didn't. I'm a close friend.'

'Right. Sorry, but we can only give confidential information to her family.'

Hale stepped around the man and held out his warrant card. 'Perhaps you'd prefer to give confidential information to me, as I'm investigating what happened to Jessica Marlowe.'

The man stepped aside and turned towards Hale. Immediately, Steph recognised him as Naz Rahman, a local solicitor she'd worked with many times in her police life. Hale must have recognised him too, but didn't show any sign of it. The solicitor stepped back, almost treading on Steph's foot, and swivelled round to apologise. 'Sorry, I didn't— Steph, what are you doing here? I thought you'd retired.'

Steph took a few steps back along the corridor and Naz followed her so they could talk away from the grumpy sister, who now appeared to be answering Hale's questions in a distinctly grudging tone of voice.

'I'm with Hale, investigating what happened yesterday. And you?'

'I've known her ever since we were at sixth form college together and—'

'Naz, whatever are you doing here?' Hale joined them and shook hands with Naz as the dragon sister bustled off.

'Hi Hale, just told Steph. Known Jessica for years and we've, well ... we've been seeing each other since she came back to Oakwood.'

Hale looked at his watch. 'Fancy a coffee and a chat? I need some background, and I'm sure you want to help find out how this happened.'

Naz grinned. 'That'll be a novel experience! I'm usually on

the opposite side of the table to the police. But, yes, of course I want to help you find whoever did this to Jessica.'

'There's a decent coffee shop up the road. Maison Mocha or something like that, I think. Car park round the back.'

'Right. I'll see you there in five.'

They walked back to Hale's car in silence. As he opened the door, he glanced across at Steph. 'Strange seeing Naz there. Doesn't seem the type to be a boyfriend of a star.'

'Oh? And what's the type?'

'You know, a glamour boy. Naz is a thoroughly nice man who does a good job, but he's definitely a small-town solicitor.'

They followed a dark blue Porsche into the cafe car park and watched as Naz climbed out.

'Maybe not quite so small town?' Steph grinned.

'I had him down as a Peugeot type – how wrong can I be?'

They found a table and waited for their orders to be taken. Hale frowned at the long menu and grunted at the waiter. 'All I want is a simple black coffee – not all this stuff – no idea what half of it means.'

When the waiter had gone, Naz looked around to make sure no one could hear them. 'You don't really think someone tried to hurt Jessica deliberately, do you?'

'Yes, I do actually.' Hale balanced the menu between the salt and pepper pots. 'The lamp that hit her was primed to hit the dead centre of the cart and it was only luck she moved it, so it missed its target – her skull. You've known her since you were both A Level students, I heard you say?'

'Yes. We were at Oakwood College together. In fact, I was with her in the play we did at Covehithe – *A Midsummer Night's Dream*. I played Lysander, and she was Hermia, or was it Helena? I forget now – so long ago.'

'But in the review, it didn't mention Jessica Marlowe.'

Steph smiled as the waiter placed the coffee cups on the table. The penny dropped. 'Ah! Was she Jessica Connell?'

'Yes. Changed her name after drama school to sound more dramatic.'

Steph glanced at Hale, not sure if he wanted her to continue, but he was concentrating on tasting his coffee. 'Did something happen to her back then? Someone threaten her?'

'How did you know that?'

'Something she said when she came round.'

'Yes, there was – I suppose you'd call it a stalker now – she mentioned some poison pen letters. What went on behind the scenes of that play was more dramatic than the performance on the stage.'

'Why didn't she go to the police?' Steph added another spoonful of sugar to her coffee.

'She was scared to. They threatened to hurt her sister if she did.'

'She must have been terrified.'

'Yes, thinking back, she must have been.'

They sat quietly, considering what Naz had said. He took a deep breath. 'It was such a sad time. There was Jessica in a state convinced someone was out to get her. She said she was pushed off the stage to stop her performing, and then there was that accident, after the play finished.'

'Really?'

'Marcus Strong – a brilliant lighting technician – original and so cool with it. I helped him hang the lights – he was so talented.' Naz took a sip of his coffee. 'Worked with Max on the lighting design. For the first time, everyone thought the Drama Award would be given to a backstage student rather than an actor, but he died after the performance.'

'How awful.' Steph wondered why Caroline hadn't mentioned him.

'Yes, a dreadful waste. He was involved in an accident, on the road between Covehithe and Southwold. Going home on his motorbike – he must have been clearing up the day after the play finished. He was found by the side of the road near South Cove church.'

Hale, who had obviously been listening, perked up. 'The police investigated it?'

'Yes, but they didn't find any evidence of a hit and run, and the coroner ruled it was accidental death.'

'How sad,' Steph sighed.

'Yes, he was a good mate and destined for the big time.'

They sipped their coffees in silence. The mood had changed.

'And Jessica. You knew her well when you were a student, you say?' Hale tore open the cellophane around the tiny ginger biscuit that came with his coffee.

'Did we go out, you mean?'

Hale nodded.

'No, not then. But since she's been back, we've spent a lot of time together.'

'And has she mentioned anyone stalking her – any phone calls or texts?'

Naz stared for a moment at a group of kids messing around at the counter and appeared to be considering his answer. 'No, not like last time ... but she was upset by the constant rows with Beverly. Jessica was convinced Beverly regretted asking her back and was doing everything she could to spoil her performance.'

Hale caught the attention of the waiter and wiggled his index finger over the palm of his other hand, miming his request for the bill. 'Like what?'

'Well, Beverly has always been top dog in Suffolk drama and Jessica was her star. She could be a bit of a prima donna too, but she knew what she was doing and whenever she suggested anything Beverly would shut her down in front of the cast and make her feel like a student again.'

Hale checked his watch. 'Thanks, Naz, you've been really helpful.'

Naz held Hale's gaze. 'Now, it's your turn. Did that sister say anything else to you?'

'The same as I heard her tell you. But the reason they have her in a coma is they think she has a bleed on the brain and want to see if it disperses or if they need to operate.'

'That sounds serious.'

'They said it could be fatal.'

CHAPTER TWENTY-ONE

SATURDAY 17TH AUGUST: 11.50AM

JUST AS THEY got back from the hospital, Steph's phone pinged with a WhatsApp message.

Mother Courage Team
I know we are all devastated by the awful accident yesterday, but Jessica would be the first to insist that we continue with today's rehearsal as planned. She is in our thoughts and prayers, and we hope she will soon return to us. The show must go on. Beverly

PS if any of you are worried about H&S, don't be. We've had an inspection, and all is safe.

Steph groaned out loud when she read it.

'Anything wrong?' Hale had kept his coat on and was hovering by the door, as he was obviously on his way out to work.

'Nothing really. Just Beverly insisting the show must go on.'

'Good. I need to come there to ask some questions.'

'You'd think she could postpone it out of respect for Jessica.'

'Well, she hasn't. I'll see you later.' With that, he swept out of the room, the door slamming behind him in the breeze.

Why had she ever let Caroline volunteer her for this? She sighed, grabbed her coat, Derek's lead, his water bowl and a bag of treats, and headed off to her car.

When Steph arrived at Covehithe, it was apparent she was not the only one shocked they were carrying on as if nothing had happened. Little groups of actors and backstage staff stood around whispering and looking up at the lighting bar, glum expressions on their faces.

Max and Jason climbed down the scaffold towers where they had been checking the lights for the umpteenth time. Standing centre stage waiting for Beverly, they appeared to be trying to hear what was being whispered about in the huddles.

A sudden hush made everyone turn to the footpath by the church as Beverly arrived. Steph giggled and nudged Caroline. 'It's the Queen of Sheba!'

'All we need is the music!' Caroline turned away so Beverly wouldn't see her trying to control her laughter.

Beverly swept across the grass, her floor length cloak flowed behind her, revealing a long grey skirt and tunic, suitably distressed.

'Someone's been in their dressing-up box.' The comment from one of the soldiers gave rise to giggles, quickly quashed as Beverly joined the lighting technicians centre stage.

'Gather round everyone. First, thank you for coming in these dreadful circumstances.' Beverly took a dramatic pause, scanned the group around her, and sighed. 'Jessica, I know, would have wanted us to continue.' Another pause fell on the total silence, which Beverly allowed to stretch just the right length before speaking in a more energetic tone. 'I will be taking Jessica an enormous bouquet with your get-well messages this evening – the card is on the prompt desk for you all to sign.'

Inevitably, heads turned to the desk where a large white envelope waited at its centre.

'We have had a formal Health & Safety Inspection this morning, and it is safe to carry on. And thank you, Max and Jason, for checking each and every one of the lights to make sure they are secure.'

She beamed a wide smile at the two men standing a little apart from the cast. 'May I emphasise in front of you all that they are in no way to blame for yesterday's accident. Max and Jason have done an excellent job but ... we do appear to have a saboteur here.' She waited until the shocked hubbub died down. 'If anyone here knows anything that will help the police, who are investigating this accident, please see me or talk to the police officers.'

Beverly held up her hand to put a stop to the panicked muttering. 'As you can see, reluctantly, I've been persuaded to stand in as Mother Courage until Jessica can be with us again, which I hope will be soon. Now, does anyone want to say something before we start?'

After a dramatic pause long enough for everyone to take in the detail of her costume but not quite long enough for anyone to speak, she gathered up her cloak, making it swirl around her feet. 'Now, places for the opening scene, please. All actors to their seats upstage or in position on stage for curtain up.'

The rehearsal limped on, with everyone except Beverly clinging to their script. Steph and Caroline sat together behind the props table, noting in the script who took what prop when and at what point they returned it. 'I can't believe it. She's word perfect!' Steph whispered to Caroline.

'Darling, this is her big break. I'm sure she only wanted Jessica for the publicity. Look at her – she's revelling in every moment of it.'

Beverly's polished performance stood out against the stumbling attempts of the rest of the cast to stand in the right place and say the right words. Occasionally she stopped to give a direction or to move the soldiers into more dramatic groups or to complain about slow entrances and exits but her accomplished, and at times, over the top acting, drove the first half of the play at a cracking pace. It was a dramatic change from when Jessica was playing the part. Beverly had stopped every other line to correct her speech or adjust her movement. Now, without those constant interruptions, the rest of the cast was beginning to get an idea of the narrative and rhythm of the play.

Beverly climbed off the cart, clapped her hands and turned to face the cast seated behind her. 'Well done everyone! Have a fifteen-minute break and we'll get on to the next part.'

As the cast went into the church for drinks and biscuits, Beverly bounced over to Steph. 'Coping all right? Told you so. You're doing an excellent job.' She swept off, humming the tune that Margaret was practising in the church with the little band.

'You don't think it was her, do you?' Steph placed the props required for the next section at the front of her table.

'No, darling, I can't believe even she would be desperate enough to do that.'

'Well, to see her prancing around the stage as if she's Judi Dench or some great dame makes me wonder. And she knows it by heart – every word.'

A shadow fell across her. Steph looked up to see Hale silhouetted against the sun with two uniformed officers behind him. 'Have you got a minute?'

'Sure.' Steph and Caroline were the only ones within hearing distance as Beverly was giving notes to the cast in the church. Hale looked around and came in closer to them.

'Not great news, I'm afraid. The hospital phoned. We're now investigating a suspicious death.'

CHAPTER TWENTY-TWO

STEPH AND CAROLINE stared up at Hale, and Steph was the first to speak. 'You mean Jessica's dead!'

An irritated Hale turned towards the church and flapped his hand, instructing her to lower her voice. 'Yes, she died. That's why we're investigating a murder.'

Caroline frowned. 'But when? She regained consciousness in the ambulance last night as we left.'

'About an hour ago. The PM will tell us more.'

'That's dreadful news. She was so ... so alive yesterday.' Caroline, now very pale, half stood, then sat down again, clearly upset.

'I'm sorry Caroline. You must have known her as a student.' Hale paused and faced her.

'Margaret and I taught her and I designed and made the sets for all her drama productions. We always knew she'd be a star. You know, total charisma – that was her. Such a talent in an outstanding year. All eyes would go to her as soon as she walked onto the stage and before she opened her mouth. I can't believe it.'

'Can I get you some water?' Steph put her hand on Caroline's shoulder.

'No. I'll be fine. It's the sudden shock. Dead? I can't believe it. After hearing her talk last night in the ambulance, I can't believe she's dead. I thought it had missed her, and she'd be out and back here rehearsing today.'

'They think when it hit the side of her head, it caused a bleed in the brain.' Hale sat down beside Caroline and took her hand. 'Sorry. I shouldn't have come out with it like that. I didn't mean to shock you.'

'No. It's fine.'

'What did she say in the ambulance again?'

Caroline closed her eyes, clearly trying to visualise the scene. 'She said she'd almost lost her life here last time and now they'd come back to finish it.'

'Did she say who "they" were?'

Caroline screwed up her eyes and frowned. 'No. I don't think she did. I asked her what she meant, and she carried on mumbling, but I couldn't make out what she was saying. Sorry, Hale.'

Hale patted her hand. 'Don't worry – worth a try. You might find something comes back to you later. Anything, however small, let me know.'

Hale stood. 'I'd better get this over with and break the news to Beverly and the cast and crew.'

He strode down the narrow pathway beside the church, then stopped halfway and glared at Steph. 'Well ... we haven't got all day, you know.'

'Sorry.' Steph scrambled to her feet and jogged after Hale. 'Didn't know you wanted me.'

It appeared he hadn't heard her, as he walked quickly on to the church porch, where she caught up with him and saw him instructing the officers to remain outside the church door. He spotted Beverly apparently having another motivational chat with the lieutenant. 'What on earth's she wearing?'

'Her Mother Courage costume.' Steph whispered.

'But ... Oh, I see. She's taken over.'

'Exactly.' Steph raised an eyebrow.

Beverly must have become aware of Hale entering the church as she gave a dramatic twirl and strode up the aisle towards him, her cloak billowing behind her. 'Is there news of darling Jessica?'

'Yes, there is. Perhaps we could find somewhere quiet?' Hale indicated the porch with its narrow benches on either side. He sat down on one with Beverly opposite, while Steph stood at her shoulder.

'Poor Jessica. Such bad luck. When do they think she can return?' Beverly re-arranged her cloak around her artistically.

'I'm afraid I have some bad news. Jessica died earlier this afternoon. I am so sorry.'

'How? I mean ... But the lamp almost missed her.'

'Apparently, it did more damage than they originally thought. She was put in an induced coma from which she didn't recover. I'm so sorry.' Hale spoke slowly and quietly, evidently realising that Beverly was having problems taking it in.

'But she's our headline. Our star. She can't be dead. Her photo is all over the posters. What'll we do?'

'About cancelling the play, you mean?'

'Sorry?' Beverly, in a daze, looked at Hale as if he was speaking a foreign language.

'You'll have to cancel the play, won't you?' He repeated quietly.

Beverly stared at the ground, apparently trying to take in the tragic news, and Hale waited for her to respond. She took a deep breath, pulled herself up and stood squarely, examining the *Mother Courage* poster on the wall opposite.

'No. We won't cancel it.'

'But in the—'

'Oh no. Jessica would want us to continue. I mean – I can...' Beverly looked out towards the acting area and her face changed as an idea hit her. 'That's it – we'll do it as a tribute to her. A celebration to her memory. We can keep the posters but put a flash across them, saying just that – a tribute to Jessica Marlowe.' Beverly moved her hand diagonally in front of Hale's face, tracing the direction of the notice she envisaged. 'That's the answer. A tribute.'

She took a step towards the church. 'Now we ought to tell the cast and crew. Could you excuse me?' Beverly made another dramatic twirl and headed for the door, but Hale reached it before her.

'Beverly. I don't think you understand. This is now a murder investigation, and your acting area is a crime scene. My job is to find out who killed Jessica.'

'And my job is to ensure her legacy and memory are protected.'

Hale blocked her way in to the church and for a moment Steph thought Beverly was going to push him aside. He appeared to grow wider, and he was getting close to losing it.

'You can do as you wish with the play, Beverly, but you won't be able to rehearse here until I tell you. And my officers will need to speak to everyone at yesterday's rehearsal to find out who sabotaged that lamp and killed Jessica. Do I make myself clear?'

Beverly took a step back and scrutinised Hale. 'Perfectly, Chief Inspector. Now if you'll excuse me, I need to inform our cast and crew of this awful tragedy.'

CHAPTER TWENTY-THREE

HALE STEPPED ASIDE, signalling with his arm that she could go past. She held her head high and floated down the aisle towards the gossiping groups. As she reached the altar, she clapped her hands.

'Now everyone, please take a seat in the front pews. I have an announcement to make. And Jo, please fetch Caroline and any of her helpers outside and ask them to join us.'

Hale and Steph walked further down the aisle from where they could see most of the faces when she broke the news. Caroline ushered in two students with paint spatters all over their overalls and pointed to a gap in one of the pews for them. Then she came and stood beside Steph and nodded to Beverly. 'That's everyone, Beverly.'

When everyone was seated and silent, Beverly stepped up in front of the altar with her head on one side, a grave expression on her face, and gave a long sigh.

'Ladies and gentlemen, it is with enormous sadness that I have to announce the death of our dear, our beloved, Jessica.'

Beverly paused, apparently to allow the astounding news to sink in to the shocked actors staring up at her from the pews.

'Yes, I'm afraid our own dear Jessica "shuffled off her mortal coil" earlier today following yesterday's tragic accident.'

Above the gasps and the growing wave of shocked mumbling, Beverly projected her voice and cut through the noise. 'Now, I am sure you will all want to join me in a moment of reflection before we continue with our rehearsal.'

A loud sob was heard from Cat, one of the college students, and some sniffs and gentle moans from some others in the pews. Caroline passed a tissue along the back pew to the sobbing girl and her friend, who put her arm around her.

Hale waited until Beverly took a breath, then he stepped forward. 'I'm afraid we are treating Jessica's death as suspicious, and we will need to speak to all of you again, so please do not leave here until one of my officers tells you to go.'

The deep voice of the lieutenant boomed out. 'We'll be cancelling the play, then?'

'Certainly not!' Beverly's voice was now much stronger, more dramatic.

'What?'

'Did she say she *wasn't* cancelling?'

'Cynical I call it—'

'Thoughtless and insensitive, more like!'

She held up her hand to stop the muttering.

'We will stage this production as a fitting memorial to Jessica Marlowe.' She waited while a buzz went around the group. 'We will do her proud.'

Once again, exclamations echoed around the church, louder this time.

'Really! That woman.'

'She can't, surely!'

'Not serious—'

'We shouldn't do it.'

Beverly raised her hand again to quieten her cast and projected her voice over them. 'You have all worked so hard and it would be wrong to cancel it now and, as I keep saying, Jessica would expect us to perform. She was a true professional and believed whatever happens, the show must go on.'

The group, now silent, listened as Beverly continued in a voice so quiet it was almost a whisper. 'This is what Jessica would expect us to do.'

The mumbling had stopped, and all eyes were on Beverly. 'No doubt the national press and television news companies will arrive soon to report on her death. Please make sure you are circumspect in what you say and ensure they know we are continuing with the production as a tribute to our very own Jessica Marlowe. I will give you each a press statement later, so we are all singing from the same hymn sheet.'

The news of press coverage caused a further wave of excited comments to go through the pews, stopped by Beverly clapping her hands. 'Now, back to work, please. We have a play to stage – for Jessica.'

Hale stepped forward, but before he could speak, Beverly pushed in front of him. 'I'm afraid as the police need to undertake their investigation here, we will have to cancel the remainder of our rehearsal today. I will be in touch to let you know where our next rehearsal will be – here or in the church hall.' She pierced Hale with a hard stare implying it was all his fault.

Hale and Steph stepped back and observed the subdued actors and crew file past into the bright sunshine, giving their names to two uniformed officers outside the porch. If they spoke at all, it was in shocked whispers. Beverly stood in front of the altar, statue still, a tragic expression on her face, waiting until she was the last one to leave the church.

'Wow! That was amazing! What a performance!' Hale threw himself down in the back pew.

Caroline rolled her eyes. 'That's Beverly.'

'But she's a vicar – doesn't that mean she should be sensitive? She was more concerned with the publicity they might get – and as for the show must go on ... I'm speechless.' He shook his head, now in shock himself.

'What do you want us to do?' Steph stepped round Caroline.

'I think you should continue to do your jobs but spend as much time as possible listening to the chatter. Someone set-up that lamp to fall on Jessica and will be surprised or pleased she's now dead.'

CHAPTER TWENTY-FOUR

SATURDAY 17TH AUGUST: 3.30PM

STEPH AND HALE picked up two chairs and walked slowly to the lighting desk, where Max and Jason sat, looking grim. Police crime scene tape encircled the acting area and Hale glanced at the two white-clad figures exploring the scaffold and the ground beneath it for any clues.

'That's the only area they can work. I don't expect they'll find much as it will have been compromised since yesterday, and as for the church, it's been trampled all over by all the cast and crew at least twice since the lamp fell.'

As they were settling into their seats in front of Max and Jason, Hale bent down to pull his notebook and pen out of his pocket and eyeballed Steph to take the lead.

The two men, lit by the bright sun, were a generation apart, but could have been father and son. They even had the same way of biting their lower lip when concentrating. She thought back to the list Beverly had given her and, although she couldn't recall their surnames, she was sure they weren't related.

'Max, Jason, I know this is an upsetting time for you but

Chief Inspector Philip Hale, who's leading the investigation into Jessica's death, would like to ask you a few questions today – you'll need to make formal statements at the station later—'

'You said in there her death was suspicious. Is that your jargon for murder?' Max interrupted her, scrutinising Hale from beneath his bushy eyebrows.

'Yes, I'm afraid it is.' said Hale.

Max leaned forward and took out a tin. 'You don't mind?'

'No, go ahead.' Steph replied. Max took out a cigarette paper, sprinkled a trail of tobacco strands along its centre, licked the long edge of the paper and rolled it into a thin cigarette. He held it up to check it was just right and lit it with an ancient Zippo lighter. Fascinated, all three watched as he took a deep drag and breathed out, visibly relaxing.

'Do you think it was an accident, then?' Steph peered through the cloud of smoke, moving her eyes between the two subdued men, waiting for either of them to answer.

Jason, who had been picking the skin at the side of his thumbnail, glanced at Max, apparently waiting for him to take the lead, which he did after another deep drag. 'No. It couldn't have been an accident. We don't make mistakes when we hang lights. Too aware of the damage they can do. That right, Jas?'

'Max is right. He's always banging on about safety. That's why we do everything slowly—'

'Slow and methodical – that's how I work, and I drum it into Jas. Always too slow for Beverly, but she knows me well enough by now. I never take shortcuts.'

'Who hung the lamp that fell?' Steph looked from one to the other.

Max nodded and smiled at Jason, giving him permission to speak. 'I climbed up there on a ladder.' He waved at the lighting rig. 'And fixed it with a safety chain and tightened the clamp. Max checked the angles from the lighting board, then I adjusted them until he said they were right and shone directly down on where Beverly said the cart would be.'

'Not as agile as I used to be, you understand, but Jas here is coming on well. Soon make me redundant.' Max smiled, reached out, and patted his apprentice on his arm.

'You must believe me, that lamp was firmly attached to the bar when we left for the night.' Jason's voice trembled.

Apparently, Max saw how uncomfortable Jason was and moved towards him, so their shoulders were almost touching. 'Someone must've come in after we left and removed the chain and undone it so it would fall down. Jas wouldn't have left it like that.'

Hale leaned forward. 'There's no security here overnight?'

Max laughed. 'This is Suffolk, mate, not Glastonbury. We're in the middle of nowhere out here. Who would think anyone would want to mess with stage lights?'

No one answered him. Someone had.

Max took a last draw on his cigarette, stubbed it on the sole of his boot, checked it was out and stowed it away in his tin. 'I unplugged the control board and took it home with me – that's an expensive piece of kit.'

'How do you think the lamp was made to fall down when Jessica was underneath it?'

'I'll tell you something for nothing, Jas and I noticed nothing that morning when we returned. Whoever took off the chain and unscrewed it left no sign. It was the only one pointed directly down over that white spot Beverly had made in the grass.'

Steph felt Hale becoming impatient beside her. 'Can you tell us how it could be made to fall off?'

This time, Jason was allowed to reply. 'Well, without the chain and the clamp, all it needed was a strong vibration to make it fall. From memory, it was early on when Jessica moved the cart and complained about the angle of one light on the side tower, so I climbed up to adjust it. That would have been enough.'

'So, if Jessica hadn't made a fuss, it mightn't have fallen when it did?' Steph's summary made Jason lower his head and Max get out his tobacco tin to roll another.

Hale leaned in, checking his notebook. 'Jason, you said earlier that you do the climbing up ladders, but Max still hangs some of the lights on the towers. Have I got that right?'

Max stopped mid-roll and glared at Hale. 'Here mate, I didn't say I can't climb, just not as good's I used to be. Jas here does more of the ladders, but I can still work up the towers – much more stable, see?'

Steph quickly defused the animosity she could feel emanating from Max. 'Let me get this straight, what you're saying is if anyone had wobbled one of the towers – like the soldiers when they are fighting around them or climbing on them – the light could have dropped at any time.'

'You've got it missus. It just happened to be when Jessica moved the cart, and we had to change the angle that Jas wobbled it.'

'And you got on well with Jessica, did you?'

'Known her since she was in that college and lit all her plays. Since she'd become famous, she was a bit up herself, but she was a Hollywood star, after all. No, it was good to see how well she'd done, but ...' Max lit his rollie and took a long drag.

'Go on.' Steph smiled, hoping to get him to open up.

'But that Beverly. Listening to the way those two were constantly needling each other, I wondered why she'd asked Jessica back.'

'Really?'

'She's good at what she does is Beverly, but you soon learn she's the queen bee – no room for anyone else.'

Having glanced at Hale and seen the slight shrug of his shoulders, she knew she'd got all she could out of them. 'Thank you both of you for your help. Could you give Chief Inspector Hale your full names and phone numbers so you can be contacted?'

Hale held his pen above the page and looked at Jason.

'Jason Strong—'

'Strong? How do I know that name?' Hale paused. 'Oh, I know, it was the lad who did the lighting for *A Midsummer Night's Dream*. I saw it on the programme. Any relation?'

'My uncle – Dad's twin brother. You'd have heard he died in a bike accident. Dad's always said the police couldn't be fagged to investigate it properly. He always thought Marcus was killed.'

CHAPTER TWENTY-FIVE

STEPH FROWNED. 'What makes you think Marcus was killed, Jason?'

Max squirmed in his seat. 'Look lad, this has nothing to do with me, so I'll leave you to it. If you need me, I'll be over there.' He patted Jason's shoulder and wandered off towards his van, which was parked by the church gate.

'Is Max OK?' Steph asked Jason as she watched his slow progress.

'He's fine really, but he's always blamed himself for Marcus's death. You see, they worked closely together, just as I'm doing with him now.'

'So?' Steph turned to Jason once more.

'Well, Max was – still is – in The Eagle's darts team and they were playing a match over in Beccles that evening, so he left Marcus to clear up the final bits the day after the final performance.'

'Was that a problem? I thought he was a lighting whizz, like you?'

A red flush moved up Jason's face at Steph's words. No doubt he'd been beating himself up ever since the light fell, taking responsibility for it, even though it appeared not to be his fault.

'You're right, he was and, according to my Dad, getting a great reputation locally. He'd already lit several amateur productions and helped out at Snape Maltings for concerts once or twice when they were short staffed. He was going into it professionally.'

'It was fine for Max to leave Marcus to clear up, then?' Steph could feel Hale beside her becoming a little irritated at the slow pace of this questioning, but she knew if she rushed Jason, he'd clam up.

'Absolutely, but Max has always felt guilty, so my Dad says. Thinks if he hadn't left, it wouldn't have happened.'

'But he crashed on the road, not here.'

Jason nodded. 'Yes, but Dad said it was dark by the time Marcus left because it had taken him longer to strike every-thing than if Max was there, see?'

Steph nodded her understanding, encouraging him to continue. 'I see.'

Jason sighed. 'It would have been pitch black by the time he left and the headlight on his bike didn't work. Dad said he was always on to him to get it checked, but Marcus said he was too busy with the play.'

He paused, swallowed, and shut his eyes for a moment. They gave him space until he was ready to carry on. 'Then just after that sharp corner before the church, they'd dug a hole in the road for water or something, and Dad thinks they must've left a large patch of oil or mud, and he must of hit it, spun out of control and that was it.'

Despite Jason not being born when his uncle had died, he was apparently seriously affected by it and his eyes were full.

Steph leaned forward and gently touched his arm. 'I'm so sorry, Jason.'

He acknowledged her comment with a slight shake of his head. 'The strange thing was, Dad said he wasn't wearing his leathers or his helmet – his helmet was the most important thing, and he always wore it. We never found it, and if he'd been wearing it, he most probably would've lived.'

Hale sat up straight, listening carefully to what Jason was saying. 'But the police investigated it?'

'According to Dad, they did, but not very well. Sorry.' Jason looked across at Hale, apparently assessing how his criticism was going down. 'He's convinced that Marcus's lights didn't work properly, and someone could've put the stuff on the road which he couldn't see and crashed.'

Hale made a note in his book. 'Did he have any evidence that someone did this?'

'Marcus was in a bad way in the hospital and my Dad managed to get there but not before ... you know ... before he passed away.'

Jason paused in the story that his father must have been recounted to him many times. Hale listened intently.

'Anyway, Dad told the police what he suspected, but they couldn't find anything to prove it. That was the problem – they couldn't find anything to back it up. Dad's always said it happened because Marcus was up for that Suffolk prize, and they got him out of the way so he couldn't get it.'

'Really? You think that would be a reason for someone to kill him?'

'Dad thinks it was.'

'But evidence?'

Jason sighed. 'Dad said after the crash the bike was mashed-up, so it was difficult to check on the lights and the ground on the side of the road showed signs of someone parking there, but as it's a place for dog walkers, it was ignored and they said it was an accident.'

Hale closed his notebook. 'Thanks Jason. I'll look into it. We'll have the files from 1989, and I'll have a chat with your Dad. I assume you live at home?'

'Yeah. He'll be pleased that someone is taking it seriously after all this time.'

'Thanks Jason. You've been really helpful.' Steph smiled at him. 'I'm sure you've got lots to do, so we won't keep you any longer.'

A relieved Jason scuttled across the field to join Max, who clapped his hand on Jason's shoulder, looking pleased.

'Maybe they didn't do a great job then. It sounds as if there could be more to Jason's story than came out in 1989.' Steph picked up two chairs, ready to go back towards the church.

'Let's not jump to conclusions. It's always too easy to blame the lot in charge before you, but it's obvious his family doesn't want to believe it was an accident.'

'And we keep getting sent back to that 1989 show, don't we?'

'Who else did you say was involved, then?'

They carried the chairs back to the stacks against the side wall of the church. Steph recalled her conversation with Beverly earlier. 'As well as Jessica, there was a girl called Lucy, Naz and his friend who played the lovers, Max and two of the mechanicals.'

'Mechanicals?'

'That's what Shakespeare called the group of workmen who performed a play at the Duke's wedding – it's hilarious even now.'

Hale took Steph's chairs off her and piled them on top of the stack. 'How did I come to be with such a cultured woman?'

He put his arms round her shoulders, and she moved in close to his body, welcoming his touch.

'You're right. We need to dig into what happened during *A Midsummer Night's Dream* to make sense of what's going on here.'

They walked towards the church porch. Steph stopped him at the threshold. 'I suggest I have a word with those involved in both plays, if that's OK with you?'

'Good idea. But after listening to Jason, I want to make it clear I'm not looking for another murder to investigate.'

CHAPTER TWENTY-SIX

SATURDAY 17TH AUGUST: 4.00PM

STEPH WATCHED Hale go up the path to his car, stopping to chat to the lead forensics officer who was packing up her van. An unexpectedly early night lifted her mood. Not that she wasn't enjoying working on the play, it just took up so much of her free time. Sometimes she wondered if Hale had encouraged her to do it to keep her occupied for some reason but banished that thought immediately. Anyway, she'd collect Derek from the dog lady and, if Hale managed to get home at a reasonable time and in a good mood, they'd sit outside with a bottle of rosé to watch the sunset.

She had taken in the last props from the table outside to lock them away in the church, when she was sure something moved at the front of the church. A slight creak of wood confirmed it. There was someone there.

As quietly as possible, she crept down the aisle and, as her eyes became used to the gloom, she came upon Beverly, her head bowed, sitting in the front pew of the church. Thinking she must be praying, Steph tip-toed back up the aisle, intending to go out and leave her in peace.

'It was a mistake, wasn't it?' The sudden sound of a voice from the front pew made Steph jump, and she hoped Beverly hadn't picked up the little squeal she heard herself make.

'What was?' Steph went to the end of the pew and saw Beverly wiping away her tears.

'Oh, today. And now I'm beginning to think I've done the wrong thing.'

Steph sat down beside Beverly and was once again surprised when Beverly reached out and grabbed her hand. 'Tell me I've done the right thing, carrying on.' She grasped Steph's hand and peered into her eyes, apparently needing re-assurance. Steph was stunned by the intense gaze of this woman and the sudden loss of the supreme confidence that defined her.

Beverly pulled a tissue out of a pocket hidden deep in the folds of her ragged cloak, blew her nose, and answered her own question. 'Of course, it's the right thing to do, but perhaps it would have been better to wait until tomorrow or Monday to bring everyone back together again.' She paused. Steph said nothing, hoping she'd learn more by giving Beverly space.

Beverly didn't seem fussed that Steph was silent. 'But then, there wasn't the slightest hint that Jessica would go and die; she was only injured when I decided to continue today.'

The silence stretched between them, only punctured by the cry of the gulls outside, circling around the bins to feast on the remnants of packed lunches overflowing after every rehearsal. 'And now you know Jessica has died?'

'Should I continue, you mean?'

'Yes.'

Beverly frowned, sat up straight, and her voice was stronger when she replied. 'Absolutely.' She explored Steph's face, apparently looking for a clue to her feelings. 'Don't you?'

'I'm not sure. On one hand, it would be a fitting tribute to her as you say, but on the other it feels ... perhaps a little insensitive?'

The Beverly she was used to emerged immediately, and Steph felt annoyed with herself for letting Beverly manipulate her again by pulling on her mask. 'Rubbish. Not insensitive at all. In this business, the show goes on whatever happens and anyway, I can play her part standing on my head.'

'Have you played it before?'

'Years ago. When I was in a student production at the Edinburgh Festival – got a five-star review, actually. You know, I'm amazed how quickly the words come back.'

Desperate to move away from theatrical reminiscences and back to the present, Steph prompted her. 'Why did you ask Jessica to come back when you could have played it?'

'She's – she was a star and would give us terrific publicity and I wanted to see how her performance had matured. Mother Courage is the part that would show it.'

As they fought over the scraps of food in the bin, the gulls were getting more aggressive and the penetrating screeching grated. 'Jessica got great reviews in 1989, didn't she?'

Beverly re-adjusted her seat, winced and moved her hand behind her back, massaging it. 'Steph, would you mind if we walked outside? Age is creeping up on me – well, at least up my back.'

Steph led them through the gloom of the church out into the bright sunlight and they walked side-by-side around the periphery of the ruins of the old church walls.

'Now, what were we saying? Oh yes, Jessica. Indeed, she was a rare talent, and I've been responsible for launching the careers of quite a few well-known actors in my time, you know. But it turns out she's been the best.'

'Really?' The heat of the sun was strong on their faces as they headed along the west-facing wall. Steph surreptitiously glanced at her watch, concerned that she would be late to collect Derek. She'd still be fine if she left at five.

Beverly appeared to be re-living the past and had stopped talking. Steph prompted her. 'And it was you giving her the Suffolk Award that launched her career, wasn't it?'

Beverly stopped, turned and stared at Steph. 'The Award caused so much trouble that year.'

'Really?'

Beverly continued walking and Steph fell into step with her. 'Yes, it was the tightest contest I'd ever seen. There was Lucy—'

'Lucy?'

'Lucy Craddock, who played Hermia. She was even more impressive than Jessica at that stage. A unique talent and so charismatic. All eyes would follow her whenever she was on stage.'

Steph slapped her neck, depriving a large mosquito of its supper. 'But she didn't get the award?'

Beverly flicked another mosquito off Steph's shoulder. 'No, the silly girl, she found love and ran off with the handsome Hugo to Paris – she said she was going to the prestigious clown school. I've often thought I'd see her name or face in France, or back here, but that wasn't to be. I presume she found her destiny in becoming a dutiful French wife – they made a lovely couple.'

'So, that left Jessica?'

'Not quite. For the first time I thought I would give the award to a backstage star – to Marcus Strong but—'

'The accident.'

Beverly stopped and searched Steph's face. 'You have done your research, haven't you?'

Steph didn't reply but waited.

'Yes. The accident. Although I've often wondered ...'

'What?'

They had reached the door of the church and Beverly, about to step over the threshold, paused to answer Steph's question. 'Was it? An accident, I mean? Marcus had a rare talent – technically brilliant, and his lighting designs were creative and so unusual. Even Max was outlit by him.'

They both stood inside the porch, allowing their eyes to adapt to the gloom. Beverly appeared to be lost in re-living the past, then sighed and continued. 'And then the accident. Such a waste. It should never have happened. I've often thought it was as if someone was getting him out of the way. Don't get me wrong, Jessica was outstanding, but so were the other two and suddenly there was no decision to make – she got it.'

They returned to the front pew to get their bags. Beverly reached in and handed Steph hers and picked up her own – a tatty ragbag to go with her costume.

'But surely Jessica has proved you were right. She was a star here and in Hollywood, not second best, surely?'

Beverly frowned before answering. 'You're right. She became a real star, but one with a tragic flaw. If she hadn't died, she would have found that her stardom would soon be in the decline.'

'Really?'

'You see, she was starting to believe in her own professional immortality and had become a spoilt, demanding woman who insisted she was right even when she wasn't.'

Beverly pulled off her ragged headscarf and shoved it in the bag with such aggression, Steph was worried she'd have to get it re-sewn. 'I'm afraid she'd grown into ... into a ... yes, a vile person. And the demands she made were absolutely ridiculous.'

Steph followed Beverly up the aisle, leaning forward to

catch each word. 'A real nightmare to work with – and it's not only me who held that opinion.'

Beverly suddenly stopped and turned – Steph just managed not to crash into her. 'Come on, you must have seen her in rehearsal putting on her parts?'

Steph remained silent.

'And the rumours of her prima donna behaviour have been swirling around for some time. I have maintained my network, you understand, and she was getting an appalling reputation.'

Having looked around to check they were alone, Beverly leaned in close to Steph to whisper. 'And it was not only her professional reputation that was tarnished. Oh no, her personal life could hardly bear close examination.'

'Sorry, Beverly, what do you mean?'

'How can I put it? She was ... yes, she was sexually incontinent. She always managed to be discrete, but I fear stories will now emerge about our Jessica ... or maybe they won't now she's gone. I hope so for her sake.'

Beverly stood back and scanned the church, evidently to check all was clear and tidy. Taken aback by what she'd just heard, Steph gripped the end of the nearest pew.

Apparently happy all was fine in the church, Beverly put her hand on Steph's shoulder, gently guided her out to the porch, and locked the door behind them.

'You know, Steph, as far as Jessica is concerned, I think her death will do her career greater good than if she'd lived. Whoever arranged for that stage lamp to fall on her did her a great favour. They really did.'

CHAPTER TWENTY-SEVEN

SATURDAY 17TH AUGUST: 6.00PM

Steph just made it to Wenhaston in time to pick up Derek from Felicity the dog woman and, despite hearing that he'd spent the day rushing around the field with the herd, parked her car at home and took him for a walk across Oakwood Common.

She half hoped to bump into Caroline walking Marlene, her fluffy-cushion dog. She could always go and call on her, but that would be making too much of a thing about the Jessica revelations from Beverly, which had appeared to come from nowhere.

So much had happened so quickly. Could it be just over twenty-four hours since the lamp fell on Jessica? For a while she appeared to have a lucky escape, but then, she hadn't, had she?

Having failed to run into Caroline on her usual dog walking route, Steph turned for home. A beep from a car pulling up beside her made her jump. It was Hale. The car stopped, and he leaned across and opened his door. 'Fancy a drink?'

His wide grin and warm voice made her feel better at once. 'Great idea. The Harbour or The Leg?'

'The Harbour. We can walk Derek along the river. I could do with some fresh air.'

Parking the car beside the river, they made their way down the three steps into the dark interior of The Harbour Inn. Steph chose their favourite table while Hale ordered their beers at the bar.

After a few gulps of Adnams' Ghostship, he placed his glass carefully on the beer mat and took a deep breath. 'What a frantic twenty-four hours!'

'I was thinking the same as I walked Derek. It doesn't seem real, does it? So much has happened. Any news on the body in the cliff?'

'We're getting nowhere fast, and now there's this.'

Hale took another long gulp from his glass and sat back, his head against the wooden settle, closing his eyes. He was relaxing at last, strange with so much going on that he should be the calmest he'd been for ages. When he opened them, he smiled at her. 'Well, did you solve it while I was gone?'

'You're joking, aren't you? It got even muddier.'

'Go on.'

Steph took a sip of the bitter beer, checked that Derek had a dog chew under the table to keep him occupied, and thought how she should tell her story. Hale picked up the laminated menu, then dropped it again – they knew it by heart. 'Hungry? The usual?'

Steph nodded and half got up, about to go up to the bar to place their order, when Hale touched her arm, stood and stopped her. 'No, let me. You look exhausted.'

She resumed her seat, watching him chat to the barman and feeling better already as his mood appeared to have lifted for the first time in days.

Hale slipped the receipt with their order number under the salt pot and placed his hand on her thigh. 'I've only been gone a few hours. Whatever can have happened in that time?'

'I was left alone with Beverly—'

'Don't tell me – she made a move on you.'

'Sorry? What are you talking about?'

'Oh, ignore me. Something someone said, that's all.' Hale took another large gulp of beer. 'Sorry go on.'

'I was putting the props away in the church and I saw Beverly sitting alone in the front pew, praying I thought, and she appeared upset.'

'That's a first. That woman is as hard as steel, or is it cold as ice? I don't know which... perhaps both.'

'She was dithering about her decision to continue with the play, but soon got over that and started saying the most dreadful things about Jessica.'

'Like?'

'That she was a prima donna, was getting a terrible reputation professionally and that – how did she put it – she was sexually incontinent!'

'What!' Hale's mouth fell open in horror. It took a lot to achieve that!

'I'm sure that's what she said and then she went on to claim that whoever had killed Jessica had done her a favour.'

'Are you sure you heard right?'

'Positive. That's what she said.'

The barman came over with their plates of fish and chips, cutlery and napkins, which he placed in front of them. 'Anything else I can get for you?'

'No thanks, that looks enough!' Hale grinned up at him.

The sizzling plate of battered fish and chips almost glowed in the gloom of the lower bar. Several times they had debated having something different, but fish and chips usually won. All conversation stopped while they crunched through the crispy batter to reveal the succulent cod inside it. Steph chose a large chip and posted it into Derek's mouth. He rested his head on her thigh and fixed her with his brown eyes, ever hopeful for another.

Having missed lunch, Steph hadn't realised how hungry she was. They both ate in silence until the plates were almost clean, apart from a few titbits to be sent down to Derek.

'Now, back to business. Beverly accused Jessica of being a nymphomaniac?'

'And a nightmare to work with.'

'And now she has the star part. Beverly certainly has a strong motive, and she also has the knowledge of how to rig the lights.'

'And the fuss she made about Jessica moving the cart from the white spot supports that.'

Hale picked up their empty glasses and plates, took them to the bar, and returned with more drinks – this time low alcohol beer for him. 'Well, that's one suspect then. Anyone else?'

'According to Beverly, anyone who had anything to do with Jessica.' Steph nodded to a couple of part-time teachers from the college and lowered her voice as they walked past her to the bar. 'It sounds as if Jessica's death is linked to the 1989 play somehow and to that award.'

Adopting the same half whisper, Hale made sure no one else could hear. 'Talking of which, I found the file from the Marcus Strong crash and there wasn't much in it. It was written off as a straightforward accident.'

'As Jason said, it was difficult to prove anything more at the time.' Steph lifted the table and pulled Derek's lead from under its leg. 'It could be a coincidence, but don't you think it's suspicious how much was happening around Covehithe when that play was being performed there in 1989, and again now?'

They climbed up the steps and walked towards Hale's car. 'Perhaps you're right. We have an unknown girl murdered there, new suspicions about Marcus Strong's death and now Jessica's death and we know two of them were murdered.'

CHAPTER TWENTY-EIGHT

SUNDAY 18TH AUGUST: 10.30AM

(

The Oakwood Chronicle – Sunday 18th August 2019

Tragic Death of Jessica Marlowe in Oakwood – Joe Denny

Star of the Royal Shakespeare Company and Hollywood films, Jessica Marlowe (48), died in hospital yesterday Saturday 17th August. Jessica, born and educated in Oakwood, returned to take the lead role in "Mother Courage and her Children" directed by Rev'd Beverly Elkin (69), to celebrate the thirty years' anniversary since she starred in "A Midsummer Night's Dream", which launched her career.

Beverly Elkin was the Suffolk Advisor for Drama when Jessica stunned the audience with her outstanding performance as Helena in "A Midsummer Night's Dream". She won the prestigious Suffolk Drama Award and studied drama at RADA, where Trevor Nunn spotted her talent and cast her as Juliet in his production of "Romeo and Juliet". Her debut in the profes-

sional theatre wowed the critics and laid the foundations for a series of starring roles at the National Theatre and the Royal Shakespeare Company before she was tempted to Hollywood. Scorsese cast her in his block buster "Silent is the Night" which ensured she became the toast of Tinseltown.

'Jessica was a unique actor one meets only once in a lifetime.' Beverly said. 'I am devastated by her death. She was to play Mother Courage in the very place where she started her career. Typical of Jessica, she freely gave us her time and talent to work with young people and inspire them. She sprinkled a little touch of star dust wherever she went. The stars will be shining brighter in heaven now that Jessica has joined them.'

It appears that Jessica Marlowe died after being hit by a stage light on Friday when she was rushed to the hospital with minor injuries, only to die of complications the next day. A police source commented that her death would be the subject of an investigation and that they were now treating it as suspicious.

If you have any memories of Jessica Marlowe, nee Jessica Connell, or experiences of working with this star to share, please send them with any photos to J.Denny@OakwoodChronincle. co.uk

———

STEPH KNEW AS SOON as she saw the headline when it had landed on the doormat, it would be a "light the blue touch paper and step back" moment. But it would be better for him to see it and explode at home rather than at work. His voice, when he looked up from the page, was so quiet she had to try hard to catch what he was saying.

'He's done it again. Whoever is the source this Denny man keeps quoting?'

'Did you find out who it was?'

'No. Gave them a five-star rollicking and scared them all rigid, so I'm surprised it's still going on.'

'Maybe it's not one of your team. It could have been Beverly. She's quoted extensively, and I bet they'd have chatted about stuff that isn't included in the piece. He could have stuck in the police source to give it credibility.'

'Perhaps you're right.' Hale sighed. 'I suppose it did come from me in that church.'

He stared at the paper again. 'What's that phrase? If you can't beat them, join them. This time I think I'll leave it for a day or two and see if he gets any new information from his devoted readership.'

Sensing a thaw, Steph seized her moment. 'Fancy taking a walk along the harbour with Derek? It's a lovely day and we could have a roast at The White Hart on the way back.'

'Sorry, love, I've got to work. Why not ask Caroline and see if she and Margaret would like to join you? I'll grab something from the fridge. Don't worry about me.'

With that, he reached for his briefcase, unloaded his laptop and fired up a website with a logo Steph didn't recognise.

'What's that?' She peered over his shoulder.

'New program we're trialling – Athena, it's called. Supposed to help us manage investigations – speed them up, you know, but it's taking all my time to get my head round it.'

He sighed and became immersed in the screen and didn't appear to notice Steph dangling the lead in front of Derek, who, after chasing his tail a few times in his excitement, rushed over and sat, waiting to be led out to the car.

She decided not to phone Caroline, as it felt like admitting defeat somehow. Although Steph had been aware of her watching them when they were together, she didn't feel like discussing it yet. No, talking about it would make it real and it could be her imagination – couldn't it?

Derek bounced out as soon as he was released from the car boot outside The Harbour Inn. Grabbing his lead, Steph led him to the bank of the river and gazed across at Walberswick, a holiday postcard in the bright sunlight.

As she watched the tide surge along the river, nudging the boats against each other, she smiled at a couple holding hands and walking along the towpath opposite. She felt numb.

How many years had it been since she'd taken this walk alone? Hale had always wanted to join Derek and her, his arm around her shoulder or holding her hand as they wandered along the river talking and laughing about nothing much. He'd always said it was his therapy, his way of calming down.

Back in June, when all was normal and whatever it was hadn't infected him, they'd stood on this spot at sunset and breathed in the magnificent pinks and peaches of the enormous Suffolk sky. A cloud shifted across the sun, forcing her into shadow. How appropriate was that?

CHAPTER TWENTY-NINE

'DIDN'T KNOW YOU HAD A DOG.' Naz realised he'd made Steph jump as she stood, head down, apparently lost in her thoughts, staring at one of the boats moored by a wooden gangplank.

Steph jerked her head up and frowned. 'Naz! Yes, I've had Derek a few years now.'

Leaning down, he patted the black and white dog on its head. He was reminded of the dog on the cover of the Famous Five books he'd enjoyed as a kid – Timmy, was it? This one appeared to be a happy dog, as his tail wagged so hard it looked like it might fall off. Happy dog? Whatever was he thinking? Dogs don't feel emotions, do they?

He'd always wanted a dog. His parents thought they were dirty and wouldn't let him have one, however much he'd pestered them. Actually, if he were ever to get a dog, it would be one like this one. Derek – was that what she called him? What a stupid name for a dog!

'I've never seen him with you before. Do you leave him at home when you're at work?'

'No. He goes to spend the day chasing around a field for hours with a herd of dogs.'

'Oh, I see. No Hale today, then?'

'No, he's stuck at home working.'

'On a Sunday?' Naz frowned.

'The day doesn't make any difference in his job.'

'And now he's investigating Jessica's murder, he can't take time off, can he?'

'You heard then?'

'It was all over the front pages this morning – local and national.'

Steph pulled Derek back from worrying a gull. 'I'm sorry, Naz.'

'Thank you. Are you walking far? I could do with some company.'

'I'm sure Derek would like to walk down to the sea for a swim.'

They turned away from the Harbour Inn and the Sailing Club and walked further along the river, past the chandlery and the fish hut. It was quieter here than he'd imagined on a holiday weekend, but then, it was lunchtime.

Naz stepped to the side to avoid a sausage dog weaving around the path on an extended lead. He certainly wouldn't like one of those – far too small. 'I know Hale said yesterday it might not be an accident, but is he now convinced Jessica was murdered?'

'Aren't you?'

He found Steph scrutinising him, as if trying to read his face. From many long hours listening to his clients' stories or sitting opposite as the police questioned them, he knew he had the perfect poker face and gave nothing away. 'There's no way it could have been an accident?'

'I'm no expert at stage lighting but – it's bound to come out so you may as well know – all safety precautions were removed, and it was immediately over her head.' Steph pulled Derek back and stopped him drinking from a puddle. 'You must be devastated to have lost such a close friend.'

Naz paused, picked up a stone and skimmed it across the river. They stood side-by- side watching a fishing boat chug up the river from the sea, creating swooshing waves that washed up the muddy shore, moving the green muck closer to their shoes. Derek sat obediently between them. Yes, a dog like him would do.

He sighed. 'Since Jessica came back, we have – had – become good friends. At first, I thought it was because she'd lost touch with most of our year group, but over the last few weeks … yes, we had become close.'

Naz stopped and pointed to a bench a few feet away from the bank on a little hump of concrete. 'Fancy a bag of chips and a sit down?'

Steph nodded. 'Sounds like a plan.'

'Good. I normally go to my parents for Sunday lunch but couldn't face it today. You bag the seat, and I'll get the chips.'

How bizarre, bumping into Steph like that. Although he'd wanted to be alone with his thoughts, he now welcomed her company. She was a bright woman, and he'd enjoyed their chats when he'd worked with her. Attractive too. Too old for him, but better than moping around by himself.

The smell of the sizzling fish and chips from Mrs T's wafted along the queue and alerted his stomach that it was empty. He hadn't fancied eating for the last two days and he certainly couldn't swallow his parents shoving yet more baby pictures at him, rubbing his nose in his brother's prolific fecundity and happy marriage. And as for their suggestion of an arranged marriage …

Anyway, he was where he was, and those chips smelled

delicious. He returned, holding two bags in faux newsprint cones, overflowing with searing hot chips and held one out to her.

'Thank you.' Steph smiled up at him and lifted the bag well away from the twitching nose of her dog.

For a few minutes they munched their way through the crispy chips, watching the girl row the ferry loaded with passengers and dogs back and forth between Walberswick and Southwold.

'Amazing that's been going for years, isn't it?' Naz finished his chips, rolled the paper into a ball and held out his hand for Steph's empty wrapper, which he expertly basket-balled into the bin to their left.

'Yes, I think they hand it down through the family. Pretty exhausting job.' As Steph made no move to get up, he relaxed back and continued observing the rowing boat. He could feel Steph tensing beside him and wondered what was coming next.

'Naz, do you mind if I ask you about the 1989 play?'

Frowning, he turned to look at Steph, a little jarred off that she had ruined the holiday feeling that had crept in and lifted his mood a little. 'What do you want to know?'

'Well, Jessica's death may have its roots in that earlier play and, as you were in it, I thought you might be able to shed some light on what happened.'

CHAPTER THIRTY

SUNDAY 18TH AUGUST: 12.30PM

Naz FELT irritated by the change of tone, but he may as well get it over with. He suspected she'd take it back to Hale and it may avoid him having to go through it all again with him.

'What do you want to know?'

'Well ... tell me anything you think is relevant to us finding Jessica's killer. Would you prefer to walk?' There it was again – the social, the let's be friends voice, but he wasn't conned. She was sharp all right, and to think he'd volunteered for this!

'Beverly was the all-powerful drama advisor then, and those who wanted to go to drama school relied on her for a reference – also there was the Suffolk Award. She'd got a large fund of money from someone in the theatre she'd worked with in her past — left in their will or something. It paid for tuition fees when drama schools didn't teach degrees, so didn't attract grant funding. It became extremely competitive.'

'Golly, that must have been tense.'

'It was. My money was between Marcus—'

'The poor chap who crashed on the motorbike?'

'Yes. That's him. He was brilliant. It was tragic. I've always thought the accident was a bit of a coincidence, as it put him out of the running.'

'Sorry, I interrupted. Who else?'

'Lucy, who ruled herself out.'

'How?' Steph pulled Derek back under the seat as he lunged towards the sausage dog on its way back.

'Only two mouthfuls there, Derek.' Naz leaned down and patted Derek on the head.

'I read the review, and Lucy got the most amazing write up. Why didn't she get it?'

He was right, Steph had been investigating *The Dream*. 'Lucy was next in the running, but we had a visiting Puck – Hugo – Hugo Dubois I think he was called. About three years older than us, from the famous Paris clown school. He was French, but he'd been brought up in England and knew Beverly somehow and he made a marvellous Puck. You know, a gymnast, leaping all over the place – perfect for the part ...'

'But?'

'How did you guess there was a but?' Naz grinned at Steph. 'He worked his way through all the girls in the cast. He was Gallic charm personified. A real romantic. Also, an amazing actor.'

'How did Jessica beat Lucy to the Award?'

'Simple. Jessica was the only one left. Lucy fell for Hugo and went off with him to Paris.'

Steph sat open-mouthed as she appeared to be taking in the complex story. 'So, Lucy didn't need Beverly's award and didn't go to drama school here?'

Naz shook his head. 'No, I think she decided to take the drama course over there and has worked in Europe, or maybe she's the happy-ever-after Mrs Dubois.'

A puzzled look from Steph hinted at the next predictable question. 'But you don't know? You've never heard from her?'

'Several of us got postcards from Paris telling us she'd found her future with Hugo and the clown drama school.'

Steph appeared to think for a few moments while she allowed a lady being pulled along by an enormous fluffy dog to pause long enough to give Derek a small dog biscuit. 'And she wouldn't need the award for a French drama course?'

'No, she'd found her patron – the loaded Hugo.'

'What did her parents think of her disappearing like that?'

Naz stood up. Steph joined him. The gentle breeze had transformed into a biting wind as the sun disappeared behind a massive grey cloud which threatened rain. They walked back towards the car park on the riverbank outside the Harbour Inn.

'Sorry – you were asking about her parents? Her father died when she was in Primary School – cancer I think – and her mother left to go to Spain with her new husband just before we took our A Levels.'

'Really?'

Naz stepped around a large pothole. 'Not the best timing, was it? But their house got sold quickly and Lucy stayed with Jessica for the last few weeks of term and during the play.'

The dense grey clouds had blown together to form an enormous lead roof, reflected in the river and banishing the bright summer day. It looked as if another big storm was brewing.

When they reached Steph's car, she opened the tailgate for Derek to jump in and he immediately lay down. Yes, Derek was exactly the make of dog he'd like. It would be good to have a reason to go for a walk after work each evening along the river or on the beach. Yes, it deserved careful consideration.

Steph stood by her door, waiting to say goodbye, frowning at him.

'Sorry. Just looking at your dog and thinking it might be time I got one.'

Steph laughed. 'They do tend to change your life. He's saved mine – literally.'

'Oh?'

'Another time, perhaps.'

Naz held the door open for her and she climbed in. 'Thank you for rescuing me and sharing my secret vice – Mrs T's chips.'

'Pleasure was all mine. See you Naz, and if you happen to think of anything else that might help us find Jessica's killer, you know where we are.'

'Certainly do.' He pushed the door to and heard it click.

He watched as Steph backed away from the river and drove off. A shiver ran through his body as the wind became stronger and the darkening clouds pressed down. He replayed their conversation. He was good at that. What had he told her she didn't already know?

As he walked towards his Porsche, he was struck by the thought that perhaps he was on the list as a suspect. As quickly as he thought about it, he shrugged it off. Ridiculous – after all, he and Jessica had been seeing each other and some of his friends were even suggesting that at last he'd found a keeper. Why ever would he want to kill her?

CHAPTER THIRTY-ONE

MONDAY 19TH AUGUST: 8.20PM

STEPH CHECKED HER WATCH. Eight twenty. He was cutting it fine. At that moment, the door crashed open, and Hale rushed in, threw his bag on the armchair, pulled out a notebook and pen and sat in front of the laptop Steph had set up on the dining table. He pulled another chair beside him, waved at Steph to sit in it, and opened the zoom link.

After several clicks, Hale's picture filled the screen, then shrunk to half size as another picture split the screen. A very good-looking, dark-haired man in his late forties or early fifties appeared on the screen sitting in front of a loaded bookcase, crammed with old leather volumes, punctuated in the gaps by small bronze sculptures and silver-framed photographs. The large window to his left showed parkland beyond.

Steph wished she'd inserted one those false backgrounds – a field of wildflowers or a sky filled with stars instead of the dull bay window and desk piled high with papers behind them. Hugo Dubois appeared to be sitting in a picture book French chateau. Naz had said Hugo was loaded – now she could see what he meant.

Hale moved the laptop ensuring Steph was in the picture. 'Good evening, Monsieur Dubois, I am Chief Inspector Hale of the Suffolk police, and this is Steph Grant, who is working with me on the case. Thank you for agreeing to talk to us.'

Even Hugo's frown made him look like a thoughtful philosopher rather than a grumpy man being interviewed by the police! Steph could see why he was so popular in his early twenties. 'Case? What case may I help you with?'

Hale had adopted his best phone voice, which made Steph smile. 'We are investigating the death of Jessica Marlowe, whom you would have known as Jessica Connell?'

The elegant frown re-appeared, along with a shake of his head. 'No ... I don't think I know this woman.'

'It was a long time ago in 1989 when you played Puck in *A Midsummer Night's Dream* here in Oakwood.' In the pause, which Hale allowed to run, Hugo closed his eyes as if re-playing his memories. 'She played Helena.'

Hugo opened his eyes, and a wide smile appeared. 'Oh, you mean the spaniel!'

'Spaniel?' Hale appeared puzzled.

'Yes, that's right, she's the one who crawled around the stage after Demetrius.' Steph interrupted, having recalled the newspaper review.

Hugo laughed. 'And believe me, he wasn't the only one she crawled after!' His smile switched off suddenly. 'Oh! I am sorry – you said she was dead?'

Hale nudged Steph under the table, which she took as a signal to carry on. 'Yes, she died when a stage light fell on her. We suspect it was murder. In our investigation, we think her death may be linked to the last play she did in Oakwood in 1989. I wonder if you can tell us anything you can remember that was strange, unusual or anything that may have led to her death thirty years later?'

Hugo closed his eyes, evidently recalling his experience from long ago. Eventually, he spoke. 'There was that tyrant woman, Beatrice? No, Beverly, I think she was called. She made sure they all suffered for their art and if anyone was asking to be murdered, it was her.' He laughed, his smile revealing perfect teeth, but just as quickly, he became serious, apparently aware that this was not a laughing matter. Hugo cleared his throat. 'But I think Beverly admired Jessica for her hard work and willingness to do even the riskiest things.'

'Like?'

'In the forest scene, Beverly made her climb up the tower to the lighting bar – way up above the stage with no safety line – she hung from it like a monkey and swung along it, arm over arm.' Hugo demonstrated the movement with the fluid grace of a mime artist. 'Even I felt nervous watching her.'

'Were you aware of any tension between the students?'

He turned slightly to look in the distance at something attracting his attention off the screen. Steph presumed there was another window to his right. 'I recall Jessica always wanted to be the centre of attention and there was the money which gave Beverly the power over them all. Jessica wanted it so badly – she didn't need it as her parents were well-off, but she wanted to be top – always first – while the others pretended it didn't really matter. But, of course, it did. She was Beverly's pet, and the others were angry with her for that.'

'Were you aware of anyone stalking her?'

Again, the philosophical frown. 'Stalking?' He paused, evidently mining his memory. 'No, I don't think so.'

'Anyone hanging around the rehearsals who shouldn't have been there?'

Again, the shake of his head. 'No. Not from what I can recall. But it was a long time ago.'

'Thank you. You have our email? Please do contact us if you can recall anything that you think may help us.'

'Of course.'

'Now, may we speak to Mme Dubois?'

A puzzled look flashed across Hugo's face. 'My wife? Why do you want to speak to her?'

'She was also in the play, wasn't she?'

'No. Why do you think that? She has never been to England.'

Hale, who was getting tense beside Steph, interrupted. 'But we've been told that Lucy Craddock, who played Hermia, left with you after the final performance and you married her.'

The extreme shock this comment stimulated was apparent on Hugo's face. 'What! I do not know what has been said, but Lucy never came back to France with me. She was lovely and good fun, but no, it was not serious. I was not in love with her. She was with that Asian boy – now, I forget his name —'

'Naz Rahman?' Hale prompted him.

'Ah! You are right, Naz. One of the lovers. He was her boyfriend.'

A pop-up box appeared, warning them the end of the talk was nigh. Steph could see that Hale was taken aback, so asked. 'Did Lucy go to your drama school? The clown school that year?'

'No. She didn't. 1989 was its last year in Paris before the school transferred to London. She may have gone to it there, but not with me in France. No.'

'Thank you so much for your time, Monsieur Dubois.'

'You are welcome.'

With that, Hale ended the meeting and sat back in his chair. 'Well, that was unexpected. I'm right, aren't I – they said Lucy had gone to the clown school with Hugo?'

Steph put the kettle on. 'Yes, Naz said she'd sent postcards from France saying she was with Hugo and I'm sure he also said they got married. How weird.'

Hale opened the fridge, pulled out the milk bottle, took down two mugs, and added tea bags ready for the boiling water. 'We keep getting dragged back to that play and we need to find out what happened to Lucy.'

'Could she be your skeleton?'

'She would certainly fit the age group we have also ... let's see ... 1989 – yes, that would be in the range.'

They brought their tea over to the armchairs. Steph offered the biscuit tin. 'Have you got an identification from the DNA yet?'

Hale chose his favourite, a Garibaldi.

Steph put the tin back in the cupboard. 'So, you need to get the French and Spanish to search their databases?'

Hale frowned. 'France, yes, but Spain?'

'Oh, didn't I tell you? Naz said Lucy's mother went to live in Spain just before they took their A Levels. I'm free tomorrow. I could come in and do a search for you if you like?'

Hale got up, took his mug back into the kitchen, and sat at his laptop. 'No, you're all right. I'll get Lizzie onto it – but thanks.'

Lizzie? Was she the new sergeant who had transferred from the Met? When she'd picked Hale up after work one evening, he was chatting to a stunning woman who looked like a model, posed on the station steps in the most stylish, designer trouser suit and elegant high heels. When she'd asked who the woman was, Hale was dismissive 'Oh her? That's Lizzie, the new detective sergeant – a breath of fresh air.'

He went on quickly to gossip about Johnson's baby – too quickly? Steph replayed the scene and recalled the way the Lizzie woman followed him with her large blue eyes, far too young for crow's feet, or the smile that she threw at him as she waved goodbye. But Steph had seen it all and knew the signs. She'd seen ambitious younger officers flirt with Hale and knew he'd be a catch. He'd never been aware of it, but this time it felt different.

'Fancy a walk to the Leg for a drink?' Her voice crammed with upbeat jollity aimed towards the back of his head.

'Nice idea, but sorry – still trying to make sense of this.' He gestured to the laptop screen with the dreaded Athena logo at the centre. 'Must get this sorted. What was wrong with the other one? That's what I'd like to know.'

'Right. I'll leave you to it. Come on, Derek – we'll go off to the common. See you later – bye.'

Sighing, his eyes fixed to the screen, then looking something up in the manual, Hale appeared not to have heard her.

CHAPTER THIRTY-TWO

TUESDAY 20TH AUGUST: 7.00PM

THE REHEARSAL HAD BEEN SUBDUED. Everyone got on with it, and the play was held together with Beverly's word-perfect performance and dogged determination. But the excitement of the earlier days had dissolved.

Having returned the props to the church, Steph assumed she was one of the last to leave. As she locked the church door and walked outside, she bumped into Jason unlocking his bike by the side of the porch.

'If you've got time, I could show you where Marcus had his accident?'

'Sorry?'

Jason undid the straps of his motorbike helmet, pulled it off his head, held it under his arm, and frowned at Steph. 'You listened to me, and if the police are now looking into it properly, you might find it useful to see where it happened.'

Steph paused. Why not? She'd arranged a late pick up for Derek, and it could be useful to see for herself. 'OK. Sounds good.'

'Climb on the back then?'

'You mean on that?' Steph pointed to the motorbike.

Jason lifted the lid of the helmet holder at the end of the seat and handed her a second helmet. Steph had assumed they'd go in her car, but she wanted to keep him onside, so reaching out for the helmet, grinned at the now buoyant Jason. 'A long time since I was pillion on one of these. Hope I remember how to lean properly.'

'That's something you never forget.'

Jason wheeled his Harley Davidson out of the churchyard and onto the road. The chrome on his treasured possession gleamed and caught the sunlight. There wasn't an oil spatter to be seen anywhere – he must have polished the engine! Steph mounted the monster bike and put her arms around Jason as he started the beast with a roar.

It was exhilarating to ride along the country roads on the bike. The hedges zoomed past; the sun flashed through the trees, and it was thrilling to revel in the thrill of the air rushing past her body.

Leaning against Jason's back, she travelled back to her late teens. She was seventeen when she'd clung on like this to her first boyfriend, Nick, who had a Honda, and she was so proud of the studded leather jacket he'd given her for her birthday.

Her memories came to an abrupt halt as Jason drew up beside a field gate and turned the engine off. They dismounted and left their helmets on the seat.

Steph fluffed up her hair. 'You always carry a spare helmet?'

He winked at her. 'Always. You never know who might be after a ride!' He pointed up the road. 'It's just along there. Be better if we walk.'

A grassy strip ran alongside the side of the road, dropping into a ditch full of bleached grasses and reeds. Beyond the ditch a dense hedge of hawthorn, punctuated by evergreen oaks and a couple of skeleton elm trees long dead, skirted a large field crowded with pigs.

A village of corrugated iron igloos ran way into the distance, each one with a grey metal trough in front of it, presumably for water. Snuffling and grunting sounds wafted over the hedge on the breeze, as the pigs sieved the soil for grubs or roots. It appeared they were eating dirt, but they must find food in it. In the right-hand field, they passed a gigantic wall of yellow rectangular hay or straw bales, at least twenty feet high. How did it remain standing against the fierce winds on this coast?

'How do you know this is where it happened?' Steph called out to Jason as he strode ahead.

'It's just along here.' He hadn't answered her question. Hadn't he heard, or was he avoiding it?

Just by the church on the other side of the road was a wider, flat area of grass that showed evidence of cars parking at right angles to the hedge. Jason could have parked there but had stopped up the road. Superstition? No, walking down it had emphasised the straight section of road immediately after the sharp turn earlier. Clever boy.

Jason stopped and waved his hand at the road in front of him. 'It was here.'

Despite the accident being way back in history, Steph found herself on automatic pilot, searching for clues. 'How do you know?'

'My dad. It's like a pilgrimage place to him. He often comes here to stand and think. Marcus is buried over there in the graveyard.'

'Tell me again what he thinks happened.'

Jason took a deep breath. 'His front light wasn't working properly, but Marcus hadn't had time to fix it. Dad said he has always regretted not doing it for him. Anyway, Marcus drove without full beam, but he knew the road well and he would have driven slowly. He didn't take risks.'

'Couldn't he get someone to pick him up if he knew his bike wasn't safe?'

Jason's face left her in no doubt of her stupidity. 'Not everyone had mobile phones then, and probably no signal here, anyway. And Covehithe is in the middle of nowhere – too far to walk. He promised Dad he would ride really, really slowly, which is why it couldn't have been an accident.'

'Right.' She scanned the road on either side. This part was Roman road straight.

'And Dad said there were roadworks that week just after that sharp turn, so he'd have slowed down even more, wouldn't he?' Jason pointed back to the point where the road disappeared around the bend and where they'd left his bike. 'No reason to crash here, is there?'

Steph nodded her head, as she was starting to agree with him.

'Luckily, no other cars were coming that way.' Jason pointed up the road to his left, then at the grass opposite. 'He must've dragged himself onto the grass verge over there and left his bike on the road. The next car come along, saw it and stopped. It was an old couple, Dad said. One of them stayed here with him, while the other one drove up to the phone box in Wrentham and phoned the police and ambulance. But they said someone had already reported it. Dad found that out when he went to talk to them after.'

'The police came, then?'

'Yes, but it was about ten and dark. The next day when they came back, there'd been a thunderstorm which would have washed any oil or mud off the road.'

They stood side-by-side in silence, contemplating the patch of road where Marcus had crashed. A car whizzed past going towards Southwold, followed by a white van. Did Marcus really have an accident? Or had someone planned his crash? Could it be a family story repeated over and over until everyone knew it by heart and embroidered it to fit in with what they wanted it to be? A talented young man with a sparkling future ahead of him, ripped from the world, might well leave his brother wanting to blame someone – anyone – but Marcus.

Jason gave her a piercing stare. 'Now you've seen it, what do you think?'

'I think there could be something in what you and your family say, but it would be helpful to have a look at the police file and the Coroner's report, wouldn't it?'

'Oh, we've got that. Well, not the police file, but the inquest said it was an accident, and that was that. But my Dad was convinced someone wanted to get rid of him.'

'Oh?'

'Marcus told him that there'd been some weird phone calls to the house. And he told Dad he thought someone was following him round when he went out.'

Where had she heard that before? Of course, Naz had said that Jessica was convinced she was being stalked. That made two of them; both in *A Midsummer Night's Dream*. She didn't believe in coincidences, but it was feeling as if someone was threatening them both. Had they killed Marcus?

CHAPTER THIRTY-THREE

TUESDAY 20TH AUGUST: 8.45PM

'Rehearsal went on late?' It was difficult to see Hale head down, working on that wretched computer program again.

Steph threw her jacket and bag on the nearest chair while she went to the dog food cupboard to get Derek's supper. 'Not really. I'll tell you about it when I get him sorted. Drink?'

'Please!'

Grabbing a bottle of Rioja and two glasses, she sat opposite him, smiling at the satisfying glugging the wine made as it came out of the bottle.

Hale took a gulp, closed his eyes, and sat back. 'That's better. Thanks.'

For a few moments, they sipped their wine and stared at nothing. Derek's enthusiastic crunching of the kibble, followed by his noisy slurping from his outsize water bowl, amplified the silence.

'Hard day?' Steph peered at the laptop screen, but he shut it down and smiled across at her.

'Yes, and no. We made some progress on the body in the

cliff. We're pretty sure it's Lucy Craddock. Right age, right place, but ...' He sighed.

'But?'

'We have DNA, but it appears she has no family left for us to check it out against.'

'I thought her mother moved to Spain.'

'She did. And Lizzie did an amazing job today, working with the French and Spanish police.' Hale took a rather large sip of his wine. 'She can certainly work, that girl. Puts most of my other officers to shame. Amazing on the phone – and do you know she is fluent in French and Spanish? Imagine that.'

'Imagine.'

'We've now confirmed that Lucy never made it to France, so all that stuff about joining the clown school was rubbish.'

'But Naz is convinced it was her writing on the postcard.'

'Well, she never went there according to the French authorities and there's no record of her studying or working or marrying or doing anything else over there.'

'Hugo did tell us that, didn't he?'

'It would be good to have a look at that card if Naz has still got it – but thirty years on, what's the chance of that? Did he say anyone else got one?'

'Don't think so, but something he said made me think there were several.'

He turned to stroke Derek, who, with his head on Hale's thigh, demanded his love and attention.

'Anyway, after we established she'd never been to France, we tried to find her mother in Spain so we could check the DNA. Eventually Lizzie discovered Lucy's mother died the September she moved out there. Mown down in a car accident, which would explain why no one reported Lucy missing. Her mother must have died shortly after Lucy did.'

Steph topped up their glasses. 'How do you know when she died?'

'We think it must have been the last night of Beverly's play. If Naz says she left that night with Hugo to go to France and was never seen again, she was probably killed that night.'

'And you're convinced it's Lucy?'

Hale closed the Athena manual and stowed it away in his bag. 'Can't be sure with no DNA match and no dental records, but the date on the bracelet fits her birthday and we now appear to have a missing person. Anyway, we're working on the assumption it's her.'

Steph got up to explore the contents of the fridge for their supper. 'That's now three deaths linked to that play at Covehithe.'

Hale stood and joined her, scrutinising the collection of oddly shaped, silver foil packets scattered around a dried-out piece of cheddar, hanging out of its cling film and a bag of limp salad that smelt of compost.

'Sorry, no time to go shopping.' She felt guilty, then irritated. Why was it always her job to go shopping?

'And I've not been much help either, have I?' Hale put his arms around her waist and pulled her back towards him, so she leaned against him. She allowed herself to relax into his chest. 'What was that about three deaths?'

'Jessica's death had something to do with that play. You think Lucy was murdered after it and buried on the cliff, and there's Marcus.' Steph gave up her quest and shut the fridge door.

Hale twirled her around to face him. 'Who on earth is Marcus?'

'You remember Jason's uncle? Motorbike crash the day after the last performance?'

'That was an accident.'

'Having been to the site with Jason, I'm not so sure, and you have to admit it's quite a coincidence.'

Hale stepped back to the table. 'Hang on here. We're already working on Jessica's murder, where we're making little progress, and now we only *suspect* the body on the cliff was Lucy. We still need more proof. I don't need another murder added to the list.'

Steph bent down to the freezer and opened the door, hoping for inspiration there. 'You've had a good look at the file, then?'

'Well, only the conclusion. It was an accident.'

She stood up and turned to face him. 'But you told Jason you would, and you'd also visit his father. You said you would.'

'And when exactly do you suggest I find the time to do either of those things? After thirty years it's hardly urgent, is it?'

Steph raised an eyebrow and stared at him. 'Well, you could say the same about the body from the cliff.'

'Look Steph, I don't sit in my office reading the paper or playing computer games all day, you know. I'm up to my eyes, as you can see.' He waved his hand at his laptop.

'OK. But you promised him and—'

'If you're that worried about it, you investigate it then. I'll bring home the file, and you can go and visit Jason's father and see if you can turn over a cut and dried case when there's no new evidence, except some gossip from a boy, who's tugged at your heartstrings and could be involved in a murder!' Derek whined and fled under a chair as Hale's voice got louder.

Steph saw red and slammed the fridge door shut. 'Right. I will. If you're too busy to do it, I'll work on it.'

'Good.'

Opening the freezer again, Steph pulled out a bag of some

tomato-coloured stuff with no label, which she assumed was bolognaise sauce. 'Spag Bol?'

Hale leaned down and shoved the laptop in his bag. 'Not for me, thanks. I'm not hungry. I think I'll turn in. Night.'

With that, he strode into the bedroom, slamming the door behind him, leaving Steph standing open-mouthed, with a lump of bolognaise sauce starting to drip in her hand. She looked down at it, then, with all her strength, lobbed it at the back of the bedroom door. It hit the wood with a thump, then slid down to the floor, leaving a trail of tomato and meat juice behind it.

CHAPTER THIRTY-FOUR

WEDNESDAY 21ST AUGUST: 9.00AM

The Oakwood Chronicle – Wednesday 21st August 2019

The Show Must Go On – Joe Denny

Jessica Marlowe (48), star of stage and screen, was to make a triumphant return to the local stage in the title role of Mother Courage in Bertolt Brecht's "Mother Courage and her Children" until tragedy struck, and she died in a freak accident last weekend.

In a tribute to their starring leading lady, the drama group has decided to go ahead and stage the play over the last weekend in August. The play's director, Rev'd Beverly Elkin (69), vicar at St Mary's Oakwood, has bravely stepped in to play the lead role a week after Jessica's death. It was Beverly in her role as Suffolk Drama Advisor who first discovered and nurtured Jessica's talent when she was a student at Oakwood Sixth Form College.

'From the moment Jessica walked into the room, I knew she had star written right through her – like a stick of rock. A glance, the tiniest movement and that voice ... unmistakable – the audience was in the palm of her hand.'

Beverly showed me her scrap-book of Jessica's reviews and newspaper cuttings charting her rise to stardom from sixth form student to Hollywood star.

'I have followed her career, as she has gone from strength to strength. She's always been in work – the theatre or the silver screen and she's shone wherever she's performed. Her appearance here would have been a celebration of her thirty brilliant years as an actor, and it's tragic that an accident has stolen her from us at the peak of her career. Instead of watching our star perform, I will have to officiate at her funeral.' Rev'd Beverly Elkin wiped a tear away as she mourned the death of the star.

You can buy tickets for the production of "Mother Courage and her Children", to be performed in the ruins of Covehithe church over the last weekend in August, at The Book Shelf in the Market Square or at Oakwood Library.

If you have any memories of studying or acting alongside Jessica Marlowe, send your comments and photos to J.Denny@ OakwoodChronincle.co.uk

———

STEPH FOLDED THE NEWSPAPER, jangled Derek's lead, which made him dash to the front door, waiting for her to fix it to his collar, his tail wagging madly and drumming against the door. Hale had left early, without breakfast, mumbling about a meeting. He appeared not to notice the tomato smear down the bedroom door. Usually, he brought her a coffee in bed before he left, but not today.

Derek was to spend the day with Steph as Fiona, the dog lady, had to go to hospital for a final scan to check her bones had knitted together, after falling over one of the dogs and breaking a bone in her foot a few months earlier. The rehearsal was due to start earlier at four this afternoon, but until then, she had the day to herself and had agreed to go for a walk across the common with Caroline, then on to lunch at The Leg of Mutton and Cauliflower.

As she drove over to Caroline's, Steph took a deep breath, admiring the brilliant blue, cloudless sky and smiled as she anticipated the day ahead. The phone jangled and made her jump. From the display on the dashboard, she saw it was Hale.

'Steph?'

'Yes.'

'What are you doing?'

'Driving, why?'

There was a background mumbling and the sound of a phone ringing. He was in the station.

'Can you get to the hospital and check that Beverly's all right?'

'Beverly? What's wrong?'

'Hang on.' She could hear Hale telling someone to continue checking some phone records. 'Sorry. Beverly's been involved in an accident on the road between Southwold and Covehithe and she's been taken to A&E. I'm up to my ears and there's no one free here.'

'Of course. I'll go now and phone you back later.'

'Thanks. You're a star.'

As she was only one road away, Steph drew up at Caroline's house, opened the boot letting Derek hop out, and rang the bell.

'I'll be about an hour, and I'll pick you up at twelve for lunch.' On the doorstep Caroline shouted back to Margaret. Marlene, on her lead, went nose to nose with Derek.

'Hang on.' Steph raised her hand to stop the enthusiastic Caroline from shutting the front door. 'There's been a problem. Beverly has had a car accident. Hale wants me to go to A&E to see what's happened and check she's OK. Would you have Derek please? He'd roast in the car, and they won't let me take him into the hospital.'

Caroline grabbed Derek's lead. 'No, but Margaret will. I'm coming with you. He'll be fine here with Marlene, and we can collect them later.'

Steph knew you didn't argue with Caroline, so watched as she pulled both dogs indoors, heard her quick instructions to Margaret and within seconds was outside and striding towards Steph's car. 'Well, what are you waiting for?'

For the forty-five minutes it took to drive to the hospital, they gossiped about the latest article in *The Chronicle*, which Caroline had spotted quoted on social media and had also been picked up by some of the London news websites. As well as taking over the lead part in the play, it appeared that Beverly was about to have a starring role in Jessica's funeral, and it was bound to hit the national news.

Having found a parking place at last, they walked into A&E and spotted a downcast Beverly sitting in a wheelchair, a folder of X-rays on her lap.

'Darling, how are you? We came as soon as we heard.' Caroline's loud voice caused several heads to turn, and even Beverly seemed embarrassed.

'I'll be fine. Just a sprain.'

Looking at her pale, bloodless face, Steph wasn't so sure.

'What do they think you've done?'

'They think I may have broken something in my arm or wrist. At least that's where they X-rayed. I'm waiting to see the doctor.'

'But you're in a wheelchair! Are your legs OK?'

Beverly blushed. Steph was relieved to see the colour flood up her face. 'I'm ashamed to say when I stood up after they brought me in, I fainted. They said it was delayed shock and told me to sit tight.'

To ensure Beverly would keep her place in the queue in the crowded waiting room, Caroline grabbed a couple of blue plastic chairs, and they sat on either side of her. Steph glanced at Beverly sideways, amazed at the change in her. Gone was the supreme confidence and control, replaced by a meekness she'd never seen before. Even her voice was at low volume, and she appeared to have shrunk into an old lady. It didn't help that Beverly was wearing her Mother Courage costume, which was little more than a bundle of rags, and Steph became aware of the curious glances directed at the two well-dressed women sitting with the bag lady in the wheelchair.

'What happened?' Asked Steph.

Beverly sighed. 'I'm not really sure. I was driving from Southwold to Covehithe, you know, on that straight bit before the church, and when I put my foot on the brake for that sharp corner nothing happened, and I went straight through the hedge and was stopped by a wooden fence.'

As Steph opened her mouth, Beverly continued. 'I can't remember how I damaged my hand. Maybe I put it out instinctively and smashed it into the windscreen or fell on it when the door flew open, and I was thrown out. It is my main hand, so I would have, wouldn't I?'

'Weren't you wearing a seatbelt?' Steph managed to ask.

Beverly coughed and caught her breath. 'Maybe I wasn't...

I can't remember. I was lucky not to hit the oak tree or go into the ditch, and then the car would have turned over and...' She paused, presumably to stop her imagination creating all the possible doom scenes. She lowered her head to hide the tears that overflowed and dripped down her cheek.

Steph passed her a tissue from the packet in her handbag, and Beverly nodded her thanks, wiped her face, and blew her nose. 'Sorry. How silly of me.'

'It's the shock.' Caroline placed a hand on Beverly's unin-jured left arm, who smiled in appreciation of the kind touch.

'You have your car regularly serviced?' Steph's gentle ques-tion made Beverly frown.

'Of course ... now, when was it? Yes, it was at the end of July before the MOT. I know it was July as I had to get all those domestic tasks out of the way before *Mother Courage* took over.'

Once again, Caroline met Steph's eye.

'Beverly Elkin!' A nurse stood at the end of the corridor, scanning the rows of potential patients.

'Thank you.' Caroline waved at the nurse, leaped to her feet and pushed Beverly towards the corridor. She bent down, level with Beverly's head. 'Shall I come with you?'

'Please.' Beverly, sounding terrified, looked up at Caroline gratefully.

'I'll wait here, and we'll drive you home.' Steph also stood and waited until they'd disappeared before going outside into the sunshine to phone Hale.

'How is she?' Hale sounded distracted.

'Sounds like a broken arm or wrist. She's been X-rayed and is seeing the doctor now. She said her brakes failed.'

'Thanks. I'll have the car brought in and I'll get it looked at.'

'From what she said, she's lucky to be alive.'

CHAPTER THIRTY-FIVE

WEDNESDAY 21ST AUGUST: 2.30PM

'You're going the wrong way!' Beverly's shout from the back seat made them both jump. Steph kept her hands firmly on the wheel and frowned across at Caroline.

'We're taking you back home. Where did you think we were going?' Caroline swivelled in her seat and gently removed Beverly's left hand to stop her from tugging at the back of Steph's seat.

'Covehithe. We must get to the rehearsal!' The panic in Beverly's voice pushed it up another octave, making their ears ring.

'Surely, after all you've been through, you need to collapse for the rest of the day at least.' Caroline accompanied her best calming teacher's voice with a smile. 'You've been pumped full of painkillers, and it wouldn't be safe for you to do anything much until they're out of your system. You need to be at home resting, darling.'

Beverly sat back in her seat, sighed, then, after a brief pause, leaned forward once again. 'Well, you two can run the rehearsal without me, can't you?'

'No, we can't. We'll cancel it today.' There was a shriek of protest from the back seat, which Caroline ignored. 'Everyone has worked so hard and one evening off won't hurt. Anyway, you won't be able to play the role with your arm in plaster, will you?'

'I was worried ... really worried about that as they were pushing ... putting it on. And I can tell you I told them to stop ... several times I did ... but they wouldn't listen.' Beverly sounded as if she'd been drinking, as her words were slurred and her voice too loud. 'No, I have a cunning plan!'

She giggled at herself. 'I can cover it with mud or paint it brown then it won't show under the lights and wrap it in ... in rags ... or put it in a sling ... or hide it under her cloak like this.' Beverly pulled the ragged cloak over the pristine white plaster so it was hidden, but gasped in pain and took in a sharp breath as she moved her arm.

Caroline turned towards Steph, rolled her eyes, and shook her head. 'Maybe you need to consider if you carry on at all.'

'With what exactly?' Beverly shot back.

'The play. I'm sure the audience would understand if it's postponed after Jessica's death and now your accident. We could do it next summer, or even in October, when your plaster's off.'

'Let me make this clear.' Beverly's voice, now loud enough to fill a large auditorium, made Steph and Caroline wince. 'We will be going ahead, and I will be playing Mother Courage as a tribute to Jessica. The play must go on!'

'Well, let's get you home and think about it after you've had a rest.'

'I don't need to think about it or have a rest.'

Caroline stared out of the windscreen, apparently deciding to leave it for now. Steph could feel the wave of tension and the anger from the back seat and knew further discussion was a waste of time. For a moment, her heart had lifted at the idea of getting her evenings and weekends back. The play had domi-nated her life for weeks and the thought of sitting in the evening sun reading a book or taking an extra-long walk with Derek or having a supper that was more than a few salad leaves thrown on a plate was tantalising.

She drove past the church and around the sharp bend, slowed down and pulled into the side of the road. 'Is this where it happened?'

Beverly turned and waved her left hand at the hedge, then held it up to her eyes to shield them from the bright sunlight. 'Yes. There. See?'

They could see a torn hedge where Beverly's car had careered off the road, the enormous oak tree to the left which fortunately she'd avoided, and the broken fence. Her car had flattened several rows of ripe wheat in the corner of the field and the soft ground on the verge was mashed up by the wide tyres of the pickup truck, along with several tracks made by the police cars and ambulance that rescued her. There were no skid marks on the road, but if her brakes had failed, there wouldn't be would there?

'You were lucky to have got out of this so lightly.' Steph turned around to see Beverly properly.

'That's what the police and ambulance people said.' Bever-ly's eyes were closed.

'Did someone see you and phone it in?'

'No. I phoned myself. I thought I was fine until ...' she moved her plastered arm a little, wincing as she did so. 'Pain didn't start until the hospital.' She sounded aggrieved, as if it was all the hospital's fault.

Steph looked through the windscreen down the road. 'I was here only yesterday with Jason to look at the spot where his uncle had his motor bike crash. Up there.' She indicated the straight stretch of road ahead of them.

All three pondered the empty road ahead of them. Beverly broke the silence. 'So tragic. That boy ... such a talent ... such a waste.'

Steph slowed down as they drove past the spot where Marcus had died. 'Well, the police will examine your car and find out what's wrong with your brakes.'

'How do I manage without a car?' Her voice blasted their ear drums.

'You won't be able to drive until that plaster comes off – six weeks?' Steph was amazed at how stupid this woman was being, but then she was full of painkillers.

They drove through the late August countryside, past a field of pigs, another where the hay was being mown, until they reached the industrial estate, where Beverly leaned forward between them.

'You've lived with Margaret a long time?'

'Yes, over twenty years.'

'Must've been difficult with ... you know ... Parkinson's?' Beverly sat back and in the driving mirror, Steph could see her head resting on the seat and her eyes drooping.

'After we got over the shock of the diagnosis, we've just been getting on with it. You don't have much choice and there's masses of support if you know where to look.'

'And people don't mind that you're – you know – you're – two women?'

'They don't seem to, but they wouldn't tell us anyway, would they?'

Caroline threw Steph a puzzled look at this sudden change of subject and Beverly's more reflective tone.

Steph mouthed 'Painkillers.' Caroline nodded but said nothing.

After a gap, an even quieter voice came from the back seat. 'Umm. I've often wondered if I ...You know ...'

Steph glanced in her mirror at a sleeping Beverly, her head back against the seat, making little snoring noises.

CHAPTER THIRTY-SIX

WEDNESDAY 21ST AUGUST: 4.30PM

DEREK DASHED into the flat as soon as Steph opened the door and rushed up to Hale sitting in his usual place at the table, his laptop open in front of him.

'Hello.' Steph hung Derek's lead on the line of hooks by the door. 'Didn't expect to see you.'

'I came home for some peace – need to get my head round this program once and for all. I thought you'd be at rehearsal.'

'It's cancelled. Sorry, do you want me to go out again and leave you alone?'

Hale shifted in his chair so he could see her. 'Rehearsal cancelled? Must be a first.'

Walking into the kitchen to put the kettle on, Steph stopped and looked at Hale. 'Remember the car crash?'

'Car crash?'

'Beverly's car crash. The one that you asked me to help with this morning?'

'Oh, that car crash!'

Whatever was wrong with him? He wasn't usually this vague.

Hale sighed. 'Sorry. Yes, I did, didn't I? Did she tell you how it happened?'

Steph made a pot of tea, which she put on a tray with two mugs and the milk jug, and brought it over to the table, where Hale made space for it by shifting the well-thumbed Athena manual.

'Beverly approached that sharp bend by the church but when she tried to slow down, her brakes failed, and she went off the road through a hedge and was stopped by a fence. She was lucky. No one else was involved, and she missed a massive oak tree.'

'Well, that's good news. She's fine?'

'A broken arm, just above her wrist. She's in plaster and out of it on pain killers. Caroline and I helped her into bed – I bet she won't remember it.'

'She'll cancel the play?'

'You're joking! It was as much as we could do to get her to cancel the rehearsal.'

Hale poured out the tea. 'She crashed on the road between Southwold and Covehithe?'

Steph took the mug he was holding out to her and sipped the tea. 'Coincidentally, just along from the stretch where Marcus Strong had his motorbike crash.'

'Where is her car now?' Hale wrote in a small notebook to his right.

'I thought you said you were having it checked? But maybe it got picked up by her garage. It wasn't at the crash site.'

'Right, I'll get Lizzie to check on where it is and get the brakes looked at. As you say, quite a coincidence. There are starting to be too many coincidences around Beverly's plays.'

Hale pulled his mobile phone out of his pocket and pressed a button. So, Lizzie was on speed dial?

'Hi Lizzie ... fine thanks. You?'

He laughed. 'Sounds as if you're settling in all right. I said you would.' Another smile. 'Yeah, really? ... Will you check on something for me, please? An RTA on the Southwold to Covehithe road this morning, only one car involved, we attended ... Yes, that's right ... Could you find out where the car is and get the brakes looked at, please? The driver said they failed ... What?' Yet another smile. 'Yes, I'll be there ... See you then. Looking forward to it ... Sorry? ... You, too. Bye.'

He finished his tea, replaced the mug on the tray, smiled at Steph, and returned to his laptop screen. Picking up the tray, Steph went towards the sink, her stomach churning.

'I'll think I'll go for a walk.'

'But you've just come in.'

'Yes, but it's such a lovely evening – a shame to waste it.'

On the way to collect Derek's lead, Hale's voice stopped her. 'By the way, we're now pretty sure the body is Lucy's.'

'Really?'

'Yes, she disappears off all the UK databases after the play. Can't find a trace of her anywhere.'

'That's good news, I suppose.' No doubt, yet again, the wondrous Lizzie had done a "great job". 'And Marcus?'

Hale sighed. 'That was investigated and found to be an accidental death.' He fished a file out of his bag and held it out to Steph. 'There's the file. It was an accident. Have a look for yourself, if you don't believe me.'

Taken aback by his aggressive tone, she stepped over to the table, took the file Hale held out to her, and placed it on top of the pile of papers on her desk that appeared to have bred since she was last there.

'Well, aren't you going to read it, now I've brought it back for you after all your nagging?'

Nagging? Had she? The knot in her stomach tightened. Deciding it was best not to argue with him, she turned on her heel and, without a word, seized the lead, opened the door and walked out, followed by an excited Derek.

CHAPTER THIRTY-SEVEN

WEDNESDAY 21ST AUGUST: 6.30PM

STEPH DROVE TO THE HARBOUR, found a space, and let Derek jump out of the boot. Still in a foul mood and feeling nauseous, she hoped that a walk by the river, then the sea, would calm her and by the time she got home, all might be well again.

It had been another hot day and the people sitting at the outside tables and on the low wall of The Harbour Inn were making the most of the glowing evening sunshine. She waved her hand in front of her face, sweeping away a cloud of tiny insects that hovered around her, pulled Derek away from making friends with an enormous poodle, and set off along the river towards the sea.

If she had hoped for solitude, then she was wrong. How stupid to have chosen this walk, which was crowded with dogs and adults sauntering along. Why not? She chastised herself – they had as much right to relish the summer evening as she did, but she still resented them being there.

As she reached the car park by the sea, she recognised the dark blue Porsche and was amazed he was happy to drive it over such deep potholes. No sign of him, so she headed through the dunes towards the sea.

Derek stopped to sniff at a fascinating clump of marram grass, and as she was turning around, she almost walked into Naz, holding out an ice cream cone, complete with a chocolate flake perched on the top.

'I thought you might like one of these.'

She laughed as she took the enormous ice cream. 'Thanks. But how did you—'

'I saw you walking Derek this way and thought you might need a sugar lift. Is everything all right?'

'Fine thanks. Just a long day.'

In casual gear of jeans and a pale blue polo shirt, he looked happy in his own skin as he pointed to the bench that over-looked the river.

'If Derek doesn't mind retracing his steps a little, we could sit there while we eat them.'

Steph smiled and joined him as he walked towards the bench, ignoring the puzzled look on Derek's face and his reluctance to be pulled away from the sea. Thank goodness she hadn't taken his lead off, or she'd never have got him.

They sat for a while watching the tide from the river rushing out to the sea, licking their ice creams. As she finished the last mouthful, Steph wiped her fingers on the paper napkin Naz had given her and glanced across at him. 'What is it they say? Do you come here often?'

Naz laughed and, wiping the dribbled ice cream drips off his pristine polo shirt, met her gaze. 'I find it's a good place to come after work to – what do they call it – decompress? After a day in court or working with those in our society who find it difficult to obey the law, I find it clears my head to walk.'

'I can imagine. I know Hale finds it difficult to switch off.'

She caught herself mentioning Hale as if to remind them he existed.

'No wonder, the amount of work he gets through.'

'Oh?'

Naz stood. 'Shall we?'

Steph smiled, stood and freed Derek from his lead, and he belted down towards the sea, chasing the ball she threw for him.

Naz laughed. 'He's got some energy, that little chap. Anyway, now Hale has the new super-woman he should get home a bit earlier.'

Steph frowned. 'Really?'

'Yes, this girl from the Met, Elizabeth, I think her name is, certainly knows her stuff and will make a great deputy. I was with her in an interview with a client this afternoon and we had a right tussle.'

Turning away to pick up the ball and throw it into the white foam at the edge of the waves, she hoped her face didn't give away her feelings. Not him too! She'd had enough of the perfect Lizzie.

Derek retrieved the ball and dropped it at Naz's feet. He picked it up and threw it an enormous distance. 'You must be a good cricketer.'

'I was once. Out of practice now. I hoped to have a quiet word with Hale about progress on Jessica, but I couldn't see him. I don't suppose you could ...' He trailed off and grinned.

Steph took a deep breath and grabbed some time to think while she bent down and threw the ball for Derek, who dashed into the sea enthusiastically to retrieve it.

'He's busy investigating the circumstances of Jessica's death.' She smiled as she heard herself sounding so formal.

Naz raised his eyebrow as he must have picked up her

tone. 'Is that code for "shut up"? Sorry, I don't mean to compromise you.'

They stood together, gazing out to sea and watching Derek splashing through the waves. Did it really matter? He'd find out anyway and she may get something more from him here.

She turned to face him. 'We've spoken to your Puck. He didn't marry Lucy.'

'Really?' Naz stared at her, obviously shocked. 'Are you sure? That really surprises me.'

Walking towards the town, they ducked beneath the fishing line of a grumpy-looking man who had set up a small igloo tent for the night and made little attempt to hide his irritation at other humans daring to step on his beach.

'Have you heard from Lucy since she left? I think you said you had a postcard?'

'Yes. It was the last I heard from her.'

'Do you think you might still have it somewhere?'

'If I have, it will be in one of those boxes in the loft full of old school reports and exam papers.' He frowned and closed his eyes for a moment. 'Yes, I'll look for you. Would it help?'

They had reached the beach huts, where dogs had to be put on their leads, so Steph turned around and threw the ball back the way they had come. 'Derek!' He dashed past them, spraying up sand, which she wiped out of her eyes. 'Sorry about that. Yes, anything to do with that play would help. It seems that Jessica's death may be linked to it somehow—'

'*The Dream?*'

'If you have the postcard or anything else from the play, I'd be really grateful to receive it.'

The wind sandblasted their faces as they trudged back towards the harbour, and it was becoming more of a challenge to throw the ball.

'Of course, I'll go home and have a look.'

'Thanks Naz, that's kind.'

'Same time tomorrow? I'll bring what I have then.'

'If you're sure you wouldn't rather drop it off at the station?'

'Not if you don't mind? It's good to have company after Jessica – well, you know – and we are on the same team after all. Anything I can do to help, you have only to ask.'

CHAPTER THIRTY-EIGHT

THURSDAY 22ND AUGUST: 9.00AM

NAZ RANG THE DOORBELL AGAIN, pressing down longer this time and heard it echoing somewhere in the bowels of the Edwardian house. He stepped back to look up at the front bedroom window. The curtains were open but that needn't mean anything; she could sleep in the back, away from the traffic. Not that there was much traffic on this side of the common.

She must still be in bed. He pulled his cuff up and checked his Rolex watch. Just past nine. He'd sent a text to his PA warning her he'd be in late, as his first appointment wasn't until eleven. Giving up, he decided he'd go into town for a coffee and come back. About to open the door of his car, he heard a shout behind him.

'Hello there. Were you after me?'

It was Beverly in a bright yellow kimono, embroidered with the most enormous red dragon spurting flames. Trust her to have such a dramatic robe.

'Yes, Beverly.'

She threw him a puzzled look. 'And you are?'

'Naz – Naz Rahman.'

Her frown transformed into a wide smile. 'My sweet Lysander!'

He cringed. After thirty years, was that all he was – her sweet Lysander? He forced a smile. 'Yes, it's me, Beverly.' As he said it, he grinned at his stupidity – of course it was him. Who else would it be?

'Of course, Rahman! How rude of me. Please forgive me – pain killers melting my brain! We are so grateful to your company for sponsoring *Mother Courage*. It's so kind of you.'

'You're welcome. Sorry to call on you so early, but I wanted a quick word – good heavens, whatever have you done?'

He was sure Beverly had deliberately displayed the plastered arm by pulling up the luxurious sleeve, and for a millisecond was tempted not to mention it.

'Oh, this?' She glanced down at it as if she had only just discovered it was there. 'It's nothing – just a small prang in my car. Would you like to come in?'

Naz walked into the imposing entrance hall, featuring a huge oak staircase with an extravagantly carved newel post of acanthus leaves and ivy. 'What a beautiful piece of carving.'

'Thank you. I've tried to keep as many of the original features as possible. Come through to the kitchen and I'll make us some coffee.'

He trailed after her along the black-and-white-tiled hall, crammed with black-framed etchings of Victorian theatre managers and actors, to a warm, modern kitchen.

'As you can see, I have replaced the Edwardian kitchen with something more practical.'

'It's beautiful.' Naz admired the pale oak cupboards that stretched away to the French windows, revealing a beautiful garden. This woman certainly had good taste, and a pile of money too.

'Please excuse my appearance. I must have overslept with

all the chemicals they gave me yesterday. Although I must say, it was the best night's sleep I've had for a long time. Espresso?'

'Please.' He watched as she fiddled with a top of the range espresso machine, obviously finding it difficult with only her left hand. Should he offer to help? No – he didn't know her well enough. He sat on one of the high stools placed around the island. The vintage cast iron tractor seat fitted in perfectly and was surprisingly comfortable.

Beverly handed Naz the elegant porcelain cup and sat opposite, sipping her coffee. 'Now, how can I help you?'

'I came to see you to discuss Jessica's funeral.'

'Oh?'

'She and I have been close for some time and I'm also her family solicitor.'

Beverly shot him an appraising glance – actually, more of a hard stare. 'Has she left instructions in her will about her funeral? That would be really helpful.' He knew she didn't mean a word of it. Jessica's funeral was to be her show, and that was that.

'Nothing about the service. Only that she wished to be buried beside her mother. I think they bought a suitable plot nine years ago when she died.'

Did he see a look of relief flash across her face? It changed quickly to one of sympathy – a look he'd seen worn so often by distant family members waiting to find out if they were to inherit anything. He chided himself for being cynical and waited.

Beverly put down her cup, aligning it precisely on its saucer. 'I have spoken to Jessica's father and naturally his wishes will be observed, but if, as you say, Jessica left no specific instructions, I'm not sure we have anything to discuss.'

Naz felt he was being dismissed. 'I wondered why it was

taking place in such a rush. Most funerals take about two or three weeks, but Jessica's is taking place next week. Why?'

'Why not? Her father is ill—'

'But not close to death, so there is no urgency.'

Beverly re-adjusted herself on her seat, sat up straight, and narrowed her eyes as she skewered him with another hard stare. 'You may be the family solicitor, but I'm not sure what Jessica's funeral has to do with you. I have agreed it with her father. You—'

'I'm sure you have, but he's hardly in a robust state. And as for arranging it for next Thursday, the day before the first performance of the play – or have you decided to cancel it?'

'Why does everyone keep suggesting that I cancel the play?' Beverly stood, stretching herself up to her full height

Naz matched her, noting that he was a good head taller. He pulled himself up to stand tall, as if in court. 'After Jessica's death and now your injury, I would have thought it respectful to cancel the show, not to link it with Jessica's funeral and turn her death into a media circus — a publicity stunt for your amateur dramatics.'

'I think it's time you left.'

'I've not finished.'

'Well, I have, and I'd like you to leave my house – now.' Beverly stood, glaring at Naz, who hadn't moved.

He held onto the edge of the island and leaned in towards Beverly. 'I will say to your face what others are saying behind your back. We've always known that everything you do is aimed at one end – to boost Beverly Elkin.'

She lifted her chin and snarled. 'Now you've had your say, please leave.'

Naz glared across at her, his powerful voice rebounding off the hard surfaces. 'Your plays are never about the actors – they're showcases for you. All you want is to get outstanding reviews to impress your London friends. When I was your "sweet Lysander", as you put it, I felt like a costumed parrot – we sang to your tune only because you had the power over who went to drama school and who didn't.'

She sat down, as if someone had hit her. Naz paused – but he'd started now, and he'd damn well finish. 'You – it's all about you. You were jealous of Jessica even then, especially when she avoided your attentions.'

Beverly's eyes narrowed. 'This is monstrous!'

'Oh yes, she told me all about that. And when she returned, a star, with far more experience than you, when she dared to stand up to you, you couldn't cope with it, could you?'

Beverly hauled herself to her feet. 'That's enough, you should leave now before—'

'Before what? You call the police? Call them and let's talk through Jessica's so-called accident together.'

'You don't think I—'

'Why not? You had the expertise and the motive. You were furious with her for stealing your limelight. She told me you regretted asking her back here and now you've got the starring role, not only in the play, but at her funeral. And the only reason you're rushing it, is to make sure your swanky London friends will stay over for your pathetic little performance.'

He stopped, suddenly ashamed of his emotional outburst. So unprofessional. But this wasn't professional, was it? It was personal, and he knew he was right. So did she from the death mask that was now her face.

He made a swift turn and took rapid strides down the hall to the front door, which he slammed behind him, presumably leaving her speechless for once. He felt better.

CHAPTER THIRTY-NINE

THURSDAY 22ND AUGUST: 7.00PM

The Oakwood Chronicle – Thursday 22nd August 2019

Jessica Marlowe laid to rest in Oakwood – Joe Denny

The funeral of Jessica Marlow (aged 48) will be held at St Mary's Church, Oakwood next Thursday 29th August at noon. Her former drama teacher, Rev'd Beverly Elkin (69), now an ordained vicar, will lead the service and it is expected that many stars of stage and screen will be there to pay their respects to the well-loved star.

Her death, which is now being treated as suspicious by the police, was a shock to all who knew her. While rehearsing the lead role in "Mother Courage and Her Children", a falling stage light hit Jessica, and she died from her injuries. She will be remembered for the many films she made in Hollywood with some of the top directors, as well as her appearances on the West End stage.

Only last year she picked up an Olivier Award for her Ranevskaya in "The Cherry Orchard", which one critic praised in her five-star review, "This is one of several great Chekhovian roles for ladies in middle age: she's gorgeous, self-deluded, has plenty of suitors and excellent frocks, and is a metaphor for the decline of the great Russian Empire itself. Jessica Marlowe's interpretation is iconic – the best I have ever seen."

"That performance was typical of her talent, and it is a tragedy that we shall not see her in some of the other great roles for women now." commented ex-drama advisor Beverly Elkin. "It would have been a rare treat to see her original interpretation of Mother Courage in my production. She shone in rehearsals and I am sure the London theatre critics would have flocked to see her. Now they will come to her funeral to bid her farewell. Such a tragedy."

In a previous article, we reported that Beverly Elkin had reluctantly agreed to take on the lead role, as she didn't want to disappoint her drama group and as an appropriate tribute to Jessica. Her brave decision has cost her dear, and she herself is now recovering from a road traffic accident.

When asked if she thought the play would go ahead with her arm now in plaster, Beverly exhibited the determination for which she is famous locally. "Good gracious, yes. This is nothing. Jessica would have wanted it, and I am doing what all those of us who tread the boards do – we get on with it whatever happens – the show must go on as a tribute to Jessica. It was her motto, and it is certainly mine."

Some of our readers have questioned the timing of Jessica's funeral as insensitive and suggest that the Rev Elkin wants to steal the limelight linking the funeral with the production.

"Rubbish!" she retorts. "It is on that day as Jessica's father requested it, and if some of the stars or the critics decide to make a weekend of it down here on the beautiful Suffolk coast and take the opportunity to come to the play, then they will be welcome. There is no intention to link the two events."

Tickets for "Mother Courage and Her Children" next weekend are available from The Book Shelf, in the Market Square, or Oakwood Library and Rev'd Elkin warned they are disappearing fast.

———

NAZ FINISHED READING the article and was about to put it down when he read it again, this time very slowly. The gall of that woman! Couldn't she keep her mouth shut and let Jessica rest in peace instead of using every opportunity to sell herself and that wretched play? Well, he wouldn't be going to buy a ticket to see her prance around in Jessica's part. She should have been there, not that dreadful woman. It shouldn't be going ahead – and as for her funeral – that would be another Elkin production with her taking the lead role.

He hoped the police were investigating Beverly as the chief suspect. She had the means, the opportunity, and the motive could have come from that secret that Jessica mentioned. What a shame Jessica hadn't shared it with him, but if she'd confronted Beverly as she'd threatened ...

Each day, Beverly was turning Jessica's death into a bigger and bigger publicity stunt to push her stupid play. Perhaps that was the reason Beverly had asked her down here? So she could kill her, while all the time learning the lines so she could step in at the last minute? And there was Beverly's starring role at the funeral. No one could ignore that ...

'Stop it!' He heard his own voice shouting and, shocked by the sound, threw himself down on the sofa, closing his eyes. Here he was, a respected member of the legal profession getting trapped in a spiral of suspicion. Based on what? Nothing but his anger. Certainly not hard evidence.

But he did have evidence, didn't he? He'd blamed her for years for bringing that French dickhead over here to steal Lucy from him, and now they couldn't find her. What had happened to her? After that postcard – he closed his eyes and could see the tourist cliche of the Eiffel Tower with her round girly writing on the back and the little daisy she always added to her signature.

He knew it by heart. "Dear Naz, by the time you get this I'll be in Paris with Hugo where I'm going to the clown school. Sorry not to have told you myself. Please don't come to find me. Have a good life. Love Lucy."

Her postcard would be up in the loft, he was sure. He wouldn't have thrown it away, would he? Lucy's last words to him before she married Hugo – or so he'd thought.

Having climbed up into the loft, he stepped over the mass of boxes, bags and piles of rubbish. Christmas decorations, an old wooden tennis racket, a broken rattan chair – whenever did he think he was going to mend that? At last, in the far corner – it could be there, couldn't it? A dusty box of his A Level exam papers and notes from Uni? He hunted through it, decanting piles of papers until at the very bottom he spied a corner of blue. That was it. He knew he wouldn't have thrown it away.

As he gently pulled out the picture, he smiled. It was exactly as he'd remembered it, the iconic landmark of the Eiffel

Tower against an unreal blue sky. About to stuff the enormous pile of papers back into the box, he paused as he spotted one of her daisies on a folded sheet of paper, and then another. Her letters? He'd forgotten all about them.

Thrilled at finding the postcard and the small cache of her letters, he went downstairs and sat down with a glass of merlot to re-read and re-create that magical time with Lucy. His first love.

CHAPTER FORTY

FRIDAY 23RD AUGUST: 6.25PM

NAZ DROVE into the harbour car park, pulled up against the metal fence that stopped cars tipping into the river, and looked around for Steph's car. He glanced at his watch and saw it wasn't yet half-past six – he was early. As he climbed out of his Porsche, her car drew up beside him.

He walked around and stood by the driver's door as she got out. 'Shall I let Derek out? He looks desperate.'

'Please. He always does when we get here.'

Naz lifted the hatch-back and Derek jumped down and licked Naz's hand, his tail helicoptering. Yes, a dog like him would do very well. He bent down and grabbed the loop of his lead while Steph locked the car.

She smiled at him. 'Good day?'

'Busy. You?'

'Mad. Spent all day arranging for students to have interviews for A level courses now they've got their GCSE results. It always amazes me how many of them do nothing about their future until the last minute.'

'No rehearsal tonight? I'd have thought Beverly would've had you hard at it.'

'No, we have the night off as we have two full days ahead of us – Saturday and Sunday – nine to five.'

He held out the lead to her, but she shook her head. 'Let him off when we get past those dunes?' He nodded, and they walked in silence through the clumps of rough grass, each one carefully sniffed, until they reached the sandy beach, where Naz leaned down and undid the lead freeing Derek to dash off towards the sea. Steph held out her hand for the lead, which she draped around her neck.

She laughed at him. 'You really should get a dog, you know, it would suit your image.'

'And what's that?'

'Oh, you know, successful solicitor, man about town.'

'Really?'

'You'd have to get a pedigree though, not a mutt like Derek. You're far too stylish for a jumble like him!' She laughed

Was she flirting with him? He didn't usually find older women attractive, but he felt comfortable with Steph and enjoyed her laugh. No, stop it! He didn't want to piss off Hale, and they were very much an item – although they hadn't married yet, which was strange for people of their age.

Her voice smashed through his fantasy. 'Did you find Lucy's postcard?'

He stopped walking and turned towards her so she had to stop and face him. 'Oh, so you only want me for a piece of evidence, not for the pleasure of my company!'

He noticed a slight blush move up her neck. 'Rubbish! It's good to have company on this walk. Derek's conversation isn't too stimulating.' She bent down and threw the ball into the waves for Derek to retrieve. They watched as he smashed through the rough waves to snap at the ball and deposit it on the sand at Steph's feet.

'Good boy!' they chorused together, laughing at their predictable reaction.

'You'll be pleased to know I found the postcard – here it is.' He fished it out of the inside pocket of his denim jacket and handed it to her. He had put it in a small plastic folder so she could read it without touching it. 'Thought it might be worth preserving it – just in case there's a print or trace of something there besides me. But after all this time it's unlikely, I know.'

Observing the picture, then turning it over, she read the message on the back. 'And you're sure this is Lucy's writing?'

'Positive. See that daisy there?' He pointed to her signature with the tiny daisy inside the Y. 'She always added a daisy at the end of her name like that.'

Steph squinted down at the tiny flower before looking up at him. 'May I hold on to it?'

'Of course.'

'And you heard nothing else from her?'

'No, as far as I was concerned, seeing her go off with Hugo after snogging him on the beach and then getting this, I assumed she was with him, and I was history. No, I heard nothing else from her.'

Steph threw the ball out, further this time, and Derek, with boundless energy, doggy-paddled after it. 'You didn't think of going after her?'

'I did at first. But it all seemed so final, and she'd been spending more and more time with him. When they went off together, I thought that was that and moved on.'

'I don't suppose you have any other examples of her writing?'

'Why? Do you suspect it was sent by someone else?'

'We're exploring all lines of enquiry—'

'Steph – it's me you're talking to! I know what that means!'

Steph paused for a moment, then looked him in the eye. 'OK. Yes.'

'You think Lucy never left England.' He stared at her, hoping to push her to tell him all. She didn't but threw the ball again for Derek and stayed silent. He wasn't about to give up. 'It's Lucy's body that's been found on the cliff, isn't it?'

'It's not been confirmed ...' What did her mother used to say – in for a penny, in for a pound? 'I know Hale will be speaking to you, but did you ever give Lucy any jewellery as a present?'

Naz looked out to sea, digesting the question with its obvious implication. 'Yes, I did. It was a bracelet, a silver chain with a heart. I gave it to her on her eighteenth birthday and had the back inscribed with her birthday on 12th September 1988.'

He bored into her with his eyes, hoping to read her thoughts. She was giving nothing away. News of the bracelet hadn't been made public. 'You've found it, haven't you?'

'Look Naz, I think you need to have a word with Hale about all this.' Her tone left him in no doubt she would give nothing further.

This time when Derek brought the ball back, she picked it up, and as he sat apparently hoping for another throw, she fixed his lead on him. 'Shall we?'

'Time for a quick one at The Harbour?'

She looked at her watch and pulled a face. 'Sorry, Naz, I ought to get back. Hale should be home about now.'

They strolled up to the cars until Derek found a particularly smelly fence post. Waiting for him, they stared across the river at Walberswick. Steph turned and frowned. 'And did you say there were others who also got postcards?'

Naz frowned. 'I didn't, but I know for certain Jessica did – she showed it to me. From memory it was the same picture with a similar "I'm going to Paris message", but as for anyone else, I'm not sure.'

Steph loaded a soggy Derek into the boot and walked around to the driver's door.

'Actually, now I think of it, there was someone else – Beverly, of course – yes, Beverly got one. I can remember Jessica saying how annoyed Beverly was with Lucy for wasting her time and she wished her "joy of the worm" – that was it!'

Steph came back towards him, 'What a weird thing to say.'

'A Shakespeare quote, I think. Jessica and I were laughing about it only the other day before she ... she ... and how Beverly turned on the worm Puck at the end. He went from hero to zero as he worked his way through the cast and caused no end of grief, which Beverly had to mop up. So yes, they both got one, but that's all I know.'

'Don't suppose you happen to know if Jessica kept hers?'

Naz thought back to their conversation. 'She didn't say she had, but maybe it's back at her father's in an old box in his loft, like mine. Might be worth asking.'

'Thanks, Naz. For this and the walk.' Steph waved the postcard at him, climbed into her car and he stood back, giving her space to drive off.

The sun went behind a cloud, and he shivered in the sudden gloom. He climbed into his car, feeling down and rather bereft.

CHAPTER FORTY-ONE

FRIDAY 23RD AUGUST: 8.30PM

As usual, Hale was sitting at the table, hunched over his laptop, when Steph arrived home. She looped Derek's lead over one of the coat hooks by the door, grabbed Hale's coat, which he'd dumped on the back of an armchair, and hung that up too.

'Sorry, wanted to get this done.' He'd swivelled round and watched her move it. 'Good rehearsal?'

'No rehearsal tonight but walking Derek. Two full days tomorrow. Let me feed him and I'll tell you all.'

'Now that sounds intriguing! Could it be that Beverly and the lighting man have got it together at last?' He came across to her as she was pouring dog food into Derek's bowl and threaded his arms around her, leaning against her, kissing her neck.

Wow! This was a change from the past few weeks! She poured the kibble slowly, much to Derek's frustration, relishing the physical contact, absent for so long. Hale nibbled her ear. 'Or could it be that pathetic little Deputy Principal, the one who's up himself, is leaving?'

'Drink?' She squirmed along the cupboard to the fridge. He shimmied with her.

'Please. Is there any of that beer left? I'm afraid I hit it hard the other night.'

She reached into the fridge, pulled out two bottles, which she opened, turned to face him, and held one out to him. He kissed the tip of her nose, took the bottle, strode over to the dining chair which he swung around and sat astride, leaning over the back, waiting for her to reveal all.

She pulled the plastic sleeve out of her bag and waved it at him. 'I've got one of the postcards sent by Lucy from France.'

'You have been busy! And how did you get it?'

'From Naz, on the walk with Derek.'

Hale reached for it and examined the postcard through the plastic. 'Don't suppose he has other examples of her writing?'

'I asked, but he thought not. He did say there may be others. He recalled Jessica showing him hers and thought it might be in her father's house. Worth a look. Oh, and he also thought Beverly got one.'

Hale continued to examine the written message. She walked across and pointed to Lucy's signature. 'You see that little flower?' She pointed to the tiny symbol. 'Apparently, she always added that daisy.'

Hale got closer to the image and frowned. 'But if she always did that, anyone who knew her could have imitated it, couldn't they?'

'Of course they could. But if Lucy didn't send those cards, and we think she couldn't have, then we're looking for someone who knew her well, aren't we?'

Hale continued frowning and staring at the card as if it were going to reveal something momentous to him.

Steph spoke slowly, saving what she was sure was the best news until last. 'And then I found out from Naz that he gave

Lucy a silver chain bracelet and a heart with her birthday inscribed on it – 12th September 1988.'

Hale gulped his beer, wiping his hand across his lips. 'Yes, we're already pretty sure it's Lucy's body, and that helps reinforce it. Lizzie did a great job tracing Lucy's uncle – her father's brother – and that provided a twenty-five percent DNA match. But I hope you didn't give too much away to Naz?'

Lizzie could do no wrong, apparently, while she had become a blundering idiot. 'How stupid do you think I am? Naz isn't stupid either and already had an idea who it is. Anyway, he told me about the bracelet, I didn't mention it.'

Hale looked perplexed, apparently puzzled at her sudden annoyance.

She took a deep breath and exhaled slowly.

Hale held out the empty bottle to her, which she took and placed in the re-cycling bin. 'Sounds as if you've made good progress on Lucy. What about Marcus Strong? Got anything since I gave you the file?'

A sudden flash of irritation swept through her. 'Hang on a minute! I've spent a full day at college doing my proper job, dealing with masses of students and Tigger-like teachers after their summer break, then got this evidence for you – so no, I've not had time to go through that file yet.' She stared around the pristine kitchen. 'Don't suppose you've sorted supper as you got home first?'

Hale frowned, evidently surprised by her question. 'No, I had to get through this.' He gestured with his thumb over his shoulder at the laptop behind him. 'Thought we could do it when you got in.'

Without a word, Steph pulled out the freezer drawers below the fridge, clattering each one free of the ice that clung to the bars, looking for a plastic bag or a baking dish with something she could prepare quickly. A grey-beige bag of something unappetising caught her eye. 'I think this may be some fish pie mixture. I can do some potatoes and veg to go with it. Ok?' She held up the beige bag and rubbed the frost off the outside. She could see some solid white bits that could be fish. Yes, it must be fish pie mix. Why didn't she ever label them?

'Fine.'

It didn't sound fine. Shitting Henry! What did he expect, a seven-course tasting menu?

CHAPTER FORTY-TWO

A CROWD three-deep in places lined the path up to the church and the road outside, standing behind metal barriers that looked more appropriate for a football match or a pop concert than a church service.

Naz felt self-conscious walking down the narrow corridor between the gawping spectators, who pulled disappointed faces and continued chatting when they discovered he wasn't a celebrity. He forced his way through to the front door through gaggles of news journalists and at least three TV crews.

Just inside the church door he found his way blocked by two security men in dark suits, thick necks bursting out over their shirt collars – bouncers at a funeral?

Beverly stood in the shadow to their right and gave a little nod to the gorilla opposite, who stepped aside to let Naz in. It appeared he'd passed the test. After giving his name, Naz waited while the usher ticked his name on the clipboard list, and escorted him to his seat, which was about half-way back on the right side of the church. The empty pews in front were no doubt waiting for the celebs to arrive.

Steph and Hale were in the row in front of him, alongside Caroline and her partner Margaret. He was just about to tap Hale on the shoulder when he froze, his hand in mid-air, deciding it might be better to speak afterwards.

He noticed the woman beside him in deepest black wearing an enormous hat, over which was draped a dense veil. There was no danger of recognising her as she wore dark glasses under the funeral camouflage, which must have restricted her ability to see anything at all.

He was about to speak to the woman in black to ask how she knew Jessica, when she abruptly twisted away, apparently concentrating on Jessica's page-long biography beneath a flaw-less publicity photo that he'd seen in magazines. It didn't capture the real Jessica at all, but a polished, doll-like version.

The overwhelming perfume of the hundreds of white trumpet-shaped lilies arranged on each window ledge and tied to the end of each pew triggered Naz's hay fever, and he sneezed loudly. The woman in black tutted and moved away as if he was contagious.

On either side of the altar were two of the largest floral displays he had ever seen. Each one must have been over six feet high and at least three feet wide, with pure white lilies woven into the two magnificent walls of flowers.

He picked up his order of service, which resembled a posh theatre programme; ivory parchment paper with embossed golden script giving Jessica's dates of birth and death, beneath the professional head and shoulders portrait of her above the detailed account of her life and achievements. Naz flicked through the inside pages – it was going to be a long service with eulogies from some of the stars she'd worked with, several musical interludes, some poetry, as well as the more traditional hymns, prayers and a sermon by the Very Rev'd Beverly Elkin.

A gentle sound floated out from the behind the flower

walls. It was the saddest music Naz had ever heard. He shut his eyes to listen as the notes poured out over the congregation, hypnotised by each pure note of Samuel Barber's *Adagio for Strings*, according to the list of music played by the Pavlov Quartet.

A whispering from behind him ran through the pews and made him open his eyes. He watched the Oscars red carpet procession of movie stars and theatrical grandees walk dramatically to their seats in the front rows, acknowledging the in-crowd as they passed. It was a Who's Who of the acting world – no wonder there was a crowd lining the way in.

Once the celebs had settled, a procession of black-robed choir boys and girls, each holding an enormous candle, followed. Then, about twenty adults snaked into the choir stalls and stood to attention, with their candles fixed in stands before them.

The flickering light of the candles reflected off the ancient glass of the diamond-paned windows, making the bright colours of the stained-glass Bible stories glow. The gentle candlelight transported him back in time to the generations who had worshipped in this church.

At the very end of the line and after a perfectly timed pause, a child about ten years old, wobbling a little as she held a cross on a pole as high as she could, walked in front of the most enormous coffin Naz had ever seen. The deep red wood – cherry? – with gleaming brass handles glowed in the candle-light and a single piercing ray of sunshine from the window to his right, created an image that could be a film sequence. Would a clapperboard appear from somewhere?

Everyone stood and watched, some with bowed heads, as the six black suited men carried the coffin to the catafalque waiting before the altar. The perfume of the enormous display of lilies covering the entire top of the coffin wafted over the mourners, making Naz sneeze loudly. He felt a nudge in his ribs from the woman beside him.

Frowning at him, she hissed loudly. 'Shh!'

As if he could help it!

At a stately pace behind the coffin, another child, a boy this time, held up a larger, more ornate cross on a pole, and led Beverly to the foot of the coffin before the altar. She stopped, paused, gave a deep bow, then moved to sit in an intricately carved oak seat in front of one of the flower walls, ensuring everyone could see her plastered arm as she took so long making herself comfortable.

The congregation appeared to hold its breath as the last bars of the music faded away to absolute silence. Beverly gave another dramatic bow to the altar as she took her place at the lectern beside the coffin and welcomed the congregation to the service.

Naz lived through the next hour in a daze, hardly hearing the three eulogies, the choir's anthems and although he stood as instructed for the hymns, he couldn't manage to sing a note.

Then came Beverly's sermon. He craned his neck to see where the camera was positioned, as he was certain that they must be filming her declamation. Her voice rose and fell, crammed with emotional expression and structured around dramatic pauses.

The woman she described wasn't *his* Jessica but a super-woman actress and film star, learning all she needed to know at Beverly's knee, before being launched to take the theatre world by storm, supported by Beverly's guiding hand. It was long and over-blown, and he stopped listening, thoroughly fed up with this show funeral.

He couldn't wait to get away to be alone with his thoughts and memories, far away from this blinged-up crowd. At last, it was over, and they trooped out after the coffin, which must have cost thousands. He was aware of the sharp-elbowed celebs ensuring they were in the best positions to be caught by the cameras and news crews as they left the church and proceeded to the graveside.

He'd had enough and he couldn't bear to watch Jessica dropped in a hole in the ground, so he crept away, keeping to the shadows created by the edge of the church wall. He left through the side gate, away from the mass gathering around the grave, and walked towards the car park. Just as he reached his car door, he felt a sharp tap on his shoulder.

CHAPTER FORTY-THREE

Naz jumped – his heart missed a beat as he swivelled round to see Hale, now an arm's length away from him

'Shit! Hale! You nearly gave me a heart attack, creeping up on me like that!'

'Sorry mate. Thought you must have seen me coming.'

Naz moved away from the Porsche and glanced back at the church and over to the crowd around Jessica's grave observing the final stage of the funeral ritual.

'Didn't fancy it? Me neither.' Hale shoved his hands in his pockets, presumably to get them out of the cutting wind. 'What a show, eh?'

'You couldn't make it up, could you?' Naz stepped beside Hale so he too could observe the crowd around the grave. 'I kept asking would Jessica have wanted all this fuss?'

'And?'

'And I thought – yeah – perhaps she would. She enjoyed being in the spotlight after all, didn't she?'

'Well, that certainly counts as a good send-off.'

Naz copied Hale. His hands were freezing. 'More like the

Beverly Elkin show. I bet she never thought she'd have this little performance to add to her programme when she asked Jessica to return to Oakwood.'

They stood side-by-side contemplating the mass of black-clothed people huddled together around the grave.

Naz frowned and gave Hale a penetrating look. It was worth a punt. 'Today's fiasco made me think of Lucy buried in that cliff all those years until the storm.'

In the slight pause, he could see Hale working out what he should say next. 'Do you know I was thinking the same thing? All this ceremony for Jessica and just a hole in the ground for Lucy, with nothing to show she was there.'

'Except my bracelet.' Naz shifted slightly to push his back towards the wind but made a sneaky look at Hale to see how he was taking the suggestion.

'Except your bracelet. And all that time you thought she was in France with ...'

'Hugo. The charming Hugo.'

'Didn't you think to go after her?' Hale shifted round too, away from the wind.

'Not much point. She sent that card and, as I told Steph, she'd spent so much time mooning after him during rehearsals, I wasn't surprised when she said she'd run off with him.'

'But didn't any of you get suspicious when you heard nothing?'

Naz felt Hale had a valid point. No one had chased after Lucy; they'd just accepted her disappearance and taken her few sentences on that card as the truth when all the time...

'It was at the end of college and the start of our new lives. We all left for uni, and she'd left for the clown school. And if that was what she wanted to do – fine.'

'But didn't you wonder when you heard nothing?'

'No. It wasn't as if she'd come home for Christmas like the

rest of us, or for the summer break. She'd got no family left here, had she?'

They watched Steph, Caroline, and Margaret, deep in conversation, break away from the crowd and walk towards them along the path from the church. The wind caught their black coats and dresses, transforming them into Victorian women.

'I think Steph said you had more of Lucy's writing?'

Naz frowned, trying to recall what he'd said. 'Did she?'

No way was he going to hand over those love letters, but then, maybe he could find a page that didn't say too much. It would be good to have confirmation that Lucy hadn't written those postcards. All these years he had hated her – no, not quite all of them. That wasn't true.

At first, her betrayal filled him with raw anger. As time passed it became covered over, but he'd found no one else, had he? Not really. He'd had relationships, many of them, but no one he wanted to commit to, to spend the rest of his life with, much to his mother's dismay. After his love, his first love for Lucy, all the others were pale shadows.

'If you've got anything, however small, it would be useful to compare the writing. Whoever sent those postcards probably murdered Lucy or was linked to it. I'm sure you want us to find out who murdered her, don't you?' Hale threw him an accusing look, one he'd seen many times, directed at one of his clients at the station.

'Of course, you know I'd do anything to find out who murdered her.' There, he'd said it. The truth about Lucy. She hadn't disappeared. She hadn't wanted to leave him, to dump him for that French dickhead. Something – or rather somebody – had stopped her from being with him. Perhaps it was Hugo? Easy enough to kill her and leave for France as planned and send those cards.

'You are looking at Hugo, I assume?'

Hale waved at Steph, who was standing at the edge of the mass of cars, trying to work out where Hale was. 'Well, he's an obvious suspect, isn't he?'

'Is that police speak for, yes?'

Hale waved at Steph, who with Caroline and Margaret picked their way over the tussocky field towards him. As she reached Hale, she pulled him aside and mumbled something about it going to kick off.

Hale turned towards Naz. 'Right, apparently, we're off to the wake. You?'

Naz hesitated. He'd planned to go home as he didn't feel like the social drinking after such a sad occasion. He'd always found wakes, or whatever they were called, inappropriate but after overhearing Steph's words decided it might be worth being there.

'Yes, I'll follow you. The Crown, isn't it? At least the car park is flat there.'

Hale grinned. 'Well, if you will have these flashy cars ... see you there.'

CHAPTER FORTY-FOUR

THURSDAY 29TH AUGUST: 2.00PM

IN THE SHORT drive to The Crown from St Mary's Church, Steph told Hale all about the fuss around Jessica's grave. After Beverly finished the formal part, she stood with her head bowed for ages, then she gazed around the assembled crowd, apparently waiting for plaudits after her performance, but the stoney silence that met her soon transformed into a grumpy mumble. Small groups formed, and Steph overheard extracts of conversations.

'Nothing to do with Jessica – more about her—'

'Using that poor woman's funeral to publicise her poxy play—'

'How dare she stand up there, all holier than thou when it was her fault—'

As they pulled up in the car park, between Naz and Caroline's cars, Hale reached over and touched Steph's arm. 'Look at that.'

Steph followed his gaze. Beverly was standing on the step in front of the wide oak door, shaking hands with the guests as if she was the chief mourner and not Jessica's father, who was nowhere to be seen. Some politely shook her hand as they entered, while others looked the other way and swanned past her, noses in the air. What was wrong with the woman? Didn't she notice?

Steph opened her door. 'If I were her, I'd keep a low profile. Those bits of conversation sounded rather nasty and after a few drinks, funerals are notorious for rows. This has all the making of quite a show.'

'Let's get in there and join the fun.' Hale waited for Steph to walk in behind Caroline and Margaret, who obediently shook hands with Beverly.

When it was his turn, Hale leaned into Beverly. 'Why don't you go in and get a drink? After all, you've had a long morning and could do with one.'

Beverly looked at Hale as if he'd sworn at her or said something outrageous. 'Thank you for your concern, Chief Inspector, but this is where I belong.'

Hale shrugged his shoulders and whispered to Steph. 'Well, I tried. Let's go in.'

The five of them opened the door of the large room used for conferences and dinner dances and walked into a wall of sound. If most of the crowd hadn't been dressed in black, no one would think it was a wake. It had the vibrant buzz of a party.

Beautifully dressed women, no doubt thespians, greeted their friends with 'Darling, you look fabulous.' and scattered air kisses all over the place. While the women sauntered around, surreptitiously noting who was worth speaking to and who should they avoid at all costs, the men were sent to the bar to collect the drinks.

Steph's party sat at one of the round tables by the wall, where they had a perfect view of most of the mingling guests working the room in a totally professional manner. And were they good at it! Most were drinking but ignoring the long banqueting table loaded with finger food and canapés.

Steph and Caroline wandered over to fill their plates and bring lunch back for Hale, Margaret, and Naz. They found little competition at the buffet table, unlike the bar, which appeared to be constantly two deep.

Not for this crowd cocktail sausages and mini pork pies, but platters of elaborate concoctions comprising oysters, prawns, delicate blini and melba toasts with squiggles of pate. Miniature Yorkshire puddings, each containing a slice of pink roast beef decorated with an elegant blob of horseradish, sat beside tiny faux newspaper cones of fried fish slices and chips. They took the plates back to their table and fell on them ravenously.

'I was positively famished, darling. Never been to such a long funeral in my life.' Caroline bit into a finger of Iberico ham wrapped around an asparagus spear. 'This must have cost a small fortune. I wonder who's shelled out for it.'

'Shh!' Margaret placed a finger on her lips. 'Your voice carries.'

'Not in this crowd, it doesn't!' Caroline retorted.

She was right. The volume of the buzz had risen so that it was difficult to hear what was being said and they had to rely on lip reading. A dramatic crescendo in the far corner of the room by the bar, cleared a space around two people, and everyone stared in that direction as a rather rotund man started shouting at someone.

They had to lean to the left around a pillar to see why everyone had stopped chatting to stare at the performance unfolding before them.

Steph whispered to Naz. 'Who is that man?'

'I think he must be Jessica's manager. She used to call him

Tweedledum, as he looks exactly like one of those pictures in the Alice books.'

The little man, about five foot nothing, was bouncing on the spot with anger and his voice, more of a loud squeak, carried through the silence. 'Are you saying you had nothing to do with it?'

'No, not at all. Just that it wasn't my fault.' Beverly, now a deep pink, appeared embarrassed by the man's anger and accusation shared by everyone.

'Then whose fault was it then?' He was so furious he bounced around to the side, making Beverly rotate to face him. 'You got Jessica to refuse a part in a West End Shakespeare to come down here to this no-man's-land and take part in your ego trip of a play. I told her it would be the worst of Am-Dram, and I was right.'

Beverly drew herself up to her full height, her plaster cast thrust forward and stared down at the little man. 'And do you know why Jessica came back to Oakwood?' She paused as the manager sneered at her, waiting for her to carry on. 'She knew who'd helped her to climb up the ladder when she first started. Me. I got her into drama school and made sure her name was known when she'd finished. I used my contacts to get her career launched, and she came back to say thank you and to pay me back for all my hard work.'

Beverly obviously thought she'd vanquished him as she posed, still and silent, apparently hoping the little man would disappear.

He didn't.

He looked up at her and grinned. Beverly turned her head to the side. Evidently, she'd picked up he hadn't finished yet.

'Oh, she came to this shit hole here to pay you back all right. You didn't know or ... did you? You found out, didn't you?'

Beverly frowned, apparently thrown out of her comfort zone for the first time. 'Found out what?'

Stressing each word as slowly as possible to ensure the entire crowd heard him, Tweedledum stood back and said in a loud squeak, 'She phoned me several times to say this was a total shit show and she was thoroughly pissed off with the way you put her down in front of these amateurs. She asked me to confirm the Shakespeare role for her, as she was going to walk out on you the day before the dress.'

For the first time, Beverly looked taken aback. 'No, that's a lie. Jessica was one hundred percent behind the production. She was a professional who would never do that.' She didn't sound too convinced. The crowd froze, listening to every word.

'That was the only reason she came down here, to get you back for claiming her all her life. Claiming her stardom was all your doing, claiming that you made her. Every journalist that came near you to do a piece on Jessica had to include the lie that you created her. She got thoroughly pissed off with it and wanted to get her own back and shut you up, once and for all.'

'That's not true.'

Tweedledum squinted and moved in closer, jabbing her chest with his squidgy finger. 'You knew! You knew all the time what she was going to do and you couldn't let that happen, could you? You needed to save your poxy reputation, didn't you? You knew, and you killed Jessica to stop her walking out! You killed her!'

CHAPTER FORTY-FIVE

THURSDAY 29TH AUGUST: 3.00PM

BEVERLY TOTTERED, falling back a step as if Jessica's manager had struck her. Some of the gawping spectators around her gasped, assuming he had. She became deathly pale as the blood drained from her face. Apparently, for the first time, Beverly realised that everyone, the entire room, was watching her reaction.

She glanced around at the silenced crowd, took a deep breath, pulled herself up, and strode out of the room with as much dignity as she could muster. Hale made eye contact with Steph and nodded towards the door, so she followed Beverly out of the conference room, through the vast oak door and out into the garden, now basking in bright sunshine.

Steph kept a little way behind Beverly and watched as she sat on a Lutyens bench in an alcove made by tall box hedges on three sides, facing away from the main entrance to the hotel. Here she'd be safe from most prying eyes.

Steph sat beside her and waited for a few moments. 'Stupid question – but are you all right?'

Beverly had her eyes closed and was inhaling and exhaling

extremely slowly, which Steph recognised as a technique she'd used herself to calm down and lower her blood pressure.

As Beverly didn't answer, Steph remained silent, enjoying the beautifully tended hotel garden. She could just see the edge of the enormous chess board that the college students had enjoyed playing on when they'd stayed there for Caroline's Arnhem project and smiled at the memory. The delicate champagne roses on the bush closest to her were in full bloom and she couldn't spot a single flower stalk that needed dead heading. The hotel gardeners certainly did a great job.

'I should go back and show my face.' Beverly's voice took Steph by surprise.

'Why should you?'

'Oh, as the funeral officiate, I should be there.'

'I think you should stay here until you feel better after that kerfuffle.'

Beverly reached into the folds of her robe, pulled out a tissue, and blew her nose. 'That man was truly vile. How could he talk about Jessica like that? It was obvious he didn't know her at all.'

Steph wasn't quite sure how to answer, as she suspected he knew Jessica rather well. Fortunately, she didn't need to, as Beverly continued.

'My Jessica would never have thought of doing such a dreadfully unprofessional act as leaving a play before the performances. It would never have entered her head.'

'Her manager seemed to think she had it all planned.'

'Yes, he did, didn't he?' Her voice expressed surprise and wonderment. 'He must have made it up.'

'Why would he do that?'

Beverly appeared to consider Steph's question and frowned. 'Of course! He wanted to make a splash in the nationals. That's what his performance was all about. As they say, all publicity is good publicity.'

'But it sounded as if he believed that was Jessica's plan – to walk out on us.' Steph included herself in the potentially abandoned group. 'If it was true, it would have been a dreadful thing to do.'

Beverly shoved the tissue back deep inside her cassock pocket. 'But typical of that woman. She had got above herself and thought the world revolved around her. No, I can see Jessica doing exactly what the vile man said just to get a headline.'

'Did you know what she had planned?' Steph quickly asked, hoping to catch Beverly off guard.

'Really, Steph, do you think she would have told me?'

Steph noted Beverly had evaded answering her question. 'OK then, did you suspect Jessica intended to walk out of the show before the dress?'

Beverly skewered Steph with a look that challenged her never to dare to ask the question again. But Steph persisted. 'I mean, when she was injured, you had already learned her lines as if you were expecting to have to play her part.'

Beverly frowned, as if trying to fathom what Steph had said. 'But, my dear, I always do that. It's a dramatic superstition of mine to learn the lead voice. It never occurred to me I might need to stand in for Jessica, so no, how could I have known she planned to walk out on me?'

Steph listened to the tone of Beverly's voice, looked her in the eye, convinced she had yet to hear the full truth. 'Jessica could have told you. You had so many disagreements. Did she ever threaten that she might walk out?'

'No, I mean ... I can't remember ... the silly girl came out with so many extravagant claims and rude comments. You saw her. She was so ungrateful and difficult to work with. She resisted all attempts at taking my direction, when all I ever suggested was designed to make her shine in that part.'

Steph shut her eyes, trying to think of yet another way to ask the question that might elicit a plain answer, but Beverly wouldn't let it go.

'Do you know I'm now convinced Jessica must have been an absolute nightmare to work with? I bet if I spoke to a few of the people I know in the business, I'd find out that she was a real prima donna with them, too. Maybe that's the story that I should tell the newspapers. Her manager wouldn't like that much, would he?'

Steph was losing her patience and had to sit on her hands to stop herself slapping this woman and was relieved when Caroline and Hale rescued her.

'Darlings, we have been so worried about where you had got to, and we find you tucked up here as cosy as anything in this beautiful bower. Margaret and I must dash. Poor Marlene has been by herself all this time and will be eating through the door.'

Steph couldn't imagine Caroline's delicate fluffy dog eating anything that wasn't mashed and heated to blood temperature.

'Will you be all right getting home?' Hale moved to stand by Beverly's side.

'Why wouldn't I?' She brushed him away with a majestic wave of her hand. 'Now, Steph, before the performance tomorrow, I need you there an hour before the others as we need to do a final check on the positioning of all the props on the table. I noticed a little fumbling at the rehearsal yesterday.'

Steph didn't trust herself to speak, so nodded and walked towards Hale, nudging him towards the car park. When she was sure they were out of earshot, she spoke. 'I got nowhere and I'm beginning to think that Jessica's manager may have been right, and Beverly did know that Jessica meant to walk out on her.'

Hale nodded. 'And while you were out here, Naz told me that Jessica kept going on about some secret she knew about Beverly – something about where the bodies were buried.'

They reached the car, turned and looked back at the empty bench. Beverly must have returned to the poisonous party.

'Did he tell you what it was?'

'Unfortunately not. But whatever it was, Naz thought she intended to confront Beverly.'

'I wonder if she did.' Steph opened the car door and got in beside Hale. 'All this makes her a prime suspect, doesn't it?'

CHAPTER FORTY-SIX

The Oakwood– Saturday 31st August 2019

Courageous Performance by Oakwood Players – Joe Denny

Last night to rapturous applause in the ruins of Covehithe Church, Oakwood Players staged the opening night of "Mother Courage and her Children". Originally booked for the bank holiday weekend but, as a mark of respect following the death of Jessica Marlowe (48), the play was postponed until after her funeral on 29th August and reduced to two performances from the original three.

This play, written in 1939, explores the horrors of war through the eyes of the people who live in it, and is often referred to as Brecht's masterpiece. Set in the first half of the seventeenth century in the 30 Years' War (1618–1648), the play presents one of the most destructive wars across Europe, which left towns and countryside alike in ruins.

The play follows the fortunes or misfortunes of Mother Courage and her three children as she makes her living travelling through the war zones selling goods to the army from her cart. She is the perfect example of a wily entrepreneur whose only purpose in life is to make a profit whatever the cost.

Rev'd Beverly Elkin (69) took on the lead role at very short notice and made a good fist of it as Mother Courage, despite her recent car crash. Her conniving, self-centred approach veered from an enviable need for survival in the midst of a war, to a cynical exploration of all around her, including her own children. If we caught for a moment the expression of emotion for her personal tragedy, we saw it disappear a second later as she haggled over the next bargain. Beverly Elkin effectively captured the tension as she manipulated her way through the tragedies of war, moving her cart from battle to battle, sacrificing her children, and watching her cart become tatty and battered.

Beverly Elkin directed the play in line with Brecht's philosophy, so all those involved were constantly on stage. Soldiers sat throughout on straw bales beside the walls, alongside the musicians and stagehands, reminding us that this was a powerful play about the futility of war.

The ruins of Covehithe created the landscape of war perfectly, and the harsh lighting design on the jagged walls by Max Bickers and Jason Strong made us appreciate the brutality and desecration of war then and today. The players performed on the ground with the audience raised on raked seating on three sides, which gave a superb view of the constant movement around the acting area.

*Duke Special's score, full of haunting melodies, played by a
talented band of local musicians directed by Margaret Durrant,
evoked the cruelty and hopeless plight of Mother Courage and
her children along with all the other victims of war-torn Europe.*

*This was a brave choice for our local group, and we can only
imagine how the great Jessica Marlowe would have led the cast.
In this tribute to her, the cast were well rehearsed, and the play
moved at a cracking pace, but it lacked that sparkle of star-dust
Jessica Marlowe would have brought to the part. A few tickets
for the final performance tonight at 7.30 pm are available from
The Book Shelf in Market Square or Oakwood Library.*

————

THE SOUND of a newspaper being slapped against a pew made
Steph jump.

'The cheek of that man! He calls himself a journalist! One
thing he isn't is a theatre critic.' Beverly nudged the newspaper
with her foot further under the pew where she'd chucked it.

'I thought it was pretty fair. It appreciated the direction,
the set, the music and made some lovely comments about your
performance.'

'But what about this?' Beverly bobbed down, gathered the
scrambled pages back into a newspaper, and made a great play
of finding the review. 'What about "it lacked the sparkle of
star-dust Jessica Marlowe would have brought to the part."
Makes me feel sick!'

Once again, chucking the paper down on the pew in
disgust, Beverly strode down the church towards Steph. Panic
swept over her as she was concerned that Beverly had only just
started to vent her spleen, and she didn't have time to listen to
an epic rant. 'Well, it's not as if he matters, is it? We had a

standing ovation from a full house last night and a sell-out this evening and, you know, I think he was right.'

Steph ignored Beverly's explosive "humph" and accompanying disdainful expression and continued. 'The cast was a little over-awed by all the famous people who had stayed on to see the play after Jessica's funeral. It felt like we were under the microscope, and they wanted something to go wrong so they could dine out on it with their friends in London.'

Beverly swept up the paper and stuffed it in her bag. 'Well, anyway, they must have been deeply disappointed as nothing went wrong, did it?'

'No, it was a great production and testimony to everyone's hard work. Now I must get—'

Beverly nudged Steph into a pew, where she gently pulled her down with her free hand on the seat and sat beside her.

'Maybe you are right. Perhaps we were a little subdued last night. I held back a little. Every time I spoke to the audience, all I could see was that slug of a manager sitting in the front row, grinning at me even when it wasn't funny. Do you think Jessica would have been any better?'

Steph was becoming uncomfortable. Last night she and Caroline had decided that Beverly was well over the top and had milked every ounce of drama out of it, to the point of melodrama on some occasions. 'No, Beverly, you were good.' Rather lame, but she hoped that would be it.

'But precisely *how* good?' Beverly was pushing hard now, and Steph didn't like to perjure herself.

'You're right, Jessica's manager was out of order, and he shouldn't have said what he did in front of all those people.'

Beverly stared ahead at the stained-glass window. Steph followed her gaze, her eyes attracted by a ray of sunshine illuminating a flying dove in the very top pane.

'And to think of all those dreadful things he said. Was Hale there?' Beverly thought for a moment. 'Of course, Hale was there and must have heard that man's lies.' Her voice changed to become whiney and petulant, like a spoilt child. 'Anyway, he can't think I killed Jessica like that horrid man suggested — he doesn't, does he?'

Steph's stomach tightened and a knot formed. No way could she tell Beverly that Hale now had her as prime suspect, convinced that she must have known somehow that Jessica was going to sabotage the play. They had agreed to interview her after the play was over. It wasn't as if Beverly was going anywhere, was she?

'I'm not sure what Hale's thinking, but he's looking at everyone involved with the play and Jessica's murder. I expect he'll want to speak to everyone again starting tomorrow. Now I really must get on and set up the props.'

As Steph got up, she caught her sock on something sharp under the pew. She bent down to release the pulled thread and found it was stuck on a screw in the bracket of a stage lamp. 'Whatever is this doing under here?'

'What?'

'It's a stage lamp. I'll tell Max.' Steph stood and started walking towards the props table.

'He probably put it there to keep it safe and then forgot all about it — a senior moment. When you see him, tell him to move it to the light store. We don't want any more accidents, do we?'

Should she take it out herself and save Max the trouble? The light store, a large metal box with an enormous padlock, would be unlocked by now, as Max and Jason would have set up the lighting desk and be testing the lights before the performance. No, she'd tell him after the play, as she didn't want to distract him. He was becoming forgetful and relying on Jason much more than he had at the start of rehearsals, but each time he'd been forced to ask the younger man for help, he'd become more and more resentful.

'Ah! There you are.' Caroline stopped inside the door. 'One of Margaret's musicians has forgotten her headscarf. Do you have a spare one anywhere?'

'Yes, in my props' basket, there are several. Hang on and I'll show you.'

Caroline took her arm as they walked together towards the wicker hamper. 'Are you staying for the party?'

'I thought I would. Could be fun. You?'

'Depends on how tired Margaret is. She never moans about her Parkinson's, but I know she gets tired after these performances. I'll let you know later.'

CHAPTER FORTY-SEVEN

THE STANDING OVATION lasted so long Steph was worried that the incessant stamping of feet on the raked seating would make it collapse. The final night's performance had exceeded everyone's expectations and had been brilliant. All the actors were on top form, the technical effects had worked their magic, and the musicians created an eerie, evocative atmosphere, while Beverly had been on fire! She gave an astounding performance, which drove them all up to a level never reached in rehearsal.

The audience helped as it comprised locals, rather than a lot of Jessica's friends who had stayed on after the funeral, so the actors relaxed and lived their parts. The day before, on top of the tension of the first night, they'd been inhibited performing in front of the professionals, including Jessica's manager, who sat in the front row scowling or grinning throughout the play – both equally off-putting.

Now it was over, and they were all the best of friends. Exhausted but exhilarated. After the audience trooped out, the party began. Long tables were pulled into the centre of the acting area, Jason and Max provided party lighting – even a glitter ball appeared on the main lighting bar – and a "get up and dance" play list blared through the speakers.

The people in the pink farmhouse opposite had been invited but declined, saying that they hoped it was a wonderful party and not to worry about the noise. Two complementary tickets had helped to seal that relationship.

The tables groaned under the enormous spread – this time plates of crisps, sausage rolls, mini pork pies and sandwiches. Everyone was smiling and congratulating each other and celebrating the many weeks of rehearsal and hard work, wishing they could do it all over again.

Steph and Hale stood together on the edge of the ebullient crowd, observing the action. Steph nudged Hale's arm. 'Look, over there, that man talking to Max is the spitting image of Hugo.'

'Maybe that's because it is.' Hale moved towards the pair. Steph followed. 'He said he'd try and make it for the play and the party.'

'Really? You didn't mention it.'

'Didn't I? Lizzie arranged for him to come over and give us a formal statement in person. Great organiser, that girl!'

Before it reached her lips, Steph swallowed the comment about the sainted Lizzie!

Max stopped talking as they approached. 'Hale, meet the mischievous Puck. Great that he's turned up, isn't it?'

Hugo shook hands and, when they'd picked up some bottles of beer, they moved across to some seats away from the crowd.

Hale pulled the three chairs into a triangle, and they sat. 'Thanks for coming over, Hugo. I really appreciate it. We can go to the station tomorrow and get a formal statement, but a chat here would help.'

Hugo looked around. 'It may be thirty years, but it hasn't changed much, has it?'

'This part hasn't, but you'd be shocked if you went down onto the beach and saw the extent of the erosion. The cliffs are right up to the edge of the field.' Steph passed around a plate of sausage rolls she'd picked up from the buffet table.

'That's how you found poor Lucy.' Hugo paused and looked towards the edge of the field and the sea beyond. 'We had the party on the beach last time.'

Steph grinned. 'The path that went down there has disappeared. You now have to walk along several fields and come along by the broad before you can reach the beach. We thought it best to stay up here so everyone could join in immediately after the play.'

Hugo smiled at her and Steph could see once again why he had been such a success with all the girls. She looked around. 'Did you bring your wife?'

'No, she has to be at the university on Monday – she teaches philosophy – and I thought if I got delayed it wouldn't be fair to the children.'

'How old are they?'

'Ten and fourteen. I'm not sure how it is here, but in France I think you need to be around more the older they are. I can stay until Tuesday before I must return to Paris.'

Hale now took over. 'Can you tell us what happened at the party on the beach?'

'Sure. We sat around the bonfire smoking and drinking and laughing for hours. It was a warm night, just like tonight, and we partied well into the night. The older actors and crew left early, but I think Beverly and Max stayed down there too.'

'You were with Lucy?' Steph handed round the sausage rolls again.

'Yes. The lovely Lucy. Such a beautiful girl and a great

actor. The best in that group.' He looked around, apparently to check if anyone could hear them, or was he concerned that Naz might be close? Re-assured, he continued. 'We'd got close during the play, you know. I was sad to leave her, but I had my career to return to and Francine, who became my wife, waiting for me in Paris, so I had to say goodbye.'

'Did Lucy mind you going back to Francine?'

Hugo looked down at the ground, and even in the pale light that reached into their corner, Steph could see him blushing. 'No, I don't think Lucy knew about her, but she knew I had to go back.'

'Was it Lucy, or you who suggested she might go to the clown school instead of drama school in London?'

Again, Hugo appeared to be uncomfortable. 'It was something we talked about when we – but it was a fantasy, you know, a dream.' He paused, his face sad as he recalled that evening, the evening they now thought was her last. 'I know she told her friend Jessica about our conversation, because she came up to me at the party and asked me if I was taking Lucy back with me?'

'Did Lucy know Jessica had talked to you?' Said Steph.

'No, I don't think so. Jessica was a tricky girl. She was Lucy's shadow and always wanted whatever she had. Naz was being chased by Jessica during the rehearsals, but he only cared for Lucy.'

Hale leaned in. 'Did Naz mind you had formed this ... er ... friendship with Lucy?'

'I never asked him.'

'Was he angry with Lucy for being with you?'

'Not angry. More sad. He kept out of the way, but I saw him keeping an eye on us. I know he followed us as we left the party – he kept out of sight, but he watched us.'

Steph took Hugo's empty bottle and dropped it in the bin beside their chairs. 'But you left with Lucy?'

'I left the party with her, and we said our goodbyes at the gate. I had called a taxi to take me to London, so she left me at the church wall and went back into the party over there where we had been performing the play.' He waved his hand towards the church.

'Where exactly?'

Hugo pointed to the enormous east window behind the acting area. 'Over there. I waited for the car, and I could see her sitting on the edge of the stones up there, looking out to sea.'

'Was she alone?'

'No. There was someone beside her.'

CHAPTER FORTY-EIGHT

SUNDAY 1ST SEPTEMBER 10.00AM

STEPH LET Derek bounce out of the back of the car and dash around the acting area, nose to the ground, tracking a smell, presumably a fox. She turned at the sound of a car and Caroline's Polo drew up behind hers, followed by Max's battered van.

Taking the flask out of her bag, a few plastic beakers, and a packet of biscuits, she set up her mini picnic on the table by the porch. The others joined her and gratefully fell on the coffee and biscuits, while Derek sat on her feet waiting for any escaped crumbs.

Max looked towards the acting area. 'I've seen worse.'

'Actually, darling, they did a wondrous job clearing up after the party last night.' Caroline held out the packet of biscuits to him.

'Yes, it leaves us the set, lighting and props to strike.' Steph grinned at Caroline's easy use of the technical jargon.

'Is Jason coming to help you?' Caroline piled the extra beakers into a tidy tower.

'He'll be along later to take down the lights from the bar. I can manage the two towers. I can manage the bar too, but I promised him I would wait until he got here.'

Steph piled some sacking into a large wicker hamper and stood as she overheard the last part of their conversation. 'That reminds me, Max. I found a stage lamp under the third pew from the back yesterday. I wondered if you'd left it there for some reason?'

'Oh shite! I'd forgotten all about that. Thanks. My memory's like a sieve. Think I put it there weeks ago. Not sure why.'

Steph looked up from folding her pile of sacking. 'Peasants in the seventeenth century were big on sacking, weren't they?'

Caroline laughed. 'Hardly Chanel is it, darling?'

Max went into the church and, after a lot of banging and crashing as he moved the cart out of the way, he emerged carrying the lamp.

'You didn't need it then?' Steph pulled another wicker hamper over towards the seats.

'Do you know, I can't for the life of me remember why it was there.' Max frowned as he tried to recall when and why he had put it under the pew.

'Eureka!' His shout made both Steph and Caroline jump. 'I know what it was. It was the first rehearsal we held here, and I thought I'd come in early to check everything before madam came and started prancing about and throwing her weight around the place. I've never been shown up by that Beverly Elkin in one of her bossy moods, and I wasn't about to give her the chance.'

As they thought they were in for the long haul, Caroline and Steph sat on a nearby wall and wound up a jumble of thin ropes and ribbons into neat coils, while they listened to Max.

'Anyway, as I said, I come in early to test all the lights and blow me, when I turned them on, a bulb blew, and I thought I'd better replace it. But when I went to my store, I couldn't find one that fitted. The lamp what blew was an older one, see? And we need to put in a special order to get them bulbs. Still works well, but old stock, see?'

'Anyway, as I was saying, I found a lamp right at the back of me van ... not sure now why we didn't use it, as it has one of the new LEDs in it. Anyway, I climbed up the bar and brought down this broken one and put the LED one in its place—'

'What! I thought you weren't supposed to climb up to the bar?' Steph couldn't help herself exclaiming.

'Poppycock – that's all I can say to that, my dear. But I was feeling good, and Jason hadn't got here yet and it was only one light, and I knew I wouldn't get dizzy, so I did it and anyway, I'm here, aren't I?'

Steph looked along the bar. 'Which was the one you replaced?'

'That one, I think it was. So long ago now I can't hardly recall.' He pointed to the fourth lamp from the left. 'Well girlies, can't stand gossiping with you all day. I want to get all the wires out and coiled by the time Jason hauls himself out of his pit.' With that, he stumbled off towards the lighting box, pulling the keys for the padlocks out of his pocket as he went.

Steph became aware of a shadow blocking out the sun and looked up, surprised to see Hale. 'I thought you were at the station with Hugo taking his statement.'

'I was, but Lizzie popped in and offered to take it. I thought I'd come down here in the daylight and have a look at that window. Coming?'

Caroline frowned. 'Sounds mysterious!'

Hale grinned, grabbed Steph's hand, and pulled her up, holding onto it as they strolled towards the window. Was this a gesture of affection or a way of shutting her up? Not being sure of anything nowadays, she gave in and let him lead her to the very end of the ruin, to the enormous hole that would once have been a showpiece window above the altar.

The bottom of it was above their heads, but Hale dragged one of the straw bales underneath it.

'What did they say the stage was like for the 1989 play?'

Steph looked around. 'The two scaffold towers were on either side of the window and that lighting bar would have been across them.' She waved her hands and created the shapes. 'And instead of being on the ground, the actors and the scaffold towers were on a stage, a good metre higher than we are now.'

'In that case, it would have been easy for Lucy and whoever it was to climb up there and sit on the edge drinking.'

'Yes. It would.'

'I'll climb up there first and give you a hand so you can join me.'

Hale, with surprising athleticism, pulled himself up onto the ledge and, when he was safely settled, reached down and helped Steph to climb up, leaving a frustrated Derek barking in circles on the ground below them.

'Hugo's right. He could have seen Lucy silhouetted even at night, sitting here with someone.'

'Well, whoever they were, they wouldn't have stayed up here for long.' Steph squirmed around.

'How do you know that?'

'It's really uncomfortable sitting on sharp bits of flint.'

'You're right. Unless they took up some cushions or something. Anyway, surely somebody must have seen them.'

Steph thought for a moment. 'I thought Hugo said that Naz followed them but kept out of sight?'

Hale smiled. 'You're right, he did.'

'Let's ask him then. Interesting why he hasn't told us he saw Lucy up here, isn't it?'

'Or maybe it was Naz who was with her.'

CHAPTER FORTY-NINE

STEPH HELD onto Hale's shoulders as she lowered herself off the window ledge onto the straw bale. It had been amazing sharing that moment with him in the sunshine, with the glimpse of the sea glinting beyond the field.

He pulled her towards him, and as he was about to kiss her, his phone rang. He rolled his eyes, but they both knew he had to answer it, even on a Sunday.

'Hi, yes, you can talk.'

But apparently not in front of her as he jumped off the straw bale and walked a little way off, leaving Steph to clamber down by herself, not helped by Derek jumping up to greet her. Trying not to show she cared, Steph returned to Caroline, who had packed away most of the costumes.

'Interesting chat?' Caroline always had a way of getting people to talk, especially students, but this time Steph avoided her prompt.

'It's incredibly beautiful here. I've been so busy during the play rehearsals I've hardly had time to notice it, but up there in the sunshine, you get the most fabulous views.'

Having finished his call, Hale strode towards Steph, beckoned her aside, and spoke in a low voice making sure Caroline couldn't hear. 'That was Lizzie—'

'On a Sunday?'

'I told you she was at the station only ten minutes ago – do you never listen?' Back in irritated mode then. The thaw had lasted less than an hour– at least there'd been one.

'Anyway, as I was saying, Lizzie has taken Hugo's statement, and he's remembered something else.'

'Really?'

'Apparently his taxi didn't turn up immediately, and he hung around at the fork up the road for ages, so he'd catch it whichever way it came. After about half an hour he gave up and walked to the phone box on the way to Wrentham, you know, the one in front of that group of cottages? Now has potted plants hung all the way down the outside and books inside?'

'I know it.' Steph deliberately chose neutral words and a flat voice to avoid irritating him again.

'Well, after he'd made the call and was waiting for his taxi outside the phone box – must have been there an hour, he thought – he saw Marcus Strong on his bike go roaring past with Jessica on the pillion.'

'So, she and Marcus had left Lucy in the church drinking alone or with someone else or she was already dead.' Steph sighed as she summarised the options.

'Indeed. I think we need to build up a detailed timeline of who was where about the time Lucy left the party with Hugo and get them to recall what they saw.'

'Quite a job after thirty years, but then, Hugo has remembered more since he found out what happened to Lucy — thanks to Lizzie.'

Hale frowned. 'Indeed, she's got more out of him than we did.'

'But he's had time to dwell on it and it must have helped to come back here again.'

'Yes. A shame Naz wasn't here last night, but you seem to have gained his trust. Why don't you have a chat about the latest info from Hugo? Maybe he'll tell you why he lied to us.'

'That's not fair. We don't know he lied. He might have simply forgotten, like Hugo.' Steph surprised herself by the ferocity with which she defended Naz. How could Hale be so snide? Surely, he couldn't be jealous?

'Right, well, I've finished here. I'm off to the station to build this timeline with whoever's there.' With a wave, he was gone.

Steph knew very well who was there, and so did he. 'Come on, Derek. Almost there. Just a few more props to put away and we can go to the beach.'

When Steph and Derek joined her outside the church, Caroline gave her that, "now why don't you spill the beans", look that Steph knew only too well. Steph ducked to ignore it and pushed the large hampers into the church, where Beverly would pick them up for storage.

When Steph came out into the blinding sunshine, she could hear Caroline chatting to someone but had to blink several times to make out who was with her. What an amazing coincidence!

'We were just talking about you!' Steph blurted out before she could stop herself.

'Who's we?' Naz had blushed a little

'Oh, just Hale and me. Going through some statements.'

'On a Sunday?'

'Come on, you know it makes no difference what day it is to a copper.'

Steph became aware of Caroline watching their chat, turning her head from side to side as if watching tennis at Wimbledon. 'Fancy a walk on the beach? Derek's desperate.'

'Great. I came to see if there was anything I could do. You know, in the way of clearing up. I felt rather lost by myself at home and thought this was where Jessica would have been ...' He tailed off and blushed, apparently ashamed of showing his emotion.

'I do understand.' Caroline's soothing voice appeared to put him at ease.

'I know, Jessica hadn't been back for long but while she was here, we ... we became good friends.'

'I'm so sorry, Naz.'

He tried a smile that didn't reach his eyes and patted Caroline on her shoulder. 'Anyway, you seem to have it all under control and, yes,' he smiled at Steph. 'I would love a walk on the beach with you and Derek. I'll change my shoes.'

Caroline's eyebrows raised and, as Naz walked back to his car, whispered. 'What are you up to? And what is wrong with you and Hale? I've never seen you like this. I thought you two were different from other couples.'

'Don't go there – I'll tell you all – promise.' Steph hissed as Naz returned.

Derek was hysterically happy and ran round in tiny circles as they walked around the back of the church and towards the east window.

'I thought we were going to the beach.' Naz looked puzzled.

'We are, but first, I wanted to bring you here and see if you could recall anything else after the 1989 party.'

'Is this a formal interview?' Naz's voice was suddenly sharp and professional, and his smile had dissolved.

'Not at all. Sorry, I didn't mean to upset you. I really do

want to go down to the beach, but we have discovered something new about Hugo and Lucy that you should know.'

Now he was interested and became friendly Naz again. 'And what's that?'

They stood looking up at the ruins of the enormous window on which Steph had recently climbed with Hale. 'Apparently Hugo said he and Lucy parted at the church gate and when he left, he looked back and saw her sitting up there drinking with someone.'

Naz considered the cloudless blue sky framed by the stone window and gave a deep sigh. Maybe something was coming back to him.

As the silence stretched, Steph prompted him. 'Did you see anyone?'

'No. I told you, I saw Hugo and Lucy leave the party together and I assumed they got into his taxi and went off together.'

'You saw them get into the taxi at the gate?'

'I think so ...' He closed his eyes, apparently visualising the scene. 'Yes, I did. I saw them get into the taxi and drive off.'

CHAPTER FIFTY

SUNDAY 1ST SEPTEMBER: 5.00PM

As usual, Steph gazed along each shelf in the fridge, looking for inspiration, then pulled out the freezer drawers, searching for supper. As she pushed each one back, she heard a sharp crunching of ice, with the bottom drawer requiring a sharp kick to persuade it to close. It needed de-frosting, but she decided it could be added to her "to do sometime soon" list.

Deep down in the bottom drawer, she had found a dark red bag of stuff, which had AC etched onto a rare white label. Great – Acapulco Chicken. It was one of Hale's favourites – a chilli-hot mixture of chicken, red pepper, tomatoes and red kidney beans. Now all she needed was some rice and there was supper.

As the microwave pinged, she heard the front door slam. 'Hi! You're home early.'

'Well, it is Sunday.' He came up behind her and wrapped his arms around her, peering over her shoulder at the dish she was stirring and then trying to replace it in the microwave without dislodging his embrace. 'Umm! My favourite!'

Not wishing to move away from him, she squirmed down to the bottom shelf in the cupboard and pulled out a pan for the rice. Hale disengaged himself and returned to the table. As she went about making their supper, she glanced across at Hale, who had rolled out a sheet of paper. Ah! The timeline. Although he was trying his best to keep up with the new technology, some things, he said, work better on paper and timelines were one of them.

'Do you want me to postpone supper while you have a look at that? It's easy to do now, but once I've put the rice on it will be too late.'

'Great idea. Stop for a few minutes and come and see where we've got to.'

Steph turned off the water, which was just coming to the boil, relieved she hadn't added the rice.

'And I've got news for you.' He leaned over the back of his chair.

'Oh?'

'There was nothing wrong with Beverly's brakes. The mechanics have checked. Crawled all over it. Nothing wrong with it, or there wasn't before she pranged it.'

'You mean she crashed the car herself?'

'Looks like it.'

'Why?'

'We'll have to ask her.'

Steph joined Hale at the table. 'Perhaps she did it, as she wanted everyone's sympathy. Although she'd landed the lead in the play and got a starring role in Jessica's funeral that wouldn't be enough for Beverly, would it? Her plastered arm was like waving a flag saying give me sympathy and watch me doing all this while badly injured after a serious accident.'

Hale didn't look convinced. 'Did it work?'

Steph thought and shook her head. 'Not really, did it? Let's have a look at this timeline of yours.'

Together, they examined the timeline on the large piece of paper spread out before them.

'So, we know that Hugo, Lucy, Naz, Jessica and the other actors were on the beach from ten thirty until midnight when Hugo left to catch his taxi. Then Hugo and Lucy walked up the cliff path together, watched by Naz who told me he saw them get into the taxi.'

Steph traced another line across the page. 'While Hugo said he left Lucy by the church and the last he saw of her was when she was sitting on the east window, drinking with someone.'

'Today, he told Lizzie it might have been Jessica, but he wasn't sure.'

Steph said nothing, but stared at the timeline, hoping it might provide an answer.

Hale frowned. 'One of them is lying. I wonder which one and why? We have Hugo until Tuesday, and it would be worth having him in for another chat. Apparently, Lizzie said he was subdued in the station, so I think I'll invite him back there.'

'But why would Naz be lying? He was in love with Lucy, unless he killed her in a fit of jealousy and made up the story that she left with Hugo?'

'And that would mean he's the one who went over to France to send those postcards.' Hale's finger traced a line along the timeline, charted in thirty-minute sections at the top of the page. 'Naz knew all about the daisy she added to her signature, didn't he?'

'True. But then Hugo suddenly remembers his taxi didn't turn up and he must have hung around for about an hour, which would have given him time to kill Lucy.' Steph paused.

'Go on.' Hale sounded interested.

Steph closed her eyes, recalling their discussion with Hugo. 'He told us he hadn't been honest with Lucy about going back to his French girlfriend – Francine? Suppose Lucy found out he was using her and became difficult. He had the opportunity, the time and the motive to get rid of her.'

'You have a point.' Hale returned to the chart and traced his finger along the line. 'When the taxi didn't come, he said he went to the phone box, and he saw Jessica leave on the back of Marcus Strong's motorbike.'

Step frowned. 'That would be the night before he died, wouldn't it?'

'Right. Have you had time to look at that file yet?' Hale narrowed his eyes as he looked at her.

'No, I've been tied up with a certain production, remember? I will, don't worry. Oh, while I remember, could I have a copy of the forensic report with all the fingerprint and data analysis please?'

'Why do you want that?'

'Just want to check on something, that's all. You don't mind, do you?'

'Course not. I'll print it off now.' Hale found the report, and the printer whirred into life. Steph went over to the desk to pick it up and slotted it in a file to go through later.

Hale gazed at the timeline again. 'Getting back to this – you're right, Hugo could be making it all up – his story's changed at least once.'

'And he wouldn't have any problem sending the cards from Paris. We must ask him if he ever saw Lucy's writing.'

'Would he have known the three addresses?'

He frowned, puzzled. 'Not as easy as now with the internet, but it would have been possible for him to find them. He could even have called Beverly and asked her, as he wanted to send them thank you cards or some other nonsense. Although that's not very male, is it?'

'What's not?'

'Sending thank you cards.'

'I can't believe you just said that!' She slapped the table, making his pen bounce onto the floor.

Hale ignored her outrage. 'And Beverly, we haven't decided where she was when all this was going on.'

Steph peered back at the diagram. 'She doesn't appear anywhere.'

'You're right, she doesn't. Was she there last night?'

Steph closed her eyes, thinking about where she had seen Beverly. 'Yes, right up to the end.'

'But it was a bit different in '89, wasn't it? They had the party on the beach.'

Steph thought for a moment. 'Yes, but she would have felt responsible for them having a party by the sea, so she would probably have been there all the time then, too. We need to ask her. But what's her motive for killing Lucy?'

'Well, you've heard the rumours. How about she tried to get off with her, Lucy rejected her, and Beverly killed her?'

'That's a bit far-fetched too. And what about Jessica?' Steph picked up the pen and replaced it on the table. 'Either she was sitting drinking with Lucy, if we believe Hugo, or she was somewhere else, presumably up to no good with Marcus and then left with him on his bike, again according to Hugo.'

Hale rolled up the sheet of paper. 'We're getting nowhere fast here. It could be Beverly, Hugo, Naz or Jessica. Although I'm not sure what Jessica would gain from Lucy's death.'

Steph turned the gas on under the pan of water for the rice. 'There's that award which everyone wanted.'

'True. I suggest we see Beverly first. If she's not involved, she may verify either Naz's or Hugo's version and we need to find out where she was at the end of the party.'

Steph turned the microwave on for the final blast. 'She may have worked it all out and has only been waiting for us to ask her.'

'Or she may have killed both Lucy and Jessica.'

CHAPTER FIFTY-ONE

SUNDAY 1ST SEPTEMBER: 6.50PM

IT WAS STILL light after supper, when Steph and Hale stood with their gifts outside Beverly's house, waiting for her to answer the door. Steph held the pile of scripts she'd picked up from the vestry inside the church. Beverly had to return them to the Suffolk Library, so they thought it would be a good excuse to turn up at her house to give them to her before they were overdue.

Also, Caroline had found the ragged Mother Courage cloak, dumped in a pew, now held at arm's length by Hale as it gave off a sick-making smell and he hoped Beverly would take it so it didn't have to return to his car.

At last, the door flew open, and Beverly appeared in a dramatic blood-red Kaftan, decorated with gold embroidery, which glinted in the setting sun. Even the sling which encased her broken arm was in a silk scarlet sleeve – did she have a different one for each outfit? She held onto the door frame, swaying a little. 'Hello, you two, please forgive my appearance. I wasn't expecting company tonight. A drink?'

'We're sorry to disturb you, but I found this pile of scripts in the vestry and thought you might be anxious to return them to the library.' Steph held them out to her.

'Ah! That's where they are. Thank you so much. Could you put them on that table?' With her un-plastered arm, she pointed to the hall table. 'It's so kind of you both to come all this way. You must join me for a drink.'

Steph left the pile of scripts on the hall table and Beverly led them down the black-and-white-tiled hall into an enormous sitting room that gave onto a large, well-tended garden. The French doors were wide open, and she must have been sitting outside on the terrace. 'A glass of wine? As you can see, I'm afraid I was drinking alone – shocking, I know – and it would be good to have some company.'

Beverly grabbed the rags Hale was holding out to her. 'What on earth is that pile? Oh, my goodness! It's my costume. Wherever did you find it?'

'Caroline found it in one of the pews. We thought you might like it back.' Steph sat on one of the cushioned garden chairs, while Hale stood beside Beverly as she examined the smelly sacking.

'The only place that is going is the bin. I don't think I'll be reprising that role for a while.'

Hale handed it over gingerly, rubbing his hands together as if to remove the smell.

'Oh, do go and wash your hands. They must be contaminated. Third door on the right.'

'What is that smell?' Hale asked as he headed for the hall door.

'A mixture of compost, pond water and sour milk!' Beverly bundled the cloak up into a tight ball and followed him across the room.

Hale frowned. 'How do you know?'

'Because I concocted it. I needed to breathe in the essence of Mother Courage so soaked it in this disgusting mixture – smell helps me play the part authentically, you know, build an emotional memory to find the truth in the character, you see?' She laughed at Hale's horrified expression. 'You don't, do you? I'll dump this and bring some glasses.'

While they were gone, Steph revelled in the garden. Nothing flash but gentle, well-designed flower beds full of hydrangeas, white and pink roses and lavender – a soothing palate of soft shades.

'Gorgeous, isn't it?' Beverly swept in with a full bottle of Chardonnay and a bottle of fizzy water balanced under her good arm, juggling two glasses in her hand. Steph leaped up and took the glasses and bottles from her.

Beverly sat opposite Steph and smiled across at her. 'I presume one of you is driving? Yes, I'm proud of my garden. I design it and Georgina, the gardener, does all the grind. No time, you see. But I do like sitting in it.'

Hale returned and made eye contact with Steph, letting her know that he'd stick to water and drive. As he sat, he observed Beverly. 'I've got some news for you, Beverly. We've had our mechanics go over your car with a fine-toothed comb and they've found nothing wrong. The brakes were fine.'

For a moment, Beverly appeared to be lost for words, but only for the briefest moment. 'Good heavens! The brakes were fine? Really? What on earth happened to me?'

Her eyes darted from face to face, as if she expected them to give her the answer. Their silence allowed her to make a melodramatic gesture as her hand rose to her forehead and she rubbed her temple as if she had a killer headache.

Then she patted her plaster, as if to re-assure it. 'Yes, I

must have blacked out for a moment – yes, of course, that day I was exhausted, totally wrecked – you know the play, Jessica and everything. No wonder I crashed. I'm so lucky to have emerged with only this.'

'So, you think you could have crashed the car yourself?' Steph hoped to prompt her to tell them more, but Beverly took another gulp of wine, placed her glass back on the table, and waited for them to continue. It appeared that particular conversation was over as far as she was concerned. Beverly poured more wine into Steph's glass.

'We met Hugo last night.' Steph accepted the very full glass.

'What a wonderful Puck he was – so gymnastic, so physical – sexy in a perverse – or is it a perverted way? I didn't know he was there. What a shame I missed him!' Beverly's booming voice projected around the garden. Steph hoped the neighbours weren't also making the most of the balmy evening.

'He goes back to Paris on Tuesday, so you may catch him.' Steph sipped the cool Chardonnay, pleased that Hale had agreed to drive. 'He was telling us about the last night party after *The Dream*.'

'Now that was a wild party! I was younger then. Oh, the fire on the beach was so dramatic and so romantic.'

'Romantic?'

'Yes, all those hormones racing around those young bodies frolicking in front of the flames! A true Grecian bacchanal!' Her voice became louder the longer she spoke. 'First love. Nothing like it, is there?'

Beverly reached over to top up Steph's glass again and spilt a dollop on the table. The empty bottle she'd pulled out of the terracotta cooler suggested that she'd had quite a few before they'd arrived. 'Always happens in a play at their age. They invariably fall in love with each other and play their parts for real.' She raised her glass in a 'cheers' gesture and drank deeply.

'Who did?' Steph nudged her quietly, exchanging looks with Hale. They were finding this easier than they'd thought.

'Oh! Hugo and Lucy – or was it Hugo and Jessica? Do you know, I'm not sure now. Let me think.' She closed her eyes, apparently visualising something of the scene. 'Yes, it was Hugo and Lucy and Jessica and that wonderful boy – the sparky – so talented – now what was his name?'

'Marcus Strong?' Steph held out her glass just in time to catch the fountain Beverly poured into it, pushing up the neck of the bottle to prevent her glass from overflowing. She took the bottle from Beverly and slotted it into the cooler.

'I can see them now, splashing into the waves – that magical phosphorescence clinging to their youthful bodies. So romantic, so evocative.' Beverly took another gulp of wine and emptied her glass.

'Who?'

'Jessica and Marcus or—' She closed her eyes again. 'Was it Lucy and Hugo? Anyway, it was one of the pairs.' Beverly reached out for the bottle and refilled her glass.

'Did you see Hugo leave the party?' Steph put her hand over her glass as Beverly was offering another top up.

Beverly closed her eyes once more, and it took so long for her to reply that Steph wondered if she'd fallen asleep. They both jumped as her voice rang through the garden. 'Yes, I've got it! Hugo bewitched Lucy. Took her off to Paris, you know. She went to the renowned clown school. Not heard anything of her since then ... Such a shame she didn't go to one of our drama schools. Such a brilliant future. Must be working somewhere in Europe now. Strange, I've never heard from her.'

Hale nodded at Steph. 'I'm afraid it was Lucy's body that

was found on the cliff fall after the storm. We believe she died after that party.'

Beverly became grey as the news percolated through her drunken brain and appeared to make her sober up immediately. 'No! I can't believe it. Not Lucy. That can't have been Lucy. She was so beautiful. Innocent and ethereal. So full of life. Are you sure?'

'Quite sure.' Steph moved Beverly's glass out of reach of her waving arms and saved it from being dashed to the ground.

'But she can't have – I mean, she wrote a card to me from France telling me she was going to the clown school.'

'Do you still have that postcard?'

Beverly paused. 'I suppose so, somewhere. Why?'

'Could you have a look and let us have it?'

'Yes. I'll look for it.' For once, Beverly appeared to find speech difficult.

'We think she was murdered and someone else sent that postcard.' Steph poured water into Beverly's glass.

'No, that can't be. Lucy sent the card. She left with Hugo. I saw her. They went off to Paris together, so romantic.'

'Can you recall the last time you saw her that night?'

Once again, she shut her eyes. 'I can see them now, Hugo and Lucy climbing up the cliff path, hand in hand, so much in love.'

'You didn't see her after that?'

'Only heard a week or so later she was in Paris. No, she left with Hugo, followed by that sneaky little snake, Lysander. So jealous he was. Not a drama student at all. He "spanielled her at the heels" – always mooning around after her, but it was Hugo she was destined to meet. I knew it from the first she meant to be with him.'

She searched both their faces in case they were joking or had changed their minds. 'Are you sure it was Lucy?'

'Sorry, Beverly. No doubt.'

'And you say she was murdered?'

'Yes.'

'Then I suggest that you have a word with Lysander, that Naz Rahman. The anger on his face that night was of the basilisk– the anger of a killer.'

CHAPTER FIFTY-TWO

MONDAY 2ND SEPTEMBER: 4.45PM

It was the first day of term for students at Oakwood Sixth Form College and Steph had been kept busy answering questions from many of the six hundred and seventy new students who had enrolled the previous week. After the emptiness of the summer break, she loved it as the students filled the college and the corridors buzzed with their laughter and chatter.

'Bye! See you tomorrow.' Steph waved at a group of girls who appeared to be quieter and more reserved than many of the students, pleased they had made friends already. Her phone rang, and she scrambled in her bag under the reception desk to answer it. It was Hale.

'Hi ... busy but good. How was yours? ... Really? ... Yes, that would be fine. Let me clear up here and collect Derek on the way. I'll see you in about forty minutes.'

Steph dashed around Reception tidying up, shutting down the students' information screen and ensuring that all the staff working in the office behind her had cleared their desks. She was sure Peter, the Principal, wouldn't mind her leaving a little early as everyone else appeared to have left for the day.

As she drove to collect Derek from the dog-lady, she felt pleased that Hale had invited her to see the taped interview with Hugo. Once she wouldn't have given this a second thought, but recently she could take nothing for granted.

The second-floor office in the police station retained the same appearance and smell as it had when she'd left it years earlier. A mixture of coffee, crisps, microwaved ready meals with a strong whiff of wood polish as the cleaners had been in. Surprisingly, it was almost deserted as she walked through the desks towards the glass walls of Hale's office. He raised his hand when he saw her, and the woman who was bending close to him, fascinated by something on the computer screen, turned her head to see who was arriving.

Hale stood as Steph walked through the open door. 'Lizzie, meet my partner Steph.'

'Pleased to meet you.' Steph shook Lizzie's outstretched hand and appraised her. Mid-thirties, confident smile, hair pulled back in a business-like bun, minimal make up but deep searching brown eyes that swept over her. Steph stood up straight and held her tummy in, pleased she'd washed her hair that morning.

'Good night, Hale. I'll be off. See you in the morning.' Lizzie gave him a wide smile, turned and walked out of his office. Her navy well-cut trouser suit would be at home in any executive board room and showed off her gym-honed figure. Steph felt a sudden wave of depression. How could she compete with that?

Before she could dip down any lower, Derek yanked his lead out of her hand and rushed around to Hale, who immediately patted him and gave him a large bone-shaped dog biscuit from his bottom drawer.

'Thanks for coming. I've got it cued up. Shouldn't take too long as I've found the important part. Lizzie was great to work with – she sensed when to push and when to hold back. Hugo obviously liked her.'

I bet he did! From what Naz had said, Hugo made the most of his good looks and sexy French voice with all the girls in the 1989 play and it appeared little had changed. As she pulled a chair round to his desk and Hale switched on the interview and froze the first frame, she could see that Hugo and Lizzie had formed a rapport. His wolfish smile and her coy Princess Di gaze from beneath her eyelashes left Steph in no doubt that they were getting on well. Hale was sitting back, observing in this shot, looking sideways at Lizzie. Shouldn't he have been looking at Hugo?

'I thought Johnson was the one who led your interviews along with Martin?'

'They do, but neither was here today, and we were up against it. Hugo goes back to France tomorrow, unless we arrest him.'

When she had settled Derek down on the floor beside her, Hale pressed the button and started the interview.

Lizzie: 'I know it's thirty years ago now, but can you tell us again what happened just before you left the party?'

Hale paused it again. 'Sorry Steph. Up to this point he told us about his growing involvement – I won't call it falling in love – more like falling in lust with Lucy – and how he was spending more and more time with her, having also taken out someone called Katie who had played Titania, then Jessica. They'd spent a few evenings together, but he decided Jessica wasn't his type and he would rather spend his time with Lucy.'

Steph felt sorry for Naz. 'Did Hugo say how Naz felt about him stealing his girlfriend?'

'Not really. He said it was Naz who was fixated on Lucy, and she wasn't that keen on him. Anyway, now we get to the interesting bit.'

CHAPTER FIFTY-THREE

MONDAY 2ND SEPTEMBER: 5.50PM

THE SCREEN JUMPED INTO LIFE.

Hugo: 'As I keep telling you, Lucy and I had spent most of the evening together before Jessica came over and made a fuss.'

Hale: 'A fuss?'

Hugo: 'Yes, I think she'd had too much to drink and in front of everyone she accused Lucy of being greedy and stealing me from her, when she already had good little Naz as her boyfriend.'

Lizzie: 'What do you think she meant?'

Hugo: 'When I first arrived, Jessica threw herself at me – literally – and wanted to spend more and more time with me. It was fun at first, but she became so dull and after a few days I got bored with her following me around. You know, she was always there whenever I turned around and monopolised me. It was embarrassing.'

Lizzie: 'What happened that evening?'

Hugo: 'I had been aware of her following me and Lucy

around all through the party – if it wasn't Jessica, we were falling over the pathetic, lovesick Naz. We found a sort of cave in the cliffs away from the crowd and we made love for the last time.'

Lizzie: 'For the last time?'

Hugo: 'We had become very good friends.' (He grinned across at Hale.)

Hale: 'Lucy knew you were going to leave her that night and go back to France, did she?'

Hugo: 'Oh yes, what we were having was just a bit of fun.'

Hale: 'Did you actually say that?'

Hugo: (Paused, looked down and fiddled with his wedding ring.) *'I think I must have done, yes.'*

Hale: 'Go on.'

Hugo: 'As we left the cave, I saw Naz lurking by the edge of the cliff, he must have thought I hadn't seen him as he crept along in the shadow. Lucy hadn't seen him, I'm sure.'

Lizzie: 'How do you know?'

Hugo: 'Come now, Sergeant, who do you think she was looking at after we'd made passionate love? Certainly not that silly little boy.'

Hale: 'You go back to join the others?'

Hugo: 'As we got to the group, Jessica leaped up at Lucy and pushed her down on the sand so Lucy lay on her back, flat on the ground. Then Jessica threw herself on top of Lucy and sat on her stomach and started slapping her around the face, shouting Lucy was a tart, a whore who would sleep with anyone and had stolen me from her.'

Hale: 'And what did you do?'

Hugo: 'I was shocked, of course, and didn't do anything. Naz pulled Jessica off Lucy and threw her to the ground. That nice boy, the lighting technician, Marcus, I think he was called, took Jessica away up the beach where they sat talking. That Marcus, he was a nice boy.'

Hale: 'And Lucy?'

Hugo: 'She was upset. All her friends were staring at her and looking shocked.'

Lizzie: 'Why didn't you tell me this when you came to make your statement?'

Hugo: 'Because you never asked me. All you wanted to know was what happened when we got to the top of the cliff and not what happened before we got there.'

Hale: 'What did Naz do then?'

Hugo: 'After he helped Lucy up to her feet, he tried to put his arm around her. I thought he was going to take her away from me, which would have been a good thing as I was about to go. But she pushed him away and fell into my arms, crying. I spent a lot of time calming her down. I was worried I might miss my taxi.'

Hale: 'To take you to London?'

Hugo: 'Yes. We walked down to the edge of the sea and along the shore until she stopped sobbing. I told her it was time to go for the cab and I had to go back to France. We walked up the cliff together and I kissed her goodbye at the church gate, and she went back and sat on the bottom of that big window drinking with someone – Jessica, it may have been.'

Lizzie: 'Really? Why do you think Lucy went to be with Jessica after all that Jessica had said and done to her?'

Hugo: 'I don't know. It was dark and thirty years ago. Maybe it was someone else then? Maybe it was Naz. It was dark, and I was worried about the taxi. I have told you the rest.'

Hale: 'How long were you waiting at the gate for your taxi?'

Hugo: 'Too long.' (Hale raised his eyebrow but said nothing. Hugo lowered his eyes.) 'About an hour. When it didn't come, I *walked up the road to the phone box where I phoned for it again and waited.'*

Hale: 'An hour by the church, and how long were you at the phone box?'

Hugo: 'Oh, let me think. It must have been another half hour waiting by the phone box for the taxi.'

Hale: 'And when did you last see Naz?'

Hugo: 'When I said goodbye to Lucy at the church gate. It was well lit there, and he couldn't hide so well and he went behind the church where he thought we wouldn't see him. I remember another taxi arrived and some of the old actors got into it on their way back to Oakwood. They wouldn't let me have it even though they were local, and I had to get to London.'

———

Hale switched the screen off and gave Steph a searching look. 'Well?'

Steph felt nauseated by Hugo's arrogant approach to everything, and everyone, including women. 'I suppose that last part suggests Naz was telling what he thought was the truth.'

'Yes, it supports his story. He could have seen the taxi pull up and assumed Lucy and Hugo got into it, not knowing it wasn't the right one, so he didn't stay or look for Lucy after that.' Hale switched off his computer.

'But Hugo's story has been like pulling teeth. He hasn't exactly been over-cooperative, has he?'

Hale pulled on his jacket from the back of his chair. 'No, not a man to be trusted, in my view.'

Steph pulled Derek up, ready to go. 'But he has given us a motive for Jessica killing Lucy, hasn't he?'

'Or Naz.' Hale gave Steph a knowing look.

CHAPTER FIFTY-FOUR

MONDAY 2ND SEPTEMBER: 7.30PM

STEPH RANG the doorbell of the cottage and stood back under the beamed porch. Hale had suggested that she should take the lead with Naz, and he would stay in the background. They were about to give up and go home when at last the studded oak door opened and Naz stood aside, looking puzzled.

'Steph and Hale – I'm honoured! But where is Derek? Is he with you?'

'He's in the car.' Steph was pleased that Naz had included her favourite dog – he really should get one.

'Do bring him in.'

'That's kind, thanks.'

When Steph returned, Derek flew over to Naz as if greeting a long-lost friend. Hale frowned. 'You two have met then?'

'Oh yes, Derek and I are old friends, aren't we, boy?' Naz pointed to two chairs and a sofa. 'Do sit wherever you like and where you think Derek would be comfortable, Steph.'

Hale chose a leather armchair to the left of the enormous inglenook hearth, while Steph sat on the sofa as the other chair appeared to be well worn on the arms, so she assumed it was where Naz usually sat. Derek settled down beside that chair as if this were his usual home.

If Steph was asked to describe what she thought Naz's sitting room would be like, this is what she would have said; gleaming antique furniture, large leather chairs, expensive-looking watercolours, and warm pools of light from three elegant table lamps on wine tables on the beige carpeted floor. A place to relax and chat with no television, unless he had hidden it in one of the cupboards on either side of the hearth.

'Now, may I offer you a drink – tea? Coffee?'

'No, we're fine, thanks. We don't want to take up any more of your time than we need to and sorry for calling so late.'

'I assume it's because you're making progress?' Naz sat back in his chair, his hand dangling over the arm so he could stroke Derek, who started licking the proffered hand enthusiastically.

'Yes, we're getting close to building up a detailed picture of what happened to Lucy, and we need your help.'

'Anything I can do, you know that.'

'Have you found any examples of Lucy's writing? I think you said you had some.'

Naz smiled. 'Actually, I recall I said I had nothing. But you're in luck. I've had another look and found this.' He got up, went over to an antique desk under the mullioned window, opened a drawer and pulled out an envelope, which he handed to Steph. From her chair, Steph could see regimented lines of pens and pencils filled the drawer.

'Thank you. That will be so helpful.' Steph slotted it carefully into her bag. 'Now I wonder if you mind me asking about the after-play party. What did you see of Lucy during the evening?'

Naz closed his eyes for a moment and frowned. Was he

annoyed at being asked to picture that evening on the beach or trying to remember? 'I spent most of the evening by myself as Lucy had made it clear that she preferred Hugo to me.'

'Really?'

'Yes. Hugo was an attractive, experienced man, and they flocked around him.'

'They?'

'Oh, you know, all the girls. It became a competition to see who would get him and keep him longest. He started with one of the fairies – I can't remember her name, moved on to Titania and then Jessica.'

He looked across at Steph, who nodded, hoping to encourage him further.

'Anyway, Jessica followed him round everywhere until Hugo chose Lucy in the end, and she lasted the longest. And as soon as he favoured her, she rejected me. As simple as that.'

Even now, the pain of rejection in his eyes was evident. At eighteen, it must have felt really raw.

'Were you angry?'

Naz frowned. 'What you mean is, was I sufficiently angry to kill her? Yes, I was angry and hurt, but no, I didn't kill her.'

Steph became aware of Hale moving in his chair as he made the leather squeak. Was he becoming impatient? If he was, tough – she'd go at her own speed.

'Where was she during the evening?'

'With Hugo, I've just said. Do we need to keep going over this?'

'Sorry, I think we do. Where were they? With everyone else around the fire? Swimming?'

'No, they didn't go swimming, but Jessica and Marcus did.' He paused and straightened the coaster on the wine table to his left. 'Funnily enough, Jessica and I were only talking about the beach party the day before she died. She admitted she only wanted Hugo so badly because Lucy had got him, and she actually preferred spending time with Marcus. She said they were best friends, and he'd always been there to take care of her, like a brother.'

'He sounds like a good guy.' She was relieved they'd got over the sticky patch and Naz was willing to continue talking.

'Yes, he was. He was a good mate of mine, too. Look at Jason and you'll see Marcus – a mirror image. Jessica took him to the wine bar a couple of times and said being with him reminded her of Marcus. The same voice, the same slightly crooked smile and he'd inherited Marcus's sense of humour.'

'Did you mind Jessica seeing Jason while she was here?'

Naz squirmed uncomfortably and she could see his defences were up again. Had she blown it? 'Look, what is this? Of course I didn't mind. She came here out of the blue. We formed an adult relationship, but I didn't own the woman. She could spend evenings with whomsoever she liked, and she liked Jason's company, not least because she re-lived her time with Marcus. Isn't that what we all like doing, re-living our youth?'

'Thanks for your patience, Naz. One last question. You say you last saw Lucy and Hugo getting into a cab at the church gate?'

'A taxi arrived and as they went towards it, I gave up and went back to the party.'

'Did you see them actually get into it?'

Naz frowned. 'I saw the taxi arrive and they walked towards it and assumed they got in it.'

'Did you see Jessica again that night?'

'No. I've no idea where she was.'

CHAPTER FIFTY-FIVE

TUESDAY 3RD SEPTEMBER: 5.45PM

STEPH LAID the Marcus Strong file on the table, ready to discuss her theory with Hale when he came home. She wouldn't start supper before he came, as he hadn't seemed bothered about eating what she'd prepared over the last few days. He said he wasn't hungry. Eating alone, she missed their chatter. Maybe it was time to have a serious talk?

Her musings were disturbed by Derek barking as the door opened and Hale came in. Amazed, she called across to him. 'Hi, good day?'

Hale came over and kissed her cheek, threw his jacket over the back of the armchair, and sat at the table. 'Oh, you know, same old, same old. Not making much progress on anything at the moment. What's for supper?'

'Sorry, assumed you wouldn't want anything. I was going to have avocado on toast. That do you?'

'No, I'm ravenous. I'll phone for a curry from The Mogul, shall I?'

Pleased that for once they were going to share a meal, Steph fished the Mogul Dynasty menu out of a kitchen drawer, brought it over to the table and sat opposite. 'That sounds a great idea, but could we have a few minutes before you phone? I've got something to show you.'

'They always take forty minutes to deliver, so why don't I order and we can talk while we wait?'

'Fine. I'd like the usual, please.'

Hale placed their order while Steph went over to the fridge, found two cold beers, removed their caps, and, sitting beside him, pulled the file towards her.

Hale finished his call. 'Told you – forty minutes.'

She pushed the Marcus Strong file towards him.

'Ah! The Marcus Strong file. Are you going to tell me you agree with Jason, and it wasn't an accident, despite the cut and dried investigation?'

Steph opened the file and pointed to one of several yellow sticky-notes she'd placed under the text. 'Look at this. It says here that the first 999 call was made by a woman who didn't leave her name and wasn't there when the police and ambulance arrived.'

'So?'

'Just supposing it was Jessica?'

'How do you make that out?'

'Hugo saw Jessica on the back of Marcus's bike, didn't he?' Why did he make her feel so stupid? She knew this was a little far-fetched, but she had a hunch she felt could work and it was more than he or the sainted Lizzie had got so far.

'But that was the night of the play. Marcus died the evening after.'

'OK. But if she was seeing Marcus, and Naz confirmed that last night, and I think Beverly also said something, why couldn't she have been on the back of his bike the next night, the night of the crash? Just let me finish where I'm going before you pull it apart.'

Hale sighed and took another gulp of beer. 'Go for it. We've nothing else to do while waiting for my Jalfrezi.'

'Let's say Jessica was there at the accident.'

'Why didn't she get hurt too?'

'We don't know that she didn't, do we?'

Hale rolled his eyes. 'Then why didn't she wait for the police and ambulance to arrive? If she was as fond of him as Naz said, wouldn't she stay with him?'

'I'll put the plates in the microwave for a couple of minutes to warm.' This gave Steph time to consider what she'd already said. His sceptical expression hadn't changed by the time she returned to the table. 'If it wasn't an accident and Jessica had caused his death, she wouldn't stay with him, would she?'

'Oh, come on! Why on earth would Jessica want to kill Marcus? They were great friends, according to Naz.'

Saved by the bell – the curry was early for once. Steph collected the foil boxes from the delivery woman and served out the food onto the warm plates. For a while they enjoyed eating the spicy curries, which were the best in Oakwood. When Hale had mopped up the last of the sauce with his naan bread, he sat back, sated. 'Where were we? You were going to tell me her motive.'

A much slower eater than Hale, Steph savoured the final forkful of the Mogul's special prawn Balti. 'There's always that award. It keeps coming up. They were all desperate to win it and Marcus was thought by several people to be the favourite – we know that.'

Hale pulled his "you could be right face." 'Let's imagine for a moment that she did all you say. How did she do it?'

Steph was ready for this. 'Simple. The crash happened on the straight part, after the bend. Jessica was on the pillion and if she leaned the wrong way and squirmed around when they came round that sharp bend, she would unbalance him enough to lose control, then she could jump off before it hit the ground, while he carried on and fractured his skull.'

'A bit high risk for her, wasn't it?'

Steph opened the file and pointed to another line in the text. 'It says here they didn't find a helmet at the crash site and assumed Marcus wasn't wearing one. And look, here it says he was wearing jeans and a tee shirt. Suppose he'd lent his helmet and leathers to her. She'd be protected and he wouldn't.'

Hale reached out for the file and re-read the sections Steph had indicated.

'And look.' She pointed to a sentence. 'There's the description of the roadworks, just after the bend, so he'd have been going slow anyway with his broken light and he'd know the hole was there so he'd slow down even more, wouldn't he?'

'There's a lot of supposition here—'

'But Jessica wouldn't be taking such a high risk, would she? She knew where the bike would slow down, and she could jump off. It was a calculated risk, in my opinion.'

Hale frowned. 'I'm not sure you'd ever be able to prove it. But I suppose it could just be possible.'

Steph paused, waiting for her big moment. She slid out the document she'd put in the file earlier, flattened it, and pointed to a section in the text. 'Perhaps this will help you see that with all I've said, it could be possible.'

CHAPTER FIFTY-SIX

TUESDAY 3RD SEPTEMBER: 7.30PM

STEPH WAS worried Hale might be done for speeding if he didn't slow down. She hadn't expected him to react to her suggestion so quickly, but she'd given up trying to work out what he might do as he'd been so unpredictable over the last few weeks.

Even at this speed, she knew she'd have ten minutes where he couldn't storm off somewhere, and with both facing forward, it was easier than talking face-to-face.

'We need to have a serious talk.'

'That sounds grim. Can't it wait?'

He sat up straight, darted a swift glance at her sideways, then looked ahead as an ancient tractor forced him to slow down to fifteen miles an hour. 'Stupid bugger. Why doesn't he move over and let us through? There was a lay-by back there.'

Just in front of their bonnet, the red lights on the trailer glowed as it came to a sudden stop. Hale slammed on the brakes and smashed his hand against the steering wheel. 'Doesn't he have indicators? Hazard lights?'

His eyes blazing, he turned to face her. 'Now we're stuck here, tell me, what were you saying?'

Steph sighed. How was she to have a reasonable conversation with him in this mood? But she'd started, so she'd continue.

'We need to talk about us.'

'Us? What about us?' He sounded puzzled – a deep frown etched on his face.

'Since we went to Latitude, things have been different – weird.'

'Weird?'

'Yes. I've had enough—'

'What on earth are you talking about?'

Steph hadn't expected this to be easy, but his blank face challenged her. Surely, she hadn't imagined his bizarre behaviour the last few weeks, had she?

The tractor had made three attempts backing its trailer into the narrow entrance of the farmyard and was making a total hash of the manoeuvre.

'For fuck's sake!' Hale slammed his hand down on the steering wheel and threw open his door. 'We'll be here all night at this rate!'

He slammed his door, making the car rock. Standing in front of the cab and waving his arms, he guided the driver through the gateway.

It gave Steph time to reflect on his apparent failure to recall all the evenings where he was too grumpy or tired to eat, or the frequent late nights at work. When he was with her, his head was usually stuck to his wretched laptop screen.

The regular walks, the spontaneous visits to the pub and the quiet evenings sharing a TV programme or film had all disappeared. It was as if she no longer existed. It had happened – she wasn't making it up – she was right, wasn't she?

Another slammed door as he threw himself back in his seat. 'Stupid, bloody man. And is he grateful? No! Now he's moaning it's at the wrong angle making it difficult to unload!'

'At least we can get past and let him get on with it.' Steph looked back at the tractor, which was edging its nose out of the gate.

Hale got up to speed and turned to her. 'What were you saying?'

'At least you're not avoiding it.'

'Avoiding what? What are you talking about?'

'Maybe that's the problem. You don't notice and don't want to bother anymore.'

'Bother about what?'

Steph opened her lips a little and breathed in deep breaths to keep down the nausea that engulfed her, hoping that Hale hadn't noticed. She'd rehearsed this speech in the bathroom mirror but found that actually saying it was much more devastating than the dry runs.

'It's been good – I mean us – the last few years, but perhaps we both need some space for a bit – or maybe we split.'

'Split? Why? What's wrong?'

'What's wrong? I can't believe you're saying this!' Her voice raised. 'You call yourself a detective and you can't see what's wrong?'

'No, I can't – what're you going on about?'

'You don't want to go out. You spend all your evenings glued to that stupid Athena programme. You don't want to eat with me, and you barely have a good word to say to me – that's when you actually come home. That's what's wrong!'

'Come on Steph! That's not true. It's been a tough few weeks.'

'It's been tough before and you've never been like this.'

'Like what?'

'Like I no longer exist. Is it something I've done?' They drove over a bridge and pulled up outside the house. Hale turned off the engine and stared out of the windscreen up the road. The silence was solid.

'Why don't you say something!' She heard herself shouting. 'You've found someone else, haven't you?' There, she'd said it.

'What on earth gives you that idea?'

'What? I can't believe you just said that! You can't even admit it. You've put me through hell these last few weeks. You want a way out? Fine. You've got it!'

'Look, Let's get in there and get this over.'

'You're right – it's over!'

CHAPTER FIFTY-SEVEN

TUESDAY 3RD SEPTEMBER: 7.45PM

ONCE AGAIN, they stood outside a front door, having rung the bell, waiting for it to be opened. This time it was a red-brick Victorian cottage in a row of three overlooking the river.

Her back to Hale, Steph stared across the river. She felt like sobbing but drove her nails into the palms of her hands to stop herself. The sunset left a deep pink glow smeared across the sky, which was reflected in the river. It had been a glorious day and Steph wasn't looking forward to the dark winter nights, especially now she'd be alone again. The door opened.

'Hi Jason, is this a good moment to have a chat?' Steph stepped forward, smiled and followed his eye, noting that he had spotted the dog-eared label on the Marcus Strong file she held in front of her. Hale remained silent. So, it was her show, was it? Fine – she'd suggested it, after all.

'Sure, come in. Dad's at a darts match with Max. You know, from the play. They think they'll be top of the league this year. He won't be back until closing time.'

'No, it was you we wanted to speak to. Just a few things to clarify.'

Jason led them into a sitting room where an enormous picture window framed the spectacular view of the dying rays of the sunset.

'Wow! What a view!' Steph stepped in front of the window.

'Yes, pretty spectacular isn't it and not an LED in sight!' He hovered by the door, apparently unsure of something. 'Would you like a drink or anything?'

'No, we've just had a curry from The Mogul – do you know it?'

'Who doesn't?' He turned on the overhead light, starkly banishing the gentle evening view, and sat on a large armchair by the window, looking across at them expectantly.

Steph sat in the identical chair opposite and started off as Hale remained silent, sitting on a chair by the door, out of her eye line. 'We think we've discovered something more about your uncle's accident and wonder if you could confirm a few things for us.'

'Right.' Jason sat up straight, paying full attention to her.

'When we talked at the site of the crash, you said that as far as you know your uncle always wore a helmet and leathers?'

'Yes. That's what Dad said.'

'Did the police ever find them, or did he?'

Jason shook his head. 'No. Dad thought the leathers could have been left somewhere as it was a hot evening, but he was surprised about the helmet. He always said if Marcus had been wearing it, he may have survived.'

'Did Jessica tell you why he wasn't wearing it?'

Jason made a sudden move and sat back, apparently taken by surprise. 'Jessica? Why would she know?'

'Well, we know that you two met several times over the weeks when she was staying here—'

'I'm not sure where you heard that.'

'She told a friend she'd seen you at least twice and we know how close she was to Marcus.'

Jason appeared to be considering what to say next and narrowed his eyes. 'Yes, we went for a drink a couple of times. I mean, she was a star, wasn't she?'

'Yes, she was. What did you talk about? Can you remember?'

Jason shifted in his seat and appeared to relax a little. 'You know, about her time here when she was at college with Marcus.'

'And the play they were in?'

He shrugged his shoulders. 'I suppose she did talk a lot about that, and Marcus. She said they'd been good friends and how much she admired him and how sorry she was that he hadn't lived to get that award.' His words tumbled out in an urgent rush to explain.

'Did she tell you he'd often given her lifts on his bike?'

He smiled. 'Yes, she said they'd go home from rehearsals together.'

'And did she say she'd been with him on the night he died in the crash? On his pillion?'

Jason lowered his head and closed his eyes and frowned, as if recalling their conversation. 'No. I don't think she said that.'

'Really? It's strange after all the other lifts that he wouldn't have taken her home on that night, too.'

'I've just told you all she said about Marcus, and she didn't mention that.' The stubborn tone of his denial and his stiff jaw made her change tack.

'Right. It was just a thought. Now could we go back to the *Mother Courage* lighting rig?'

'Sure.' Jason nodded, visibly relaxing.

'You put all the lights up on the bar for Max?'

'Yes.'

'And he didn't put any of them up?'

Jason frowned. 'Well, you must have seen him. He's getting a bit ... well, a bit doddery. Not always firm on his feet and we agreed I'd do the bar to stop him climbing the ladder.'

'And who did the side towers?'

'We both did.'

Jason appeared to have lost his defensive attitude at last. 'He said in the next play I could be the chief designer, and he'd help me out. He was really pleased with what I'd done.'

Steph opened the file and held it slanted towards her making sure Jason couldn't see it, and pretended to peruse the page, tracing her finger down the margin. It was actually Marcus' coroners' report, but Jason wasn't to know that. She looked up at him. 'Tell me – which lamp fell on Jessica?'

'I think it was the middle one, the one directly above her cart. You were there, weren't you?'

'Yes, I was. But you're the expert and I just want to check. And there were – how many?'

'Seven.'

'Seven in total on the bar, so the middle one?'

Jason frowned and gave her a look, suggesting she was being particularly dense. 'Yeah, as I've just said, the one in the middle.'

'It would be the fourth one? Yes?'

'Yes, the fourth, the middle one of the seven.' Sounding impatient, Jason rolled his eyes at her.

Steph shut the file, holding his gaze.

'So, can you explain how your fingerprints were on the fourth lamp, the middle one that fell on Jessica?'

Jason rolled his eyes and tutted. 'Simple. I've just said – I hung it up there. Of course, my fingerprints are on it.'

'Yes, but we also found Max's fingerprints.'

'Of course you would. He and I handled all the lamps.' Jason now sounded confident and replied without hesitation.

'Not this one, you didn't. You see, after you left the night before that first rehearsal, the bulb blew in the lamp you'd hung. Max found an old light right at the back of his store, one that you didn't know was there, so couldn't have touched. He climbed up and replaced it himself.'

She paused and allowed this news to sink in. 'It should only have his fingerprints on it, but yours were found around the clamp where you loosened it later that night.'

A brief flash of panic flushed across Jason's face. 'But I could have gone up there to adjust it for him in the rehearsal.'

'But you didn't, did you? The rehearsal had already started when you arrived that morning – you were late, remember, and Beverly had a go at you in front of everyone. So, the only way your finger-prints would be on that lamp would be if you'd gone up there the night before, after Max had hung it, and removed the safety chain and loosened the clamp so it would fall on Jessica.'

Shocked into silence, Jason appeared to be letting the news she'd just given him sink in and working out what she knew and could prove.

Steph placed the file on the table. 'And it was you deliberately jumping off that tower and shaking it that made the lamp come off the bar, wasn't it?'

Jason studied the carpet, then stared at Steph. 'Not much evidence, is there? A few finger-prints that could have been left there at any time. And anyway, why would I have killed Jessica?' He sounded cocky.

Steph stared him out. 'Jessica told you she'd been on the pillion that night, didn't she? She was wearing his helmet and leathers, and she wobbled the bike near that church and they both fell off. That's what she told you, didn't she?'

He said nothing but stubbornly stared her out. She won.

'I'm right, aren't I? Jessica felt guilty, didn't she? And after a few drinks, that's what she told you, didn't she?'

Jason cleared his throat. 'I need the loo.'

'Is it through there?' Hale, by the door, gestured towards the kitchen.

'Yes.' Jason swiftly strode into the kitchen, followed by Hale.

Steph heard a scuffle and the back door slam. She rushed into the kitchen. On the floor lay a body. It was Hale, an enormous carving knife stuck in his chest.

CHAPTER FIFTY-EIGHT

TUESDAY 3RD SEPTEMBER: 8.05PM

For a moment, she froze and heard herself scream. 'No! Hale!'

Throwing herself on the floor beside him, she examined the place where the knife had penetrated. Not a drop of blood has escaped. It looked like one of those joke knives, but this was no joke. It was an enormous carving knife, pushed into his chest almost up to the hilt.

The revving of a powerful motorbike slammed into the silence, roared past the house, and disappeared as it sped away.

'Jason. Escaped.' Hale tried to lift himself up as if he was going after him but gasped in pain.

'Stop moving, Hale. Stay as still as possible. They'll get him, don't worry.'

She knew she mustn't touch the knife and resisted the urge to put pressure on the site where it was sticking out of his chest in case she made it worse. He have serious internal bleeding.

She dashed into the sitting room, grabbed some cushions from the sofa and put them under his feet elevating them above his heart to slow down the bleeding then pulled a seat pad off a kitchen chair to give his head something softer to lie on rather than the cold tiles. His breathing was becoming shallow, but at least he was conscious.

'Hold on, Hale, I'm calling it in.'

Steph sat on the floor beside him, leaning against a cupboard, holding his hand, and dialled 999. 'Police and ambulance, it's urgent ... A police officer is seriously wounded ...Yes, needs immediate help ... Stabbed but not bleeding externally ... Yes, conscious and breathing, but getting more difficult ... Right, the address is 2, River Cottages, Rectory Lane, Blythburgh ... Yes, I'll keep my phone turned on and please tell them to hurry.'

She bent down to Hale, pushing his hair away from his eyes. 'They're on their way. I'm just going to open the front door and leave the lights on so they can find us.'

Hale tried to smile, which became a wince as he moved slightly.

'Keep as still as possible.'

On her way to the front door, which she left wide open, Steph turned on every light switch she could find until the house would probably be visible from outer space. She rushed back to Hale.

'Hold on, my love. You'll be fine, I know it.'

He didn't look convinced, and his breathing was becoming laboured. She shoved the kitchen table against the wall and dragged the two kitchen chairs out into the sitting room giving the paramedics sufficient room to treat him as soon as they arrived.

Steph sat on the floor beside him, holding his hand and stroking it. 'They'll be here soon.' They created a bizarre tableau, both sitting so still while they waited. There was little more she could say or do, but she kept her eyes fixed on his, willing him to stay alive.

Where were they? It seemed hours since she'd phoned. Probably only a few minutes. It could take ages for them to arrive. She mustn't show her panic.

'It's not bleeding, which is good, and they'll soon have it sorted.' She smiled down at him, suspecting his thorax was probably filling with blood and he needed attention as soon as possible. He'd know that too.

He closed his eyes, squeezing them, and gasped. 'Pain in—'

The pounding of feet drowned out his whisper as two paramedics stormed in. The front one threw his bag on the floor and dropped beside Hale, staring at the knife penetrating deep into his chest. Steph hauled herself up and stood at Hale's feet allowing the second paramedic, a woman, to take her place.

Steph became aware of a movement behind her as Johnson and two uniformed officers peered over her shoulder. She was pleased it was Johnson, now a sergeant, who had been her protégé when he first joined the service and was now Hale's right-hand man – or he had been until Lizzie had arrived. Thank goodness she wasn't on duty.

'So sorry, Steph.' Johnson patted her arm. All four of them stared in silence, not wanting to distract the paramedics working on Hale. She recognised the male paramedic and knew he was the best.

'Well done, Steph. Exactly the right thing to do.' The bearded paramedic turned and grinned at her as he fixed an oxygen mask over Hale's face. The woman added an oximeter to his middle finger and carefully placed packing around the knife making sure it wouldn't move. When she had finished, she left the kitchen to go back to the ambulance; Hale's colleagues making room for her to pass.

The bearded man stood. 'That's great Hale. We'll soon

have that out. Now we need to move you onto the stretcher. OK?'

Hale nodded, finding speech difficult as his breathing was now in shorter gasps than ever.

'Have you any pain?'

'Back ... between shoulder blades ...' Hale sounded as if he'd run a marathon.

Beardy, his head tilted, raised his eyebrow to Steph, so that Hale couldn't see. Steph's stomach knotted. It was serious. What did they know? What did Hale's comment mean?

With consummate skill, they lifted Hale onto the stretcher and took him out to the ambulance, joggling him as little as possible. Steph stood at the door watching while they fixed him up to a cardiac monitor and a drip with a transparent liquid in it, presumably saline.

She became aware of Johnson standing beside her. 'It was Jason Strong. The lighting tech. He escaped on his bike after he stabbed Hale. He can't have gone far. When you get him, arrest him for Jessica Marlowe's murder.'

Johnson frowned, nodded and turned to walk away. 'We'll get him, don't worry. You'll let me know how Hale gets on?'

'Of course.'

She climbed into the ambulance, the doors slammed shut and they zoomed off, the siren screaming and blue light flashing.

CHAPTER FIFTY-NINE

THE NURSE HANDED Steph a mug of tea. 'Why don't you go home and get some sleep? We'll phone you when he comes round.'

'No, thank you. I'll stay, so I'm here when he wakes up.' Steph placed the tea on the bedside cabinet, waiting for it to cool a little.

The nurse put her hand on Steph's shoulder. 'Right. You know where I am if you need me.' She walked out of the room and shut the door, blocking out the noise and bustle of the hospital as it woke up.

Hale's slow breathing through an oxygen mask and the rhythmic beeping of the machines dominated the room. Steph stood at the window, watching an ambulance siren blaring, blue light flashing, pulling up at A&E and felt for the person inside. A moment was all it took for your life to change forever.

What a nightmare it had been. A picture of Hale, struggling to breathe on the red tiles of the kitchen floor, pushed its way into her mind. A moment was all it took for him to be here in this bed, fighting for his life.

The door opened and the surgeon who had operated on Hale the night before came in, unhooked the chart from the end of Hale's bed and stared at the monitor.

'Morning. That's a good sign.' He indicated the regular beeping and green flashing graphs chasing across the screen. Steph followed his gaze.

'Sorry I couldn't see you myself after the operation – it was one of those nights – but I think sister spoke to you?'

'Yes. But I'm not sure I understood what she told me.'

The doctor, who looked about sixteen but must be in his late twenties, smiled and spoke slowly. 'That knife – Christ, it was a big one – penetrated his diaphragm, perforated his stomach and the internal bleeding led to blood clots on the stomach and the liver. We cleared it all up and mended the tears, so now it's up to him. He should come round soon.'

'Thank you so much. How long will he be here?'

Having scribbled a note on the chart, he stuck the pen in his pocket and re-hung the clipboard on the bed rail. 'A fit man like him, not too long. We'll know in a day or two, but he'll take at least six weeks to get over this and several months before he's fully recovered.' With that, he left the room, closing the door behind him.

Hale lay still, his eyes closed, and his face relaxed. He showed no signs of waking up but at least the regular beeps and constant green graphs crawling across the screen were re-assuring. Steph sat and stared at his face.

What if he'd died last night? He still could, couldn't he? It was her fault. It was her idea. She'd goaded Jason with her mad theories instead of waiting until they had him safe in the interview room at the station and presenting the evidence to him, logically and calmly.

And Hale. He must have been distracted to let it happen, and it was all her fault. No way would Jason have managed to stab him if he'd been fully alert and not worrying about what she'd said. Why had she gone on at him like that? And had she really told him it was over? She squeezed her eyes shut, trying to replay the final bit of the argument, but she couldn't remember what she'd said, only that she was angry and had said far, far too much.

He'd have every right to blame her for what happened. That's if he woke up. Everyone was being so positive, but they didn't know for sure, did they? It was her crazy idea to go and confront Jason and push him into admitting it all, which he didn't, did he? Of course, his attack on Hale would scream out his guilt, and at least they could charge him for attempted murder when they caught him.

Hale's hand fell out of hers and rested on the bed. Suppose when, or if, he woke he wouldn't forgive her? What then? Would he want to leave her and move in with her rival to recover? If only she hadn't chosen that drive to confront him but had done it calmly, when they were safe, at home. But he'd hardly been present when he'd been at home, had he?

Her head was spinning. She had lost him, she was sure, and even worse, put his life in danger. How was she to live with herself if he didn't recover? If only she could turn the clock back to last night and do things differently.

Steph sighed. The beeping speeded up a little. She looked at the monitor and down at his face. His eyes were wide open, and he was staring up at her.

CHAPTER SIXTY

THURSDAY 5TH SEPTEMBER: 2.00PM

THE DOOR OPENED to reveal Johnson balancing an enormous pile of magazines and a box of chocolates with a beige file on the top. Steph winked at him, while Hale, propped up in bed watching football on the TV, grinned.

'All right for some, lying around watching TV!'

Hale smiled. 'Indeed!' He muted the sound on the football.

'Good to see you looking better than last time I saw you, boss. The team sent you these.' He dumped the pile on the bedside cabinet and pulled out an enormous "Get Well Soon" card from the file. which he passed to Hale, who laughed at the picture of a miserable Derek look-alike dog, with a bubble saying, "At least you don't have to wear a cone!"

Johnson, obviously pleased at Hale's reaction, whispered. 'Didn't think they'd let you have this medicine yet, but just in case ...' He slipped a large bottle of Scotch inside the back of the cupboard and hid it behind a sponge bag.

Hale laughed, opened the card, and glanced at the mass of signatures and comments written inside. His eyes filled. He was evidently touched. 'Thanks. Please thank them all for me. It's very kind of them.'

Steph pulled a second chair beside the bed, gave hers to Johnson, and sat back a little. Hale had been desperate for news, and Steph had agreed to Johnson's visit to update him.

'It doesn't look too bad in here.' Johnson looked around at the room. 'Food all right?'

'Not had much chance to try it yet. Light diet, they call it. Soup so far and not much of that. May need an emergency call out for a burger or fish and chips soon!'

'You know the number!'

Hale pushed himself up a little higher. 'Right. Tell me what's happened.'

Johnson opened the folder revealing a few typed pages stapled together. 'Jason turned himself in and —'

'He what!'

'I'd just got back to the station to organise the search, when as cool as you like, he walked through the front door and said he wanted to turn himself in.'

'Bugger me! After what he'd done to me!'

'I asked him why, and he said he knew we'd get him so he may as well come in. Oh, and he said to tell you sorry.'

'That's good of him.'

'He said he panicked and didn't mean to hurt you.'

'That's all right then.' Hale shook his head in disbelief. 'Go on.'

'He wanted his brief and after they'd had a talk, he said he wanted to make a statement and confessed – just like that.' He looked down at the file in front of him. 'His story chimed exactly with Steph's briefing. Jessica had spent several evenings with him in the wine bar and apparently, she didn't take her drink too well. He thought she'd felt guilty all these years and wanted to get it off her chest and she dropped enough hints for him to be able to piece them together and reach the same conclusion you had.'

'So, Jessica told him she'd caused Marcus's accident?' Steph plumped Hale's pillows up to give him more support.

'Yes, she told him about the pillion ride, said Marcus had given the leathers and helmet to her and she claimed it was an accident.'

'Presumably he didn't swallow that?' For the first time in weeks, Steph recognised the old Hale, who, despite his pallor, appeared alive again.

Johnson shook his head. 'No, he said she hadn't waited for Marcus to be rescued, so he knew she'd been guilty.'

'And Jessica's death?'

'When we told him we'd got a statement from Max, he admitted the lot. Just as you said,' Johnson nodded to Steph. 'He'd gone up the night before, taken off the safety chain and undone the clamp on the light knowing it would fall on her when he wobbled the rig. He wanted to get her back for killing his uncle, but claimed he only wanted to scare her, not kill her.'

Steph couldn't help herself interrupting. 'That's ridiculous. He's an expert. He knows very well that a lamp that heavy will smash a skull and it only fell to the side because Jessica moved the cart.'

'That's that, then. Well done!' Hale sat back, looking very pleased.

Johnson closed the file. 'But it was you did all the work.'

'Actually, it was Steph who wouldn't give up. Like a dog with a bone, she was.'

Both men turned towards her, and she felt herself blushing. 'Well, it helped I was on the spot, you know.'

Steph moved a little to allow Johnson to leave, but he leaned towards Hale. 'And there was something else. Apparently, in her drunken state, Jessica told him that Marcus was always there to help her and got her out of a very big mess. That night when he died—'

'Killed him, you mean!' Hale was back on the ball!

'The night after the play – she said the reason Marcus came back with her was to bury a girl's body. Lizzie and I wondered if it could be our skeleton – you know, Lucy? Jessica told him it was an accident. The girl had fallen and hit her head and that was it. She was dead.'

'Another accident? Rubbish! Jessica killed two people in twenty-four hours!' Hale's voice was so loud a nurse passing by popped her head in the door, looked around and, evidently seeing all was well, closed it again.

'Anyway, she hid the body under the raked seating and the next night they dug a hole and buried her on the edge of the field, on top of the cliff.' Johnson closed the file.

Steph added. 'They'd have no idea that the erosion would reveal it thirty years later, would they?'

Hale frowned and closed his eyes. Was he getting too stressed? Steph took over. 'Well, that would support what Hugo told us. He said he saw Lucy and someone sitting on that high ledge of the east window. It could have been Jessica. Did Jason say anything about how the accident happened?'

'No. That was it. Jessica just talked about a girl's body Marcus buried, and it had been an accident – something about falling and hitting her head and no one must know, or it would be the end of their futures.' Johnson opened the file again to make sure there was nothing else.

'It certainly proved to be the end of his future!' Hale sounded annoyed.

Steph replaced one of Hale's pillows, which, in his excitement, had slumped beside him. 'I suppose it could have been an accident. That ledge is high up – we sat on it – and if Lucy lost her balance and fell, she could have smashed her skull easily enough.'

Johnson nodded. 'Good point. But why didn't Jessica phone the police instead of hiding it and involving Marcus?'

Steph sighed. 'From what I've seen of Jessica, she wouldn't risk anything getting in the way of her ambition, and any investigation or scandal could have ruined her career before it got started.'

'That meant the ever-helpful Marcus had to disappear too.' Hale closed his eyes for a few moments, and his voice had dropped. 'Then, with Lucy and Marcus out of the way, there was no one else to get that award.'

Johnson looked puzzled, then caught on. 'Oh, that prize thing! But it can't have been that important, can it?'

'Apparently it was to Jessica.' Steph took over. 'We now know she murdered Marcus and possibly Lucy too and even took the trouble to go to France to send a bunch of postcards claiming Lucy had run away with Hugo.' Steph stood, hoping that Johnson would take the hint. He did.

'That's all, boss. Two – no, three cases cleared up in one fell swoop. Now all we need is for you to get better.'

No reply from Hale – just a little snore.

CHAPTER SIXTY-ONE

WEDNESDAY 11TH SEPTEMBER: 5.30PM

'I'M HOME!' Steph threw her keys in the bowl by the front door and was almost knocked over by Derek dashing past her to greet Hale, who was sitting in an armchair doing a crossword. Steph had bought him several puzzle books and Johnson had lent him a Play Station and Fifa 19 to stop him getting bored while she was at work. He'd only been home for two days and was already desperate to be going out and getting back to work.

'Good day?' Hale patted Derek on the head. 'Five letters, first one S, holiday memories.'

Steph paused by the back of his chair, peering over his shoulder at the crossword grid. 'Snaps?'

'Brilliant!' He wrote it in the squares. 'Any chance of a beer?'

Steph went to the dog food cupboard and fed an anxious-looking Derek, then opened the fridge and brought over two bottles of Peroni, handing one to Hale.

She sat opposite and raised her bottle to him. 'Cheers.'

It was no good. This had gone on long enough, and he

hadn't mentioned anything about their row since that evening – well, she'd have to then.

'Now you're getting better, we need to sort something out.'

'What do we need to sort out?' He sat up straight, apparently aware that she wasn't messing about.

'Remember that discussion we had in the car on the way to Jason's house?'

'Er – not really. I know you arrived in a bad mood and pushed him over the edge—'

'What!'

'Which was a good thing – you got him to admit to it all.'

Steph took a deep breath, trying to keep her patience. 'I wasn't in a bad mood, simply annoyed you wouldn't admit things had been wrong for weeks.'

'Whatever—'

'No, don't interrupt. Let me finish. Let's be straight with one another. Even since you've been home from the hospital, you've been taking secret calls, going into the bedroom so I can't hear. There's someone else, isn't there?'

'Whatever are you talking about?'

'It's Lizzie, isn't it?' There, she'd said it.

'What? I've no idea where you've got that idea from.'

Was he really going to play it this way? She thought he'd have more dignity than denying it. 'Right, I'll spell it out. Ever since that woman joined your team, you haven't stopped talking about her. It's Lizzie this and Lizzie that and how you couldn't manage without her. To be honest, I'm totally pissed off with hearing about her and quite simply, if you'd rather be with her than me, just say so and we'll call it a day.'

Steph had held onto this speech for well over a week now, not wanting to resurrect their argument while Hale was ill. Now he was getting better, she had to get it over with. Why didn't he say something?

'I'm honestly not sure what you're talking about.' Hale appeared confused or was he taking the piss, working out what to say?

'Come off it. We've been great together. Let's not spoil it with lies and childish denials now. It's been good, but you obviously feel it's time to move on. That's fine.' Trapped between searing anger and wanting to cry, she struggled to keep her voice steady.

'Lizzie?' He laughed, a real belly laugh, and held onto his stitches. 'Ouch! You can't be serious! Me and Lizzie?' He laughed again, placing both hands over his stomach, tried to get up, but fell back in his chair, sucking in his breath against the pain. 'Ooh! I've no idea where you got that from. Lizzie's gay and very happy with a long-term partner she met at university. I'm only interested in her excellent professional skills and what she's contributing to the team.'

Now it was Steph's turn to be taken aback, and she felt herself blushing. 'Oh! She's gay, is she?' She paused to let this sink in. 'But ... but if it isn't her, who is it?'

Hale leaned forward as far as he could and winced. 'Steph, please believe me, there's no-one else.'

'Then why have you been so vile and weird for weeks?'

Hale frowned, and when he didn't reply, she continued. 'You've not wanted to spend time with me, been in a foul mood and avoiding me by working on that computer every night. If it isn't her, then who is it?'

Hale closed his eyes and let his head droop. When he looked up, she could see his eyes were full. 'Steph, I'm so sorry. I thought I was managing to cope with it and wanted to protect you.'

'Cope with what? Protect me from what?' Had he been told he had cancer? What was it? Why wouldn't he tell her?

His shoulders slumped. 'That phone call at Latitude was to

tell me they're reorganising the force – that's code for making cuts – and I was offered early retirement. Since then, there've been so many meetings and organisation charts you wouldn't believe it. In some of them I'm there, while in others, I've disappeared.'

'Why didn't you—'

'Share it with you?'

Steph nodded. Her anger now melted to sorrow for what he must have been going through.

'How could I tell you that you were going to live with an old age pensioner rather than a Detective Chief Inspector?'

'What! You think I'm only attracted to you for your job? Your status? You don't know me very well if you think that.'

'Sorry Steph. I should have told you, but when they mentioned retirement, I felt so old, so useless and then there's that new computer program I can't get the hang of it. I thought it proved I was ready for the scrapheap.'

'Don't be ridiculous. We're more than our jobs. That's not how we should define ourselves – learned that myself the hard way a few years ago. And are you?'

'What?'

'Going to retire?'

'Well, according to the latest family tree, I'm not. Well, not until the next chart comes out.'

'And so what? What if they make you retire? You'll find something else. It's not the end of the world.'

He didn't look convinced. 'Sorry Steph. I've been wrong not to tell you and you're right, it would have helped.'

'Honestly Hale. I was thinking all sorts. How I've suffered all these weeks! You owe me, mate!'

She reached behind her, found a cushion and, forgetting his stitches, lobbed it at him. He caught it and she ducked as she expected its return, so was surprised to find him slowly coming towards her. He perched on the arm of her chair, his arm around her shoulders.

'You're right. I should have shared it with you. I will next time – promise.'

Steph sighed and stroked his thigh. 'I really thought we were over.'

'Never. We make a good team, don't we?'

'Yes, we do.'

Hale leaned over her and kissed her. Derek squirmed between them, joining in the group hug.

'And I think it's time this team found a permanent base with a larger garden for Derek, don't you?'

The End

READ THE STEPH GRANT MURDER MYSTERY SERIES

'This wonderfully fresh take on a crime fighting duo, expertly explores dark, contemporary themes brought to life by a fabulous cast of characters who will stay with you long after the last page.' GRAHAM BARTLETT

Blood Notes
Blood Lines
Blood Ties
Blood Ribbons
Blood Spots

Buy now from book retailers or the Hobeck Books website.

ACKNOWLEDGMENTS

Thank you:

Rebecca Collins and Adrian Hobart – the talented, tireless power-couple behind Hobeck publishing, for their excellent feedback, editing, inspiration and constant encouragement.

Jayne Mapp, for a creative and evocative cover design.

Brian Price, author and crime science advisor, for ensuring all the technical details postmortem are correct.

Matt Maller, a talented lighting technician, for all of his suggestions on turning a spotlight into a murder weapon.

Rev'd Alan Perry for explaining the ordination and role of a priest in the Church of England.

Jo Barry, Gerry Wakelin, Freda and Bob Noble, Julie Mursaleen, Debby Hurst and Mary Luke – my first readers for their enthusiasm, critical appreciation and helpful suggestions.

LIN LE VERSHA

ABOUT THE AUTHOR

Lin Le Versha has drawn on her experience in London and Surrey schools and colleges as the inspiration for the Steph Grant crime series which now includes five books and a novella.

Lin has written and directed over twenty plays exploring issues faced by secondary school and sixth form students. Commissioned to work with Anne Fine on *The Granny Project*, she created English and drama lesson activities for students aged 11 to 14.

While at a sixth form college, she became the major author for *Teaching at Post 16*, a handbook for trainee and newly qualified teachers. In her role as a Local Authority Consultant, she became a School Improvement Partner, working alongside secondary headteachers, work she continued after moving to the Suffolk coast. She is the Director of the Southwold Arts Festival – an eight-day celebration of the Arts.

Creative writing courses at the Arvon Foundation and *Ways with Words* in Italy, encouraged her to enrol at the UEA MA in Creative Writing and her debut novel, *Blood Notes* was submitted as the final assessment for this excellent course.

Lin is now working on the sixth title in the series.

HOBECK BOOKS – THE HOME OF GREAT STORIES

We hope you've enjoyed reading this book by Lin Le Versha. Lin has written a short story prequel to this novel, *A Defining Moment*.

Hobeck Books offers a number of short stories and novellas, including *A Defining Moment* by Lin Le Versha, free for subscribers in the compilation *Crime Bites*.

- *Echo Rock* by Robert Daws
- *Old Dogs, Old Tricks* by AB Morgan
- *The Silence of the Rabbit* by Wendy Turbin
- *Never Mind the Baubles: An Anthology of Twisted Winter Tales* by the Hobeck Team (including many of the Hobeck authors and Hobeck's two publishers)
- *The Clarice Cliff Vase* by Linda Huber
- *Here She Lies* by Kerena Swan
- *The Macnab Principle* by R.D. Nixon
- *Fatal Beginnings* by Brian Price
- *A Defining Moment* by Lin Le Versha

- *Saviour* by Jennie Ensor
- *You Can't Trust Anyone These Days* by Maureen Myant

Also please visit the Hobeck Books website for details of our other superb authors and their books, and if you would like to get in touch, we would love to hear from you.

Hobeck Books also presents a weekly podcast, the Hobcast, where founders Adrian Hobart and Rebecca Collins discuss all things book related, key issues from each week, including the ups and downs of running a creative business. Each episode includes an interview with one of the people who make Hobeck possible: the editors, the authors, the cover designers. These are the people who help Hobeck bring great stories to life. Without them, Hobeck wouldn't exist. The Hobcast can be listened to from all the usual platforms but it can also be found on the Hobeck website: **www.hobeck.net/hobcast**.